CONSTABLE IN THE FARMYARD

More tales from Aidensfield, where Claude Jeremiah Greengrass is having trouble with a billy-goat and a traction engine, and the local postmaster disturbs raiders on a lonely farm. The constable too has crimes to investigate – who is stealing gardening equipment and leaving more behind, and who is the phantom milk bottle thief? Meanwhile romance flourishes in an un- likely setting, and Tabitha Gumlock can't remember what day it is!

Constable Nick deals with this and more, even when someone wants to build a nudist camp on the moors, and Greengrass is mistaken for the new chief constable!

CONSTABLE IN
THE FARMYARD

CONSTABLE IN THE FARMYARD

by

Nicholas Rhea

Magna Large Print Books
Long Preston, North Yorkshire,
BD23 4ND, England.

British Library Cataloguing in Publication Data.

Rhea, Nicholas
    Constable in the farmyard.

CI 52866431

A catalogue record of this book is
available from the British Library

ISBN   0-7505-1573-2

First published in Great Britain by Robert Hale Limited, 1999

Copyright © Nicholas Rhea, 1999

Cover illustration © Barbara Walton by arrangement with
Robert Hale Ltd.

The right of Nicholas Rhea to be identified as the author of this
work has been asserted by him in accordance with the
Copyright, Designs and Patents Act, 1988

Published in Large Print 2000 by arrangement with
Robert Hale Ltd.

Magna Large Print is an imprint of Library Magna Books Ltd.

Printed and bound in Great Britain by
T.J. (International) Ltd., Cornwall, PL28 8RW

1

One of the most inaccessible houses on the North York Moors was called Rigg End Farm. It was situated on my beat, but the beautiful and spacious stone-built premises were hidden in a deep fold among the hills above Aidensfield. The miniature dale which contained the farm was fertile and green, but the lofty moors which surrounded it were covered with acres of open heather to create a somewhat bleak and forbidding landscape. There was not a single tree upon those moors, not even a solitary mountain ash or stunted pine. The only concession to beauty came from rippling moorland streams, dense bracken, clumps of gorse with brilliant yellow blossom, huge granite boulders and the ever-present sound of curlews and skylarks. It was a wild and lonely place, rarely seen by other than the occasional passing hiker.

The only road to the farm – the sole habitation in that small valley – was an unmade rock-strewn track which twisted its way between tall dry stone walls via several five-bar gates and remarkably steep inclines. In wet weather or wintry conditions, the road was impassable to vehicles with the possible exception of a tractor. Even in summer, few drivers risked their cars' exhausts or underparts by driving along that stony, rough track. Deliverymen, who were duty-bound to make the perilous trip, ensured their vehicles had a high ground clearance – they included people like the coalman, vet, doctor and others who made periodic visits to Rigg End.

Several visitors had had pieces wrenched from their vehicles by immovable rocks lurking among the grass which thrived in the centre of that primitive road, consequently few people ever went to Rigg End unless it was absolutely necessary – even then, many never ventured right down to the farm, preferring to leave their wares in a small shelter at the end of the lane. The grocer and postman were just two of the people who adopted that system. Even the daily milk lorry did not go all the way to the farm. The resident farmer had always carried his day's output in churns, using a tractor and trailer to take the milk to a stand near the main road. That system still applied.

My early visits were by police motor cycle. I would stand on the footrests of my Francis Barnett and guide it over the rough terrain as if I was competing in a rough-riders' outing or scrambles event. Later, when I graduated to an official Mini-van, I drove as close to the farm as I dared, bearing in mind the low-slung underparts of the vehicle, and then I would park in a suitable place to walk the rest of the way. Making an official visit to Rigg End wasn't something one did in a hurry; it was more of a mountaineering expedition than a case of popping in for coffee.

Rigg End Farm was a relic of former times, a living reminder of the days when horses and carts used such tracks, not motor vehicles. Probably as recently as World War II, those who lived here rarely ventured out and no one had seen fit to have the track surfaced. It was just as rough in the 1960s as it had been in the 1860s and its chief users seemed to be hikers who enjoyed the panoramic views from its elevated route.

There was a public footpath around the edge of one of the fields and it joined the farm track on its journey to the top road. Any attempt to convert the track into a serviceable road would be extremely costly because it was over a mile long with a most difficult surface to contend with. Massive rocks would have to be moved, rivulets diverted, walls moved to widen the carriageway and steep hills made more manageable by zig-zagging them down the slopes. Few hill farmers could afford to surface their front doorsteps let alone build and maintain a private road of this kind.

To reach Aidensfield village or Ashfordly market from Rigg End, these being the nearest centres of population, entailed a long, arduous trek, but in times past, the occupants of this farm rarely made those journeys because there were few reasons to leave the premises. Leaving Rigg End to go anywhere required such a long and difficult trek that few bothered to make the effort. People who lived and worked on remote farms like this were, of necessity, very self sufficient – they had to be to survive – but Rigg End enjoyed one vital ingredient: it was a non-stop supply of pure, fresh moorland water which tumbled from the hills in a series of becks, waterfalls and rivulets. This water enabled the farmer to keep hens, pigs, cows and sheep and to grow his own food because it made the valley very fertile and enabled the land to be comparatively easily worked. Even though the farm had neither electricity nor piped water, nor indeed a telephone, it could provide a good living for those prepared to work, very hard, over a sustained and prolonged period. The snag was that there was nothing else one could do here but work. Days off, holidays and sparetime interests were non-existent – survival at Rigg End meant non-stop work.

Even when I began to call in the 1960s, modern amenities were not to be found within its walls – the water still came from a moorland spring, there was no hot water on tap, but the farm now had electricity which was produced by a generator. Every time I visited Rigg End, however, I found myself admiring the magnificent setting and the unrivalled solitude while wondering how on earth Reuben Collier managed both to survive in such conditions and to make a living. But he did survive and he did have money to spend; as I was to learn, this was usually spent in the village pub although he possessed some very up-to-date farm machinery.

Reuben was a cheerful pink-faced character with twinkling eyes and a ready smile. He was a tough and wiry man of average build but of indeterminate age, who wore black leather clogs and an old grey trilby hat along with an ancient Harris tweed jacket, a thick shirt and corduroy trousers. I think he was in his late forties or early fifties, but I was never quite sure. He was one of those people whose appearance changed little over the years; he could be anywhere between thirty-five and sixty. My first encounter with Reuben had happened a long time earlier, very soon after my arrival at Aidensfield as the village constable. The encounter took place during one of my outings with Sergeant Blaketon. It was just after midnight and we were in the Ashfordly police car, crossing the moors on a dark autumn night as the sergeant showed me the extremities of my beat. At that stage, I had never met Reuben and most certainly had never visited his farm at Rigg End, but we came upon Reuben in our headlights. He was half walking, half trotting along the dark moorland verge with his head down and his legs twinkling along in his famous clogs.

He had no torch and seemed to be finding his way across the wild heights of the moors in complete darkness.

'That's Reuben Collier,' Blaketon explained. 'From Rigg End. On his way home from the pub. Never give him a lift, Rhea, especially not in an official police vehicle.'

'Why, does he smell?' I laughed.

'Worse than that,' the sergeant told me. 'He gets car sick. If you offer him a lift, he'll accept but within minutes, your car will receive the full treatment from him. He'll be sick all over the place and after a night in the pub, the stench and volume of his output is considerable. Let him walk, Rhea. Everybody else does. Some have learned their lesson from bitter experience.'

'Right, Sergeant.' I made a mental note to heed this advice.

'And never take an official vehicle down to his farm, you'll have the bottom ripped out of it. Walk to Rigg End, if you have to go, Rhea.'

'A rough track, is it?'

'I'd say it was easier motoring up Helvellyn, Rhea,' he chuckled. 'But at least Reuben's not a hermit like his ancestors, he does get out of the place, even if it's only to the pub.'

And so, on that occasion, we did not offer Reuben a lift even though I thought it was rather late for him to be out in such an exposed and deserted place. I wondered why he was walking along such an isolated part of the road because he was nowhere near the pub at Aidensfield, and nowhere near his farm at Rigg End.

The place we'd seen him did not appear to be anywhere close to his route home. In the months which followed, I became more closely acquainted with Reuben's unusual lifestyle, chiefly through occasional official visits to his farm in its spectacular setting but also because he came into Aidensfield every evening for his nightly pint or two – or more – in the pub. I rarely spoke to him there – he would pop into the bar, sit in his favourite corner seat and order a succession of pints interspaced with a pickled egg or bar snack of some kind. Other farmers and villagers would join him and he'd remain there talking and drinking until closing time, then he'd go home. That was his evening's entertainment – every day. Reuben was by no means a Friday-night drinker or a Saturday-night regular – he went to the pub in Aidensfield every night of the week because there was nothing for him to do on the farm. It seemed he was bored at Rigg End.

This had happened because developments in farm machinery and equipment had made the work easier. Probably, he was the first resident of Rigg End who had no need to spend twenty-hours a day working on the farm simply to survive. Now he could complete his work more easily and more speedily. But Reuben, it seemed, had no idea what to do with his spare time. Regular visits to the pub provided the answer.

It was some time before I realized he walked all the way from Rigg End to the pub and walked all the way home afterwards. Furthermore, he did so by not using acknowledged roads. Instead, he cut across the moor by the network of footpaths he knew so well. A trek which would take seven or eight miles by road was shortened to about four miles by a direct cross-country route.

But a four-mile walk, particularly one across some of England's most dramatic and testing scenery, was no mean achievement – and to do it twice a day, every day, was even more astonishing. By making such a determined effort to sink a pint or two, I reckon Reuben must have loved his beer.

As I learned more about him, I discovered he did not always take the most direct route home, even if he did use the shortest route to reach the pub. I calculated it would take roughly an hour to walk from Rigg End to

Aidensfield by the shortest route across the moors. However, his circuitous trek home, I was to eventually learn, varied according to how much he had drunk, but like a determined homing pigeon, he always managed to find his way back to base. I must admit there were times I wondered how on earth he achieved this triumph of navigation.

I discovered this foible after countless sightings of Reuben at different places on the moorland roads around Aidensfield and Ashfordly. Whatever route he took through the wilds, he had, at some stage, to cross one or other of the surfaced routes which criss-crossed the moors. That's when people spotted him. That's when people saw Reuben in the middle of the deserted moors and wondered how he'd got there. He'd be seen, sometimes singing, sometimes staggering and sometimes merely talking to himself, as he made his unerring way back to Rigg End and everyone living locally knew that the mysterious figure on the moors was Reuben because he was unmistakeable in his trilby hat and clogs. To my knowledge, he had been observed crossing roads in all manner of unusual places, often miles away from his most obvious route and sometimes apparently heading in the wrong direction.

But those who knew him were wise enough never to offer him a lift even if it was raining heavily or blowing a blizzard. The local people knew that Reuben was best left to his own devices even if visitors to our district were frequently puzzled by the appearance of a cheerful drunk in the middle of nowhere with not a public house or indeed any other house within miles. Sometimes, as a means of teasing visitors, we'd explain it was the power of the moorland air, or the quality of the moorland spring water which had that effect upon the fellow, explaining that he was a moorland shepherd tending his far-flung flock. I think some gullible tourists believed us.

From time to time, however, Reuben did not reach his isolated home until six or seven o'clock next morning, by which time he was quite sober if a little short of sleep. No one knew where he'd been and I don't think he knew either – but sometimes early morning visitors to Rigg End, like the postman, or even myself, would see him staggering down his lane from some unknown place on the moors. By then, of course, he was stone cold sober. There is no doubt his long, roundabout route across the hills was a fine way of clearing his head and restoring him to sobriety before he tackled his day's work. On such occasions, he began work immediately, with never any thought of going to bed. And then, that same evening, he'd walk all the way back to Aidensfield for another long session in the pub. He must have had a formidable constitution.

Once when we met at his farm, he told me he walked to the pub for two reasons: first, because he did not own a car, and second, because he did not believe in driving his tractor after his regular drinking session.

He had no wish to damage the vehicle because he depended upon it for most of his other excursions – every Wednesday, for example, he drove into Aidensfield at twelve noon precisely to call at the shop for his provisions, to buy stamps at the post office, post his mail and collect his *Farmers' Weekly*. We called it the Twelve O'clock Tractor – one could set one's watch against Reuben's regular appearance in the main street. On a Friday too, he took his tractor into Ashfordly where he did his banking, sold some produce and eggs, and bought whatever he needed by way of clothing, tools or other necessities.

I was not entirely surprised to discover he was a bachelor. He'd inherited the farm from his parents and I think their canny husbandry had enabled them to save a lot of money. They would never have earned a large amount, but they seemed capable of existing on very little; certainly, they had not spent anything on the house. For all its eight bedrooms, four reception rooms, kitchen, larder and countless outbuildings, it had barely had any money spent on the building for decades, and yet it was in splendid condition, if in need of a lick or two of fresh paint and a spot of elbow grease. The cash saved by his careful parents had been left to Reuben which explained why his tractor was always fairly new and well maintained, why his machinery was modern and why he could afford to buy a generator for his electricity supply. And, I suspect, it helped to fund his visits to the pub.

With a useful sum of money to his name and the means of increasing his wealth if he was so inclined, he lived alone in that wonderful isolated place, with no one to help in the house, on the land or around the buildings.

Although he had a cousin living on another moorland farm some eight miles away, no member of his family or anyone else lived with him. It was difficult to believe that a woman would enjoy living in such a remote and primitive place. It was equally difficult to imagine Reuben ever having an opportunity to meet a potential wife. By the very nature of his lonely existence, he was one of life's single people, destined never to know the love of a woman even though he was as masculine as a tom cat. His entire world comprised his farm and his visits to the pub in Aidensfield, albeit with occasional outings to Ashfordly. Romance would never come his way.

Then one morning in late August, I was patrolling in my Mini-van along the top road which ran across the moors when I was flagged down by a couple of sturdy young men in hiking gear. They'd be in their early twenties, I guessed, university students by the look of them. It was early – around 8.30 – and I could see they had been camping; they were carrying their tents and other gear such as a frying pan which dangled from the belt of one of them.

'Yes, lads?' I climbed out to speak to them.

'We've just come over that hill.' said their spokesman. 'Over by Rigg End. The cows look distressed, they're waiting at the gate and making an awful noise. I think they want to be milked.'

'How long ago was that?' I asked.

The second man looked at his watch and said, 'Oh, threequarters of an hour, I'd say. We wondered if the farmer was ill, there's no sign of life. We knocked on the kitchen door but got no reply and he's nowhere in the outbuildings.'

'Thanks; I'll go and have a look,' I promised them. 'I can't radio my office to arrange anyone to ring him, he hasn't got a telephone.'

Half an hour later I was bouncing along the uneven track towards Rigg End and parked in a convenient place to walk the final half-mile or so. That was the worst section, particularly the steep descent into the dale with its rock-strewn track. It was a memorable walk – with the August sun shining from a clear sky, the air was crystal clear with just a hint of autumn coolness. A shower of rain during the night had settled the dust in the atmosphere and the views were astonishing; mile after mile of open purple heather adorned those moors like a lush coverlet of royal silk and in the far distance, it was just possible to see the blue North Sea between the high and low points of the coastal dales and moors. Views of forty miles or so were commonplace from these deserted moors, but I could not wander around all day admiring the scenery – I had work to do. Soon, I was treading that part of the track which formed my descent to Rigg End Farm. As I walked down the steep slope, I looked for the distressed cows, but saw none. It looked as though Reuben had come home after all. Nonetheless, I had to make a positive check and so I continued into the farmyard and soon heard the distinctive sounds of the contented cattle in their byre.

I could hear them munching their cattle cake and hay; I could hear their tethering chains rattling against the skelbeasts (the name used on the moors to describe the wooden partitions in cow byres), and the occasional sigh from a patient animal.

As I drew closer, I could hear Reuben talking to the animal he was milking by hand, and I could hear the swish of the milk as it streamed into the pail he held between his knees. When I entered, I saw him, his head resting on the flank of the cow, as he skilfully teased the milk from the teats. His trilby hat was hanging on a hook in the wall, I noticed, and he still wore his clogs. He must have come straight here from his night's activities. Then I saw a cat was waiting nearby; it was rewarded by the occasional squirt of warm milk which it caught with amazing dexterity in its mouth. It was a nice friendly gesture, I thought.

'Now then, Reuben,' I said as I entered.

Looking up, he saw me in the doorway, but continued to draw the milk as he said, ''Morning. What can I do for you, Mr Rhea?'

'I was hailed on the top road,' I began. 'By a pair of hikers. They thought you might be ill or something.'

'Me? Ill? Why would anybody think that? I'm never ill, Mr Rhea. All this fresh air keeps me fit. Germs can't tolerate our moorland air, you know, it's far too strong for 'em.'

'They said your cows were overdue, hanging around waiting to be milked.'

'They were, Mr Rhea, because I was late back. But I'd never forget 'em, you know, and I wasn't all that late. Half an hour mebbe, no more, but cows do like to be regular ... they'd have been all right for a while yet in spite of the noise they'd be making. I'd have got 'em milked in time for the milk lorry coming. I need my milk

23

cheque, you see ... I daren't miss yon lorry.'

'OK, that's good enough for me. I didn't want you lying there desperately ill with nobody knowing about it and no one to care.'

'Thanks; I appreciate your concern. Now, if you've the time, I'll be finished here before too long, and we could have a coffee made with fresh milk. And if you can wait a bit longer, I could run you back to your van when I take my milk churns up to the top road.'

'I'll settle for the coffee, Reuben, then I'll have to be off.'

It was the first long chat I'd had with Reuben and I found him to be amazingly knowledgeable about the wildlife which surrounded him on the moors. He knew the domestic habits of the grouse and partridges; he had an affinity with the peregrines and hen harriers which sometimes hunted near his farm: he knew the habits of all the other moorland birds and animals; he recognized the worth of all the herbs which grew beside the beck and, of course, he was totally familiar with every aspect of his farming profession. He was a thoroughly professional man of the moors.

In listening to him, I decided not to refer

to his late-night wanderings – after all, he was not disorderly; his wanderings were chiefly away from public places; he committed no nuisance or damage; he offended no one and his private life was his own affair. He loved animals, both domestic and wild, and could never be cruel to his precious herd of cows. I left him to process the milk before he conveyed it to the top road and set off to walk back to my van.

As I struggled back up the hill from his farm, I did wonder if he was a happy man.

His heavy drinking suggested he was frustrated in some way, unfulfilled perhaps, and it was abundantly evident that he had a good brain and a wonderful knowledge of wildlife which he could use to advantage. But he was stuck on this lonely farm, one person in a far-off place which would accommodate dozens as it had surely done in the glorious past as a busy working farm. It would have had live-in workers, even numbering up to a dozen. Now, it was a place some townies might consider idyllic in spite of its lack of amenities and access, and yet it was here that Reuben seemed destined to spend the rest of his lonely days. He was by no means an old man – there was little wonder he found solace in the pub.

Then one Tuesday evening in September, Reuben did not turn up for his nightly pint. I happened to pop into the pub early that evening, on duty, because I wanted to alert George Ward, the landlord, to the theft of some spirits from an Ashfordly off-licence. He said he'd look out for offers of cut-price bottles, and would call me if such an approach was made; he had no wish to buy stolen property. I thanked him, and then he said, 'Reuben's not in tonight, Nick. He's usually here by now. You've not heard whether he's away or sick or something, have you?'

'No,' I admitted. 'Not a word.'

'Well, there's no reason for him to call me if he can't make it, but this is the first time he's not been in for months. It's not like him to miss.'

'I'll keep my ears and eyes open,' I assured George. 'Thanks for the tip. We don't want Reuben to come to any harm. I can't ring him, he's not on the phone, but I'll ask around.'

'I hope he hasn't fallen and broken his leg on his way here, or on his way home last night. It could happen, it's a rough old route he takes across those moors, and nobody would find him up there. I've told him to

26

come on his tractor and drink a bit less so he could drive it home, but he won't. He'd be safer if he did. He could even take it across country most of the way if he wanted to avoid the roads.'

'I'll look out for him as I patrol the area,' I promised. 'I'll make sure I pay a visit to his part of those moors!'

I did not feel it was right to pay a late evening visit to Reuben's remote farm; that might appear as if I was spying on him, poking my nose into his private affairs especially so soon after my earlier check on his presence, but I must admit I felt some concern for him. It was a slight concern, certainly, but I hoped I was wise enough to realize there was no call for a dramatic intervention when Reuben had missed just one night in the pub. I felt my instincts were correct because next day, as the parish church clock struck noon, Reuben motored along Aidensfield main street on his tractor bang on time as usual, as he made his way to the shop for his *Farmers' Weekly* and groceries. He was all right, I was pleased to note, and I refrained from rushing over to him to ask where he'd been. I told myself it was nothing to do with me if he missed the occasional session in the bar with his mates.

But I did wonder what he'd been doing!

The odd thing was that he missed again the following Saturday without explanation. Furthermore, George told me that Reuben had still not offered any explanation for his absence the previous Tuesday.

Even though his drinking mates had quizzed him, he had simply smiled in response, adding coyly that he'd fancied a night or two at home. Somehow, that did not impress his pals as a truthful answer. They suspected some other reason. There was wide speculation that he was getting too old to cope with the long walk into the village, or that he'd had some nasty sobering experience on one of his lengthy return trips, but no one managed to elicit the reason for his absences. And when the same thing occurred the following Tuesday and again the next Saturday, it caused something of a rumpus in the pub. People began to lay bets on Reuben's reason for these absences and the likely answers included: he was getting too old for the walk; the doctor had told him to drink less beer; he was frightened of the long walk home; he'd seen a ghost; he was running out of money; one of his cows had been ill; he'd eaten something that disagreed with him;

he'd started bed-and-breakfast accommodation for hikers in his huge home; he'd bought a car and was taking driving lessons in secret; he'd had visitors; there'd been a relative's funeral...

The guesses were many and varied, but I felt sure none was the right answer and although Reuben never gave a clue about the reason for his absences, I was as curious as the others. Things almost reached fever pitch when he absented himself the following Tuesday evening, and this time I was due for a late patrol – 10 p.m. until 2 a.m. I discovered his absence from the pub as I paid an official visit just before closing time, but because I was due to patrol the area for the next four hours, I reasoned I might encounter Reuben during his late-night moorland crossing. After all, I thought to myself, he might be visiting another pub!

I daren't suggest that to George Ward, but Reuben's home was as close to Ashfordly as it was to Aidensfield; it was possible he might have discovered some interesting people during his visits to the small town on market day and he might be meeting them in one of the town pubs. I knew he hadn't a car and I knew he would never risk driving his tractor, especially if he intended to enjoy a heavy boozing session in town. He could be offered a lift home by someone unfamiliar with the risks involved, but the chances were that Reuben would walk home from whatever destination he had chosen. If so, he would have to cross one or other of the moorland roads at some point, or walk along them for a short distance which meant there was a fair chance our paths would cross. But they didn't.

That night, I did not set eyes on Reuben, but I know he was at home to milk his cows next morning – the postman told me. Clearly, an element of mystery had now developed in Reuben's life and while it could be argued that his domestic affairs concerned no one but himself, everyone who knew him was intrigued. But, as if to deepen the mystery, Reuben was providing no explanations to anyone.

Then a quite separate incident occurred. I had no cause to associate it with Reuben's activities, but in fact it had some bearing on his recent behavioural changes. I was performing a four-hour spell of office duty in Ashfordly Police Station when a lady, a visitor to Ashfordly, walked in to report finding a small haversack. Apparently, it had been abandoned on the steps of the market cross and appeared to have been left by a hiker who'd rested on the steps for a while. It looked as if the owner had unintentionally walked away without it.

Following the very rigid procedures involving found property, I opened it in the presence of the finder to check the contents with her and to make an appropriate entry in our Found Property Register. It contained a lot of official-looking papers, both handwritten and typed, and although I did not read these closely, it was evident they formed part of an academic appraisal of the environment upon the moors around Rigg End. One piece of paper was an internal memo which contained the heading 'Keasbeck College', albeit without any address, and there were some other items such as ballpoint pens in various colours, a compass, a map, a flask of hot coffee and some sandwiches. The heat of the coffee in the flask told me that the haversack had been lost very recently. There was nothing in the haversack that might quickly identify the loser and it made sense to retain it at the police station in the hope the owner would report its loss. In any case, it might be possible to trace Keasbeck College and restore it to the loser.

Within an hour, however, a woman came to the counter to report its loss. She was in her mid-forties, a confident woman with dark-brown hair, a round happy face and a quick smile who was dressed in walking boots, jeans and a thick woolly sweater designed to beat the chills of autumn.

'Officer.' She had a loud, well-spoken voice. 'I would lose my head if it wasn't fastened on so securely. Have you, by the remotest chance, had a haversack handed in? I've lost mine and I think I left it on the steps of the market cross.'

After obtaining a description of her lost article, I was in no doubt I had her property in my possession and was happy to restore it to her, against her signature.

She asked for the name and address of the honest finder, and I was happy to oblige; she said she would write a thank-you letter. During our conversation, she seemed most affable and friendly, chatting to me enthusiastically about her project and stressing the importance of the recovered papers. When I asked for her name and address for my records, she said, 'Karen Hartley. Miss. Or Professor Hartley, if you have to be very formal. I have rooms at Keasbeck.' It transpired that Keasbeck College was in the

Midlands, not far from Nottingham, and after providing her address there, she added, 'But I have a weekend cottage in Aidensfield, Peat Spring Cottage. That's where I'm living now. Until the new term begins.'

'Peat Spring Cottage?' I had never heard of it and she recognized my puzzlement.

'It's not far from Rigg End,' she said. 'To the eastern side of the top road, in a dip in the moors over the hill from Rigg End. There's no village, not even a hamlet. It's all by itself: it's a former gamekeeper's cottage. You get to it by turning off the road and following the track that leads to Lairsbeck; you turn right at a little packhorse bridge. Very pretty and very remote, Constable, but just what I need to recharge my batteries from time to time. I come to Peat Spring as often as I can. Most weekends in fact.'

There was a map of the area on the office wall and so, while she was there, I went across to it to locate her cottage and she followed me, eventually stabbing the map with her finger and saying, 'There it is, beside Peat Beck. Idyllic, Constable, utterly idyllic.'

'I've never been there,' I told her. 'Now, when I looked through your belongings hoping to find an address, I noticed you were doing a project about Rigg End.'

'I am indeed; fascinating place. You know it?'

I told her as much as I could about the remote dale and the isolated farm it contained and after a few moments of discussion, I added, 'You've met Reuben Collier, have you?'

'I have indeed, Constable. Fascinating fellow. So knowledgeable about the wildlife and the topography of the area. I've started to invite him in for dinner, you know; he comes on a Tuesday and Saturday. He's only recently started to join me and I can fit him in during the holidays. I feed him well and he provides me with information about Rigg End ... it stops him getting pie-eyed at the pub, too. When term resumes, though, he'll go back to the pub, I suppose, unless I can get up here for weekends.'

I laughed, and couldn't prevent myself saying, 'So that's where he gets to! We've been wondering where he was!'

'We?' she asked.

'Me – and his cronies in the pub,' and I then told her about Reuben's nightly visits and his long walks home afterwards. I explained that sometimes these were undertaken in a fairly advanced state of inebriation, but stressed that he always managed to arrive back at his farm in time for morning milking, and to recover in time for the following night's outing.

'That's how I met him,' she laughed. 'He was wandering past my cottage late one night, singing happily to himself and I happened to be in the garden working very late on my borders, using a torch in fact ... anyway, he stopped for a chat. He was fairly well plastered but he talked lot of sense. He likes a chat, Constable, and well, after that he started to come past my house most nights. Sometimes I saw him, sometimes I didn't, and of course, sometimes I wasn't there anyway. But when I got to know him better I discovered he lived at Rigg End and began to realize he was a very interesting man and quite harmless. I felt he had a lot to offer, a wonderfully deep knowledge of moorland matters. So, on one occasion when we got talking, I decided to invite him in for a meal.'

'So Reuben's being secretly seeing a lady and none of us guessed!' I smiled.

'I think he likes to keep himself to himself, Constable. But you may know that our college is interested in his farm as a field study centre? I can tell you because the planning application for change of use has been published in the *Gazette,*' she told me. 'It's no secret, although I don't suppose Reuben has told anybody. However, over recent months, I've been several times to look at it and so have my colleagues. We think it's ideal. It's got the necessary space for accommodating students; there's enough outbuildings to make lecture rooms or display centres; it's established in wonderful surroundings; it's away from any centre of population so we'd not make a nuisance of ourselves, and we would resurface that awful road....'

'Reuben would never leave Rigg End!' I interrupted.

'He won't have to,' she smiled. 'We intend to get him involved in our work, his knowledge is so great, he'll be a wonderful asset for us. I'm not saying he'd make a lecturer, but he will be a superb guide for our students, giving them the real depth of knowledge they require, genuine rural knowledge and not something gleaned from reference books. You can see why I became so interested in Reuben Collier.'

'And all because he stumbled past your house on his roundabout way back home from the pub.'

'Yes, one thing did lead to another. He's got so few people to talk to. He likes talking to people with brains, Constable; he can't tolerate small talk – which I think is why he drinks so much in the pub. His brain needs to be occupied, Constable; he soon gets bored out of his mind. He never had a drink while he was with me, and I know that when we get him involved with our work, he'll stop drinking – well, drinking to excess, I mean. He's not an alcoholic – he's a long way from that – he drinks out of boredom, and for companionship ... so when we turn his farm into a field study centre with young people and mature students around him for a lot of his time, I can assure you he'll blossom into a very interesting man.'

'A new beginning for Reuben?' I said.

'Yes, exactly,' she added.

'He'd stay there?' I put to her.

'Oh, yes, the farm will remain in his hands; we've come to an agreement about a suitable form of rental for the parts we use and it will make life easier for him.'

'It is tough, living at Rigg End,' I said.

'We'll make it easier for everyone. We'll get a telephone installed and provide a good road to Rigg End, and we'll upgrade his

37

premises with things like flush toilets, showers and baths – and he can keep his cows and sheep as well. It's an ideal way of utilizing all that space he's got. It will give him companionship and I know we will all learn something from him – and he'll learn from our students.'

Professor Hartley remained with me for some time, happy to chat about Rigg End, Reuben and her exciting plans for his place on the moors, then she said she must dash because she had a meeting on site with both Reuben and one of the college advisers. I wished her luck – and wondered, just fleetingly, whether there was a spark of romance in her eyes. She and Reuben?

It seemed unlikely, but nothing is impossible!

Those proposals, while not being particularly far-reaching or innovative, were one of the first of their kind in that region so far as diversification by moorland farmers was concerned. The farmers themselves, so often without any capital other than their farm premises, could never contemplate or finance any other form of use for their homesteads and yet in the years which followed, more isolated farms were turned into other businesses. Some became living museums, bed-and-breakfast accommodation, small hotels, pottery manufacturers, carpentry workshops and study centres for all kinds of arts, crafts and academia. Others began to use their unproductive land for caravan sites and their unwanted outbuildings for holiday cottages; some turned to the rearing of exotic or rare breeds, the growth of new crops like flax and oil seed rape, or the sale of barns for conversion into splendid homes.

But Reuben Collier was one of the earliest in our region to authorize the conversion of his farm into a place of rural study and relaxation. Keasbeck College moved onto his premises about eighteen months after my chat with Professor Hartley and Reuben began to play a vital role in their work, thanks to his extensive knowledge of the moors and wildlife about him. Eventually, the road was surfaced, the telephone was installed and the house was modernized. Reuben kept his cows and sheep and continued as a working farmer with all that bustle and activity going on around him. And I do know that he taught some of his students to milk his cows!

And, not totally unexpectedly, he got married.

Professor Hartley gave up her work at the college and moved into Rigg End with Reuben. She started to breed heavy horses, specializing in Clydesdales, and she won prizes at major shows, while Reuben gave up most of his nightly visits to the pub. However, he did not totally give up his former life because he continued to trek over the moors on a Wednesday night, and to walk home afterwards – now sober of course, and always making use of the shortest route back to Rigg End.

When the long track to his farmhouse was eventually surfaced with tarmacadam, he learned to drive a car and this seemed to cure his car sickness. He even gave up wearing clogs.

The inception of the Collier Field Study Centre at Rigg End represented a time of great change in Aidensfield.

2

Scattered across the moors and throughout the expanse of my Aidensfield beat were lots of smallholdings. These were farms in miniature; some were privately owned and some were rented from larger estates. They were worked by the families who occupied the house which formed the domestic accommodation of such spreads but the size of these fertile areas of cultivation varied considerably. Some were very small – as tiny as four or five acres perhaps – although most of them seemed to extend to teens of acres, perhaps boasting fifteen, sixteen or even twenty acres plus a family house. I am not sure when a smallholding becomes categorized as a small farm but there were small farms of fifty and sixty acres on the moors. I would guess a smallholding could be generally regarded as being less than fifty acres.

In most cases, there was not sufficient land to provide an independent living for the resident family. Smallholders reared and

41

sold a variety of livestock such as pigs, goats, sheep, hens, geese or ducks and even kept a cow or two for milking; they grew marketable crops such as potatoes, turnips, cabbages, sprouts and other vegetables, but as this did not generate a living wage, most of the menfolk and sometimes their wives had to supplement their income by other work. Many men hired themselves out for what was known as datal work. This was the term used when men were hired by the day to work on neighbouring farms, undertaking such labours as hay-making, hoeing turnips, sheep-shearing, rabbit-catching, mole-hunting, dry-stonewalling, ditching, thatching, milking, harvesting, potato-picking and a whole range of other necessary and sometimes seasonal tasks.

It was customary for the smallholder's wife to remain at home, tending the livestock and working on the land, but some did leave the premises for the odd hour or two to earn extra money in domestic service of various kinds as well as seasonal work in the hayfields or at harvest-time and during sheep-shearing.

Casual labouring for other people enabled smallholders to spend fruitful time working on their own holding but even so, this was not easy without the help of their wives and even their children. Running a successful smallholding was certainly a family business. Few expected to make a full-time living from such a small patch of land; it was not an easy life but many found it enjoyable and fulfilling because it provided a means of working for themselves in pleasant rural surroundings while growing their own crops and rearing their own livestock. A smallholding provided a means of achieving the popular 1960s dream of being self-sufficient, but equally it demanded hard work and an unwavering dedication not found in everyone.

One man who had always wanted to run a smallholding was called Edward Cowton. He lived on his little spread at Elsinby and was known locally as Ted. He had come to Beckside Cottage, Elsinby, from the suburbs of York, having seen the smallholding advertised in a local paper. He'd liked it, sold his suburban semi-detached house and bought it with the intention of rearing pigs for sale in the local livestock marts. He knew he could not make a complete living from pigs, and so he had half a dozen cows, a flock of hens and some ducks from which eggs would be produced

43

and sold, and a large vegetable patch which would provide potatoes, cabbages, carrots and other popular household necessities.

In his enterprise, Ted was fully supported by his wife, Dorothy, known as Dot. Both were in their early forties, with no children, and initially both of them appeared rather too idealistic to make a practical success of their chosen career. With no country knowledge and no background of country life other than the occasional hike across the North York Moors, they regarded their enterprise as some kind of dream. In spite of their naïvety, however, they were keen to learn, they were very nice people and they were very hardworking.

From the outset, they realized the smallholding would not generate sufficient regular income to keep them. Even when buying the place, Ted knew he would have to find other supportive work and he found part-time employment selling cattle food to farmers. For this he was paid a modest wage of around £8 per week, plus commission. The work suited him because he could make his own hours and it kept him in touch with the complex world of farming; there is no doubt he did learn a substantial amount from his farmer customers.

Furthermore, he could generate a few livestock deals while on his rounds, occasionally earning extra pounds from the sale of a pig to a farmer or buying a bargain-priced piece of second-hand farm machinery or selling a cartload of potatoes to an hotel.

While Ted was performing these money-earning duties, however, it meant that Dot had to remain on the smallholding during the day to feed the livestock, milk the cows, clean the pigs' styes, gather the eggs and wash them, weed the crops or harvest the fruit. But even her selfless help was not sufficient – Ted felt that, in order to maintain their lifestyle, Dot must go to work, if only for a few hours a week.

It would generate some much-needed cash. Accordingly, she cleaned at a bank in Ashfordly for two mornings a week; she worked behind the bar in the Hopbind Inn at Elsinby on Sunday lunchtimes, and helped behind the counter in the village post office from time to time. In short, life was hectic for both Dot and Ted and their endeavours were based on an old Yorkshire saying that there is no money in small-holdings.

I did not have many dealings with the

Cowtons, except a quarterly visit to check their livestock register, and once every three years to renew Ted's firearm certificate. Apart from that, my only contact was when I passed them in the street or saw either of them in the village shop or at one of the local markets. They were a nice pleasant couple, I realized, perhaps on the quiet side but very capable of working hard for themselves and causing trouble to no one. As I got to know them better, I realized they had no spare time; all their energy was directed towards survival on their small-holding. When Ted finished his salesman rounds there was always work to be done on his piece of land, and even his weekends were spent repairing buildings and fences, maintaining machinery, attending to his livestock, and doing the paperwork. And because he was so busy, Dot's assistance was always required – apart from keeping the house clean and tidy, doing the washing and preparing the meals, she was responsible for dispatching the milk, feeding the poultry, collecting eggs, cleaning the henhouses and rearing chicks. I must admit there were times when I wondered if Ted and Dot were happy in their new life. It seemed they never had any spare time for social activities; their life was all work.

They never emerged for an evening in the Hopbind Inn over a drink and a bar snack, they never attended events in the village hall or on the sports field, and did not go to church. The smallholding, it seemed, was their entire life and I must admit that, on the occasions I had to visit the establishment, it always looked as if more work needed to be done. Wire netting needed replacing, woodwork needed a coat of paint, paths needed weeding. I got the impression that the Cowtons were chasing their tails – paddling fast and getting nowhere, treading water, or whatever cliché fits the bill! For all their hard work, they did not appear to be making any kind of progress. I did not think that was their original plan – I think, when they left suburbia for a life of rustic bliss, they saw themselves sitting quietly on their land with lots of spare time while surrounded by clucking hens, contented cows, pink piglets and pretty flowers. Instead, they were surrounded by a permanently demanding, time-consuming business which did not appear to be paying for itself.

And then one morning, just after ten o'clock, I received a call from Dot.

'Can you come quickly, Mr Rhea?' She sounded breathless on the phone. 'Somebody's broken into our house.'

My heart sank. 'Has much gone?' I asked.

'Yes, all Ted's money...'

'Cash, was it?'

'Yes, but I don't know how much. Several hundred pounds, I'd say.'

'In notes?'

'Yes, most of it.'

'I'll come straight away,' I promised her.

Fortunately, I was on duty and had been spending an hour in my office, catching up with my own paperwork and report writing. Dot had caught me moments before I departed for a patrol of my patch. I was able to reach her smallholding within six or seven minutes of her call and found her waiting anxiously at the back door of the house. She was a pretty woman in her forties with short fair hair, blue eyes and a round, pink face. She was wearing a blue overcoat when I arrived, she'd not even removed that in her anxiety. I noticed the broken glass in the window to the left of the doorway – it seemed chummy had smashed it, reached inside and opened the catch before climbing through and gaining access to the house.

'I'm sorry.' She looked so miserable and tearful that I felt I ought to express my own sorrow at this shock. 'Have you touched anything?'

'No.' She shook her head. 'I just got back from Ashfordly, I've been to work at the bank and then did a bit of shopping. I got home to find this smashed window, so I checked the money straight away and saw the box open, then rang you before doing anything else.'

'Well done. Did you see anyone leaving?'

'No, no one. They'd gone before I got here.'

'Was the door open? Did he let himself out by the door?'

'No, it was locked, just as I'd left it.'

'So it seems he left by the same way he got in, via the window. Ted's on his rounds, is he?'

'Yes, it's his Brantsford day. I don't know how to contact him, I have no names of his customers. But he said he'd be back about three o'clock.'

'What time does he leave for work?'

'He usually goes out about nine o'clock,' she said. 'But I leave at seven, for my little bank job, so I'm gone before him. I can't be sure what time he left but it would be about nine, he always leaves at nine.'

'And you returned at ten or thereabouts?'

'Yes, just before I rang you.'

'So they broke in between nine and ten – they can't be far away.'

I decided to radio Ashfordly Police Station from my Mini-van, just in case any of our patrols came across a vehicle speeding away from the Elsinby area or someone on foot trying to thumb a lift; if so, it would be worth stopping and subjecting such a vehicle or person to a swift search with a request for an explanation about their recent movements. Alf Ventress responded to my call, and although I could not provide any description of a suspect person or vehicle, nor even give details of what precisely had been stolen, he said he would circulate the fact that the housebreaking had occurred within the last hour or so and that a large amount of cash had been stolen. All suspects would be checked and asked to account for their whereabouts since nine o'clock this morning.

The smashed window was hidden from the neighbouring houses and the road; the villain would have been able to work unseen. I looked at the broken window pane. The window had not been forced open with a jemmy or other tool.

Slivers of glass lay on the window ledge inside and a few had dropped to the ground outside the house; it had been a simple job to break the glass, probably with an elbow or gloved fist, release the catch and open the window. It was large enough to admit a full size person. She led me to the back room which they used as their office. It contained a small desk covered in papers and file jackets, two four-drawer filing cabinets, a couple of chairs and rows of shelves on the walls, all containing files. One of the filing cabinet drawers was standing open; inside was a large metal cash box, also standing open. It was empty but did not appear to have been forced. With Dot, I made a search of all the other rooms just in case Dot had returned while the villain was in the house and he was hiding here, but we drew a blank. He'd gone. No other drawer or cupboard had been searched; it appeared that the thief had known exactly where to find the money. I completed my own examination of the premises before calling the Scenes of Crime officers.

'The filing cabinet drawer was not forced open?' I put to Dot.

'No, we never locked it. Or the money

box. You never think you're going to get broken into, do you?'

'Who knew the money was there?' I asked. 'The thief seems to have known where to find it. He's not searched any other room or looked anywhere else for the cash box – he's broken in and gone straight to your office.'

'I don't know.' She sounded weepy and upset. 'People have been in, when we sell a pig or want to pay for something, Ted brings them in here ... he would know who they were; he'd know better than me.'

'So several people, other than you and Ted, would know that your cash was kept in that drawer?'

'Yes, I know we should have banked it, but, well, Ted didn't want to ... he kept them all, unopened.'

'Unopened?' I was puzzled by her remark. 'He kept all what unopened?'

'His wage packets. He kept them all unopened, he gets paid in cash, you see, with his commission.'

I was astonished at this. 'So how many pay packets would there be in here?'

'I don't know, Mr Rhea. A year's wages, maybe.'

'A year? All in unopened pay packets?'

'Yes, with his name on. Little envelopes

with cash in them, with holes in the front so you can count the notes and coins before you open them.'

'So if a year's wages has gone, how much money are we taking about?'

'I don't know really, Mr Rhea. Five hundred pounds maybe.'

'Five hundred pounds?' My own wage was around twelve pounds and I knew Ted was only working part-time. This was a huge sum to lose. 'But why was Ted keeping all this money here, Dot? Why hadn't he banked it, or spent it?'

'He always said the smallholding should earn us a living, Mr Rhea. He wanted to show that it could actually pay its way, even when other people said it wouldn't. So he got the sales job just in case – and said he would not use those earnings to supplement our income from the smallholding. And it worked you see, he never had to use his sales income ... it was completely separate; he was keeping it for a rainy day.'

'He should have paid it into a bank account or building society,' I sighed. 'He's lost the lot now.'

'He wanted his bank statements to show we were living entirely on our earnings from the smallholding, Mr Rhea. I think he wanted to prove to the bank manager that we could make a go of it without the need to take a job.'

'But you work as well. You've got part-time jobs.'

'Yes, Ted said I should do that, so I could get myself nice clothes and things. A bit of spare cash, pocket money for me, for little extras. But everything else came from the smallholding's income, Mr Rhea. You see, we *can* earn a living from a smallholding, if we work hard and act sensibly. We've proved that.'

I did not want to get into a discussion about this illogical way of running a business but I did need to circulate details of those stolen pay packets, and I did need to call the Scenes of Crime department and ask them to come and examine the place for fingerprints or other evidence.

'Dot,' I said, 'can you put the kettle on? I could use a coffee – and I'm sure you could. You can use the kitchen and other parts of the house. Just keep clear of the office and that broken window. I'm going to radio for our Scenes of Crime team to come and examine the site of the break-in and your office for fingerprints and any other evidence, and I'm going to circulate a description of those missing pay packets. If you like I can ask our office to ring some of the farms in the Brantsford area, to see if Ted can be contacted and asked to come home. We have a list of farmers in this area; we keep notes of those whose stock registers we have to check.'

'That would be nice,' she said, looking a little more cheerful. 'I want him to know as soon as possible.'

Preparing the coffee would occupy her while I went about the business of radioing Ashfordly Police with an update and with my further requests. Alf Ventress cheerfully agreed to telephone a few farmers in the Brantsford area with a view to tracing Ted Cowton and said that the fact the stolen money was in pay packets would help enormously if we traced the culprit – it seemed as if the villain had considered them a convenient way of transporting the haul. He could have stuffed them all into the pockets of his clothing or he might have used a carrier bag of some kind. Having notified the Scenes of Crime department and completed those calls, I returned to Beckside Cottage where Dot had made two mugs of coffee; she'd also produced some home-made jam tarts. I settled at her side to await the arrival of our fingerprint experts – about forty minutes, they assured me.

I explained what my colleagues would be doing now – circulating details of the crime, keeping observation for suspects and so forth, and I told her what to expect when the Scenes of Crime officers arrived. I also questioned her about the people who had come into her office and who might have known about the unopened pay packets and succeeded in obtaining a few names. They'd all be interviewed as soon as I could trace them.

The ginger-bearded Ted returned to Beckside Cottage just as the Scenes of Crime van was arriving, and I was able to brief both about the break-in.

Ted was able to provide us with a more detailed total of stolen money – £675.15s.0d. to be precise, all in those small buff-coloured pay packets, fifty-six of them containing slightly different amounts – and while Detective Sergeant Brownlow and Detective Constable Parkin embarked on their scientific examination of the scene, fortified with Dot's splendid coffee made with fresh milk, I obtained the necessary written statement from Ted. It was not within my brief to criticize him for not

56

spending his salesman's wages and for working so hard for so little return, but it *was* part of our general crime prevention role to advise people, particularly those in business, to take greater care of large sums of cash. He listened patiently as I produced my well-rehearsed advice about using safes that were impossible to move from their mountings, and were locked securely with the keys hidden from potential thieves. Also, I told him about making sure all his surplus cash, particularly large sums, was banked, and that his premises were strengthened against intruders.

He said, 'I did intend banking it eventually, Mr Rhea, but I had to prove to myself that I did not need the money ... by leaving the envelopes unopened. I could tell myself the cash was not available. I suppose I just let the system continue week after week without really thinking about it. Even if I'd banked it, though, I might have been tempted to dip into those funds when things were tight and, by not banking it, the bank manager would never know about it. He'd see that I was making a success of the smallholding without any outside income. My own system, daft as it might appear, worked for me and Dot. You must admit it has proved I don't need that cash, hasn't it?'

'It's proved you don't need to work at your salesman job,' I said. 'Just think, though, you could have spent all those hours on your smallholding instead of chasing farmers to sell cattle food; the extra time with your business would have increased your income from the smallholding and given you more time to relax ... and think of the income tax savings too. Anyway, those are my thoughts. Now, are you insured for larceny, housebreaking, burglary and so forth?'

'Yes, I am.'

'Good. Contact your insurance representative and he'll contact our headquarters for an abstract of our crime report. I hope they compensate you....'

'They might not, if it wasn't locked up,' he said gloomily. 'Besides, it wasn't business money, was it? It was personal – and some companies aren't happy about making compensation for stolen cash.'

'I can't really help you with that side of things, but at least you can prove how much was really stolen!' I smiled. 'Not many people keep their pay packets unopened for a whole year or more.'

'If I'd been working full-time on the

smallholding, he'd not have broken in, would he? I'd have been there to keep an eye on the place.'

'Right,' I said. I could see that he was already rethinking his entire philosophy; the shock of the break-in had caused him to reappraise the whole idea of working at one job while trying to juggle that work with the demands of his smallholding and its complement of livestock and plants. But I had to leave.

I had done what was necessary from my point of view, and the Scenes of Crime officers would soon complete their examination. We would continue to search for the thief and I would begin by asking questions around Elsinby, just in case someone had witnessed a visitor anywhere near Beckside Cottage. Meanwhile, Ted and Dot would have to repair the damage and adopt a new and more sensible method of dealing with *all* their cash, not just Ted's income from selling cattle food.

To cut short a long story, we did trace the thief. It was a small-time pig dealer who lived at Stovensby. In his late forties, he was struggling to survive on his own smallholding, supplementing his income by dealing in second-hand agricultural machinery along with a spot of labouring work during the harvest or potato-picking time.

He knew Ted; he knew Ted's routine and the fact he and Dot would be away from his premises that morning. He'd also known that Ted's cash box contained all those unopened pay packets and had paid a visit to Beckside Cottage that morning, ostensibly to ask about buying another of Ted's pigs. Happily, he'd been spotted driving his rusting pick-up truck in the village by Gilbert Kingston, the postman, and he told me. A visit to his rundown smallholding at Stovensby quickly recovered most of the cash, still in its neat little pay packets.

As a direct result of that raid, however, Ted did see the sense in not working at his supposedly spare-time job. He gave it up and concentrated full-time on his small-holding, eventually developing a thriving market garden. Later, this modest but thriving spread expanded into a busy garden centre.

He branched out into selling seedlings, flowers, fruit bushes, shrubs, garden tools, ornaments and so forth. This was such a success that the pigs, cows and other livestock were eventually sold and I must admit that, at times, I felt a little envious of Ted and Dot. Their dream had come true, even if it had changed course slightly and even if it took the actions of a petty thief to provide the impetus.

Another smallholder of local renown was Claude Jeremiah Greengrass. His ramshackle ranch on the edge of the moor could be described as a smallholding, although few people regarded it in a very favourable light. Most thought it was a rubbish tip which happened to surround a battered old house. The land was always full of rusting machinery, rotting cartwheels, discarded household furniture ranging from beds to easy chairs, old car seats, damaged pieces of car bodywork, old tyres, oil drums and spare parts, discarded pots and pans, tin baths and anything else that no one appeared to need or want. The site boasted a small complement of hens and stray cats plus, of course, Alfred, the flea-ridden lurcher. From time to time Claude also purchased a large animal such as a pig or a calf or even a few moorland sheep, invariably hoping to make a small profit by selling these animals; but, for Claude, his plans rarely worked as he hoped.

Residents of the village found it odd, therefore, when a billy goat appeared on the ranch. Had the goat been a nanny with kid-bearing potential and an ability to produce rich, health-giving milk for ailing humans, none of us would have been particularly surprised. That would have been quite sensible.

But the unheralded arrival of a fierce-looking billy goat with massive horns created something of a stir. It was of the English breed with a handsome fawn coloured coat, a black stripe down its spine, a black tip to its tail and a black smudge down the front of its forehead, this somehow emphasizing its wicked-looking horns. The snag with billy goats is that they can become rather rampant and uncontrollable and that's when they display inordinate strength and determination. Also, they produce a rather offensive smell, particularly in hot weather, although, as one villager pointed out, 'It couldn't be any worse than the smell in Greengrass's kitchen, especially after he's been cooking sausages.'

I had to call at Hagg Bottom, the home of Claude Jeremiah Greengrass, one morning and noticed the goat tethered to a stake in a paddock at the side of the house.

'Whatever it is, I didn't do it and I know nowt about it,' he said, emerging from the house at the sound of my approach. 'Whenever anything's gone wrong, you coppers always come here blaming me....'

'I'm not here to blame you for anything, Claude,' I laughed. 'I just wondered if you'd like to buy a raffle ticket.'

'A raffle ticket? First prize a week in a police cell, second prize two weeks in a police cell, or do I win a meal for two in the police canteen or a chance to throw rotten codfish at Blaketon ... now there's a thing. I might enjoy that.'

'It's for the Police Widows' and Orphans' Fund,' I told him. 'Threepence a ticket, but to you – a book of ten for half a crown.'

'I don't support the work of the police, Constable. You ought to know that by now.'

'First prize is a week's holiday in a nice hotel in Scarborough, and then there's the usual things like bottles of whisky or sherry, cakes, a meal for two at the Royal Hotel in Strensford, a voucher for ten pounds to spend in the Co-op and lots of other valuable prizes still to be announced. It's drawn in a month's time.'

'I don't support the police,' he repeated.

'Didn't you hear me first time?'

'This is not for us, Claude, it's for the widows and orphans of policemen killed on duty while doing their best to keep society calm and secure so that you can go about your lawful business with confidence.'

'I haven't got half a crown to spend on raffle tickets, I'm just a poor self-employed businessman, struggling to earn a crust for me and my Alfred.'

'I see you've just bought a goat.' I nodded towards the animal in question. 'How much did that cost you?'

'Nowt,' he said. 'It was given to me. By a mate of mine. He can't cope with it, not after it ate his wife's best knickers when they were drying on the line, and I happened to want something to keep that rough patch of land in order, summat that would eat anything, especially nettles and briars and elderberry bushes. I reckoned if it could cope with Alice Hamilton's knickers, it would soon clear my rough patch. So he gave it to me. I've called him Oscar, after Sergeant Blaketon.'

'He'll give you a load of trouble,' I warned him.

'Blaketon's always giving me trouble!' he replied.

'I meant the goat,' I retorted. 'Billy goats are strong; give him half a chance and he'll be off down the village after those nanny goats that live near the beck.'

'I've got him staked in, Constable, and that rope'll hold an elephant. It'll take more than a love-crazed billy goat to uproot that stake and get away from me.'

'These chaps have been known to do that, Claude. Give them the scent of lust and they'll move heaven and earth...'

'He'll have to move my stake before he moves heaven and earth,' chuckled Claude. 'When I hammer a stake into the ground, it stays hammered in. Now, was that all? I have work to do, you know, I can't stand about here talking all day. Us busy entrepreneurs have to make use of every minute of the day, just to keep our heads above water.'

'Right, I'll go, Claude, when you've bought a raffle ticket.'

'I've told you, I haven't any cash right now...'

'I see your truck's licence is overdue for renewal, Claude,' I smiled.

'Well, I might just have one book, then, for half a crown. It's in the house, my money, I mean. Just wait there and don't touch my goat.'

He returned with half a crown and I gave him raffle tickets, wishing him luck in the draw.

'You should have got nanny goats, Claude, and let them earn money for you. There's a big demand for goats' milk, for making cheese and for giving to invalids; it's very good for poorly people, Claude. You could make a good income – and you could breed from the nannies.'

'Aye, well, that's my long-term plan, you see. Breeding goats. When Oscar's settled in and got to know me and is friendly with Alfred, I'll introduce him to some nanny goats. He'll be at stud, you know, like a prize stallion. Or a bull. He'll earn his keep, Constable, you mark my words.'

I left Claude with his dreams of wealth and success, then continued my patrol. It was a quiet spell so far as police work was concerned and I managed to sell useful numbers of tickets for the Christmas raffle as I made my routine calls. It would be several nights later when I received a frantic telephone call from Mrs Roe at Heather Cottage. It was eleven o'clock and I was about to climb the stairs to bed, but I could not ignore the call.

'Aidensfield Police,' I announced.

'Jessie Roe, Mr Rhea, can you come? Somebody's trying to break my gates down!'

'I'll be with you in two minutes,' I assured her and after shouting upstairs to Mary with the news, I raced from the house and leapt into the Mini-van. I arrived at Mrs Roe's place within a couple of minutes and in the light from my vehicle headlights found Claude Jeremiah's billy goat repeatedly ramming the solid wooden gates with his head. He must have been there for ages. As I watched from the safety of my vehicle, I saw that a length of rope was attached to the goat's collar but that it had a frayed end. It looked as if Oscar had chewed through the rope to gain his freedom. For a moment, I wondered why Oscar was battering these high solid gates, then remembered that Mrs Roe kept nanny goats.

They were inside those gates and when I wound down the window, I could hear them bleating. The plaintive sounds served only to excite Oscar even more and encouraged him to batter the stout gates with even greater vigour. The problem was how to cope with Oscar when he was in such a determined mood. The loose end of rope offered what was perhaps the only solution, but if I tied him to the tree which stood nearby, he might chew through the rope again, and repeat his performance. And if I left the security of my van to physically discourage Oscar's lustful efforts by dragging him away, he would turn his violent attention to me and I had no desire to be butted by an angry and frustrated billy goat.

As I contemplated the scenario, I realized that the person responsible for this animal was Claude Jeremiah Greengrass, and so he should come and deal with it. But I felt it was necessary to provide the worried Mrs Roe with an explanation for the rumpus and the only way into her house was through those gates – and the goat was making sure I did not pass. I couldn't ring her from the police van and so, believing that Oscar would not stray from here, at least during the next few minutes, I returned home. It took only a minute or so. From there, I rang Mrs Roe to explain the hammering at her gates and to reassure her it was not a violent criminal wanting to rape or burgle her. I explained that I was on my way to get Claude to deal with the ramming raider and then drove out to the Greengrass ranch. I wondered if Claude would be in the pub, enjoying a late drinking session, but he wasn't; I caught him just after he'd climbed into bed and he was in his pyjamas when he responded to my heavy knocking.

'If you're selling more raffle tickets, I don't want any!' he spluttered. 'Why are you frightening the wits out of decent folks by knocking them up at this time of night?'

'Because your billy goat is frightening the wits out of decent people by knocking *them* up at this time of night,' I said.

'Oscar?' There was disbelief on Claude's whiskery face.

'He's down at Mrs Roe's, and if he's there for much longer, you're going to be faced with a big bill for the repair of her gates.'

'It's not Oscar, Constable, he's tied up. He'd never get loose from here.'

'He has, Claude, I've seen him. I think he's chewed through his rope. If you want to keep him on your premises, you'd better use a chain from now on, or lock him in a shed.'

'Somebody's let him loose, that's what. Vandals, folks wanting to get me in bother.'

'You'll be in deeper bother if you don't go and deal with him,' I said.

'I shouldn't have introduced him to Mrs Roe's nannies,' he muttered. 'It's gone and put ideas into his head ... will you give me a lift to Mrs Roe's?'

'I will, but I'm not running you back, nor

am I giving that goat a lift in my van. He's making a dreadful stink...'

'That's goat lust for you, Constable. Them lady goats love it. Hang on while I put some wellies on, and a top coat.'

I drove Claude to his reunion with Oscar who was still battering the gates with his head, and the animal's concentration on the job in hand was so intense that it enabled Claude to creep towards him in the light of my vehicle's headlamps and grab the loose end of the rope before the goat realized he'd been caught. Claude tugged it and shouted, 'Come on home, you daft bugger...'

The goat responded immediately. It was abundantly clear that Oscar did not wish to be interrupted during his courting ritual, and he turned towards Claude with his head down and his hooves hammering the tarmac of Mrs Roe's drive. It looked like the prelude to a bull fight. Claude ran. Somehow, he managed to retain a grip on the end of the rope and I saw him galloping along the street, weaving from side to side as he tried to dodge those terrible horns as the goat sought to wreak its revenge on Claude's ample rear portions. Within a few yards, however, Claude found the security of a lamp post and, dodging around it to keep the angry goat at a safe distance, he quickly wrapped his end of the rope around it while avoiding Oscar's head butts. In a few seconds, the goat was secured.

'You can't leave him there!' I shouted as I pulled up, still not leaving the safety of my van.

'Where else can I put him?' beseeched the panting Claude.

'In your compound ... if you run up the village, he'll follow you like a little dog; he'll not let you get away with this,' I laughed, and prepared to drive on as Claude dealt with his problem.

'He won't come quietly. He'll knock hell out of me ... look at those horns and that gleam in his eyes. He's mighty angry, Constable, can't you stay and help me?' he begged.

'Do you want to buy any more raffle tickets?' I asked.

'You can't expect me to fork out for raffle tickets every time I see you...'

'Good night, Claude,' I said, engaging first gear.

'All right, then. You win. Another book. Half-a-crown's worth.'

'Right,' I said. 'I'll reverse the van towards that tree with the rear doors open. I'll get as

71

close as I can, then I'll stop. You undo your end of the rope and get into the back of my van as fast as you can, keeping hold of the rope. Then shut the doors quick before Oscar has chance to leap in after you. That'll keep him outside at the end of the rope, won't it? With the closed doors between you and him.'

'I'm not letting him inside with me!' spluttered Claude.

'Right, but remember the doors won't shut properly because the rope will be in the way, so you'll have to hang onto the doors as well as the rope, and so long as you don't let go, you'll be safe inside and Oscar will be outside. Then I'll drive back to your place at walking speed – you keep hold of the rope and draw Oscar behind you. We'll have him back home in no time.'

And so the plan was put into operation and within minutes, we were back at the Greengrass ranch where Claude's only job was to get the goat inside a building of some kind.

He had plenty of spare outbuildings and persuading Oscar to enter one of them proved no problem because the animal was now docile. It seemed as if his amorous urges had evaporated and I watched with some relief as the door closed behind him.

'I'll see you tomorrow about the raffle tickets,' I said, grinning at Claude. 'Keep an eye on that goat of yours; keep him locked up otherwise you might have to buy more raffle tickets!'

During the next couple of weeks, Oscar managed to escape several more times. I have no idea of the actual number of explorations he achieved, but he made a return trip to visit Mrs Roe's nannies, he ate an entire cabbage patch in one garden, demolished the contents of a greenhouse in another, invaded the village shop, chewed some washing on a clothes line, and butted several ladies in the high street. Happily, they all complained to Claude, not me.

Then one Saturday night, I paid my usual duty visit to the pub and saw Claude at the bar with his cronies.

'Ah, Constable,' he hailed me. 'I've got some good news for you. That goat of mine, Oscar, I've got rid of him. He was too much of a handful, so he's gone. I thought you'd be pleased.'

'I am, so your scheme for breeding goats has ended, has it?'

'I think I'll stick to hens,' he chuckled. 'But old Arthur Robinson reckons he can

73

deal with Oscar.'

'Arthur at Lower Keld?'

'That's him. He's got plenty of space and he knows a thing or two about billy goats. I got two pounds for him, an' all. A bargain, I reckon – but I'm glad he's gone. He was getting to be a bit of a handful, you know.'

'So peace will reign in Aidensfield, Claude?'

'It will,' he smiled with some relief. It was shortly after receiving Claude's welcome news that the raffle for the Widows' and Orphans' Fund was drawn at the annual police Christmas dinner-dance in the Spa Ballroom at Strensford. There had been a good response with lots of tickets being sold and lots of useful prizes being donated. Mary and I went along to the dance, having secured the services of Mrs Quarry as baby-sitter for our four youngsters, and during the orchestra's meal break, we listened as the prize-winners were announced.

Other than the main prize, a week's holiday in Scarborough, it had been decided to pull the name of the other prizes out of a hat too. This was due to the large number of donations, many of similar value, and so as the name of each winner was announced, the master of ceremonies dipped his hand into a hat and extracted a card which identified the appropriate prize. Mary and I did not win anything, although a couple of people to whom I had sold tickets did win prizes – one got a bottle of whisky and another a meal for two at a Strensford restaurant. But the shock of the evening came when I heard the master of ceremonies announce, 'Claude Jeremiah Greengrass of Aidensfield. Ticket number 466. Is he here?'

'No.' I stood up and caught his attention by waving my hand. 'No, Mr Greengrass is not here, but I am PC Rhea, the Aidensfield constable. I can make sure he gets the prize.'

'All right, PC Rhea,' said the MC. 'Let's see what he has won.'

He dipped his hand into the hat and pulled out a card bearing the name of the prize. 'This is a late prize, donated by a Mr Arthur Robinson of Lower Keld. One billy goat in prime condition. You'll inform Mr Greengrass, will you, PC Rhea? The goat will be delivered free of charge.'

'I'll tell him to expect it very soon,' I said, thinking it might be best if Oscar was delivered while Claude was out. That would be a nice surprise for him. But I didn't think he'd ever buy another raffle ticket from me.

3

One Thursday morning, I popped into Aidensfield shop-cum-post office to buy a book of stamps and was in time to see the proprietor, Joe Steel, loading his small green van. He was stacking the rear section with boxes of groceries and seemed to be making hard work of the chore. He was slightly breathless and perspiring with the effort.

"Morning, Joe,' I greeted him. 'Off on your rounds, are you?'

'My weekly delivery to outlying farms and houses, Nick,' he panted, pausing to straighten and ease the ache in his back.

'There's not many village stores do that any more,' I commented.

'No, but I think it's important and I know it's appreciated,' he smiled. 'It's a service started by my predecessor. I make nothing from it – in fact it costs me money to continue it – but it helps the old folks and those who can't get into the village for various reasons. But it's hard work, all this heavy lifting. It gets tougher by the week.

I've got to the stage where I'm thinking of retiring. It's days like this, with all those heavy boxes to load and then unload, that makes me think I'm getting too old for this sort of thing.'

'Rubbish! You've years of good service left in you and besides, the place wouldn't be the same without you,' I said. 'But if this side of the job is too much, you could always give up these deliveries. They're almost a luxury these days and stopping them would make things easier for you.'

'I know; it's expensive and time consuming, and it means finding someone to look after the shop while I'm out, but some of my customers depend on it. I can't overlook the fact that it wins me customers who might decide to shop somewhere else. I cover a very wide area, Nick, and the goodwill is important to me. I still do two deliveries a week – Tuesdays and Thursdays.'

'It's a question of finding the right balance, I suppose.' I could understand his dilemma. 'Giving up something worthwhile is never an easy decision to make. I suppose you could consider a small charge for this service.'

'It's a thought, but I wouldn't want to stop

my deliveries. They're part of the service I provide, but humping these boxes around does give me twinges and back ache. Seriously, Nick, Betty and I are considering retirement. We're approaching retirement age and our dream is to sell this place and move to the coast. In a few months' time, I mean, not immediately. Strensford maybe, or even Filey.'

'Well, I must admit lifting heavy loads is something I wouldn't want to do if I was nearing retirement. But I do know your efforts are appreciated, Joe, and you will be missed if you leave here.'

'I'll be passing the word around any time now, Nick, so it's no secret. If you know anyone who wants to buy a post office and thriving village store, well, tell them to get in touch. I'll be happy to talk business.'

'It's odd you should mention that,' I said. 'Sergeant Blaketon was saying only recently that he fancied a post office when he retired.'

'You chaps retire early, don't you?' Joe commented.

'Constables and sergeants have to retire when they reach fifty-five,' I explained. 'Inspectors and those of higher rank can stay on until they're sixty, although it is

79

possible for some officers to be granted an extension of service, usually one year at a time. Whether or not that is approved usually depends on their health.'

'So, provided his health holds out, Sergeant Blaketon could battle on until he's sixty?' smiled Joe. 'I can't see him wanting to take on something like a post office or shop at that age.'

'Not many of us want to stay on with an extended period of service,' I told him. 'After plodding the beat for thirty years or so, we're usually glad of a rest and a change. What most of our officers do is find a cosy little job of some kind, just to give them a reason for getting out of bed on a morning during their retirement. Nothing too demanding.'

'Well, I can't say a shop and post office is very relaxing, but it's not too difficult for a fit person, so if the post office idea appeals to Blaketon, tell him to get in touch. If he wants the place and is willing to give me a firm commitment, it'll mean I don't have to advertise it.'

Joe closed his doors and drove away to complete his deliveries while I went in and bought my book of stamps from Betty, his wife. The church clock was striking ten when I emerged and today was my day for patrolling the area around Crampton village. I had my flask of coffee and some sandwiches in the van and would spend a full day's duty in and around that area.

I'd be checking some stock registers on local farms, arranging the renewal of firearms certificates on others and attending to various other duties. One of those duties was the never-ending crime prevention advice we provided, and I know many people took not the slightest bit of notice. In that respect, while visiting farms on my patch, I made a point of warning the house-holders about a current series of unsettling raids which were taking place in our area. They'd been prevalent over the past year or so, and comprised spasmodic raids on isolated farm-houses while the owners were out. The only common factor, apart from the fact the target premises were all farms, was that the attacks were always on a local market day. It had long been customary for a farmer and his wife to vacate their premises for a day to attend the local market, whether it was a livestock or fruit and vegetable market.

Although this was part of their work, when many of them bought and sold their produce, it was also regarded as a relaxing day out but it meant that the premises were left unattended for most of the day. Many farmers never locked their doors which meant that thieves could take almost any-thing they wished, whether it was something from the outbuildings like tools and equipment, or something from the house like a grandfather clock, antique chair, valuable piece of pottery or even jewellery and consumer items like television sets and radios. As a consequence of the market-day raids, as they became known, it was our continuing policy to warn farmers about them, advising them to lock their doors, safeguard their valuables and report any suspicious people or vehicles wandering around their land. Ideally, someone should remain on the premises throughout the day.

Our criminal intelligence network had identified two suspects – a couple of brothers called Starling, Derek and Kevin, who were in their thirties and who lived together on a smallholding on the outskirts of Galtreford. We had never been able to secure any positive proof of their activities, certainly not enough to present to a court of law to ensure their conviction. The brothers had been interviewed countless times and always denied any involvement with the market-day raids and in spite of repeated searches of their premises, not one piece of identifiable stolen property had been found in their possession. They were very clever thieves and appeared either to have fast outlets for the stuff they stole, or a secure place of storage well away from their home. We suspected they had a lock-up of some kind which they used to accommodate their stolen items. one which did not appear to be associated with them. There were lots of likely places in the area – disused barns, lock-up garages for rent, deserted buildings, abandoned hangars on former airfields but we had never traced any of them to the brothers' possession. The brothers knew we were interested in their activities and if we had placed a tail on any of their vehicles, they had always managed to dodge it.

Today, I would maintain my usual observations for the Starling brothers because it was Eltering market day – and Crampton was within easy driving distance of that market town. Apart from that on-going problem, the only other outstanding matter was a statement which I had to obtain from a lady in Crampton village – she'd witnessed a hit-and-run traffic accident while shopping in Leeds and had left her name and address with the victim.

Leeds City Police had asked me to interview her. It promised to be a quiet and very routine day's duty.

It was early that same Thursday afternoon, around 2.30, that the radio in my van burbled into life with my call sign and I responded.

'Delta Alpha Two Six receiving,' I acknowledged.

'Delta Alpha Two Six, location please,' said the unmistakeable voice of Sergeant Blaketon from Ashfordly Police Station.

'Crampton village,' I responded. 'Stationary outside the primary school.'

'Delta Alpha Two Six,' continued Blaketon. 'I have received a call from Mrs Steel at Aidensfield post office. It seems her husband has not returned from delivering groceries to his customers; he was expected back around half-past twelve and she has had no word. Two of the farms on his round are near Crampton; she's rung them but got no reply. I've rung too, but got no response, they might be out at market or working down the fields. As you are in the area, could you check? She's worried because he always rings her if he's going to be late home and in any case she thought he wasn't feeling too well this morning. He was complaining of back ache. I know this isn't within the normal scope of our duties, Rhea, but I'm sure we can accommodate this modest request.'

'Two Six to Control. No problem, will co,' I acknowledged, wondering if poor old Joe had suffered a heart attack or crashed his van or worse. 'Which are the farms?'

'Throstle Nest, the Bartrams' place, and Aspen Hall, Appleby's place.'

'I know them,' I confirmed, then finished the transmission with, 'Delta Alpha Two Six out.'

I had not visited either of these premises today and as Throstle Nest was the closer of the two, I drove there first. The well-surfaced lane leading to the farm rose steeply from the riverside road about a mile out of Crampton when travelling towards Lower Keld. It crossed a couple of rising fields, none of which had anyone working in them, before dipping into the hollow in which the beautiful mellow stone farmhouse was situated. This farm was clean and well maintained, specializing in wheat and barley rather than dairy produce and livestock, and as I drove into the yard, I could see the place was deserted. There was no immediate sign of Joe's van either. It seemed that Alan and Ruth Bartram were out, but I parked on their forecourt and walked around the deserted buildings, calling their names and looking for any sign of Joe Steel. I searched for his van, wondering if he had parked it behind the house to unload his box of groceries directly into a lobby or outbuilding but he was nowhere to be seen. Eventually, however, I did find a box of groceries tucked under a seat in the porch which graced the back door. Clearly, Joe had been and gone while the family were out and I was satisfied he was not still here.

The second farm, Aspen Hall, lay some distance away. It involved a drive of about twenty minutes and, in spite of its rather grand name, this was an average sized working farm with a double-fronted stone house almost hidden among cattle sheds and barns. Lots of local farms were called Hall.

Aspen Hall stood high on the moors above Crampton in a somewhat exposed position so far as the weather was concerned although the buildings themselves were concealed from the approach road by a dense barrier of Scots pines and spruces.

The road to the farm was a long, twisting and rather narrow lane, neatly tarmacadamed but weaving between dry-stone walls for almost a mile before it emerged into the farmyard. This farm, which belonged to Dick and Grace Appleby, was more traditional than Throstle Nest for it had a range of livestock including some Highland Cattle, Aberdeen Angus beasts and dairy Friesians as well as sheep, pigs and poultry. Although I could see the farm buildings behind the curtain of trees, they were indistinct from this distance and I lost sight of them several times as I traversed the dipping and rising track into Aspen Hall.

Soon, however, I was approaching the cluster of buildings but the yard was at the far side of the complex; I could not see from this approach whether or not Joe's van was there, but soon I was rounding the corner past the eastern end of the house and noticed Joe's distinctive green van in the yard. It appeared to be parked perfectly normally, but as I eased to a halt beside it, I saw that its rear doors were standing wide open and it contained a solitary box of groceries. But I could not see Joe anywhere. My first reaction was that he was inside the house, perhaps chatting after having had lunch with the Applebys; inviting visitors to stay for a meal was a perfectly normal gesture by the farmers of this region, but it was odd that Joe had not notified his wife and odd that he had left his van doors standing open.

I went to the back door of the farmhouse – farmers of this region rarely used their front doors – and it was standing open. Then I saw the signs of a break-in. A jemmy had been used to force open this door and its marks were in the woodwork.

'Dick? Grace?' Without touching the evidence on the woodwork, I hurriedly stepped inside and called their names. There was nothing, merely a deathly silence. 'Joe?'

A feeling of impending doom swept over me at that stage and the hairs on the back of my neck stood on end; I had no idea what I might find although the only vehicle in the yard was Joe's little van. It seemed the villains had departed – there was no other vehicle in the yard and I'd not passed any on the drive up to the farm. There is always a feeling of helplessness in these cases, but I knew I had to make a provisional search of the premises, just in case the thief or thieves were hiding. First, though, I radioed

Ashfordly Police Station from my van. They had to know my location just in case I suffered some form of attack. When I explained the situation, Sergeant Blaketon said he would come immediately and bring PC Alf Ventress with him. He'd also notify the Scenes of Crime department and instruct them to attend.

As it would take about twenty minutes for Blaketon to reach the farm, I knew I had to make an immediate search of the house on my own. It was, of necessity, a cursory inspection because the full scientific examination would be done by the Scenes of Crime officers, but I had to try and establish what had happened here, then find Joe, Dick and Grace. I had to know if this raid had been completed or whether Joe had interrupted it.

With a range of concerns on my mind, that hurried search told me the raiders had succeeded in entering the house; drawers were standing open, cupboard doors were standing wide, clothing was scattered across the floors, glass cabinets had been forced ... there was a lot of damage and distress but no sign of Joe, Dick or Grace.

At this stage, I had no idea what had been stolen – judging by the intruders' areas of search, it looked as if the thieves had been targeting jewellery or money, but the furnishings of this farm included some fine pottery and glassware, both antique and modern, and there was some beautiful antique furniture, large and small. I had to try and locate the owners as soon as possible, but human life is more important than goods and chattels and so I turned my attention to the outbuildings. As I hurried across the yard where I'd parked, I noticed an odd thing – a smashed bottle of tomato ketchup lying on the ground, but I left it alone for the time being as I continued my search. Minutes later, I found Joe. He was lying on a bed of hay on the floor of a loosebox with his hands and feet bound with rope, and a gag over his mouth.

'Joe!' I called his name and quickly went to him, realizing he was conscious. As rapidly as I could, I loosened the gag, then the ropes.

'Thank God...' he croaked. 'I thought I was a goner, Nick. I thought nobody was going to come...'

'Rub your hands and feet,' I said before quizzing him. 'Stand up and stamp around for a minute or so, get your circulation moving.'

'I was getting pins and needles...'

'How long have you been here?' I asked, wondering how long a lead the villains might have gained.

'Just before twelve,' he said. 'I thought I'd get this last delivery done, then get back in time for lunch.'

'They'll be miles away by now, but you need a hot drink,' I told him as he stomped and marched around the place, clapping his hands and stamping his feet.

'We can't use the farm's kitchen, we might contaminate the scene of the crime, but I've some coffee left in my flask. Come and sit in my van until the others get here, and tell me what happened. What about seeing a doctor, Joe? Are you injured at all?'

'No, just a bit shaken. I got a thump on the head but it hasn't drawn blood. No, I don't need a doctor. Thanks for asking.'

Under my gentle questioning, Joe told me that he'd driven into the yard and noticed an old ambulance standing there. Thinking something had happened to Dick or Grace, he was about to approach the back door when two men rushed out of the house carrying chairs. Within seconds, they had been placed in the ambulance which was parked close to the back door. As Joe was

91

endeavouring to make up his mind whether these were legitimate furniture removers or not, he saw the break-in marks and realized he had stumbled upon a couple of housebreakers in action. He'd then decided to stop them, but they had regained their vehicle, started the engine and were moving off. In a desperate attempt to stop them, he'd grabbed the first available thing and threw it.

It happened to be a bottle of tomato ketchup from the box of groceries in the back of his van and he flung it after the departing vehicle; it hit the side and smashed, but at that point, instead of continuing to race away, the ambulance stopped. Both men got out and came for him. He tried to gain the security of his own van, but they caught him, thumped him over the head and hauled him into the loosebox where they managed to tie him up.

'Did they say anything?' I asked.

'One of them said they had to get away before the alarm was raised. That's why they tied me up. I couldn't do anything, couldn't ring anybody but I got their number and think I would recognize them again if I saw them.'

'It's probably carrying false number

plates,' I said. 'Was there anything unusual about their truck?'

'Just the fact it looked like an old ambulance, a sort of pale-tan colour,' he said. 'With all the rear seats and internal things removed.'

'And it will have a tomato ketchup stain on it now!' I laughed. 'Where did the bottle hit it, exactly?'

'The nearside, near the window closest to the back. It hit the frame of the window, and I saw some run down the side of the window and onto the bodywork.'

'Even if they clean it off,' I said, 'there might be residue in the window seals. Let's hope so. Now, let's see if our patrols can come across the ambulance, although I think it will have gone to ground by now. You'll have put the wind up them!'

I wrote down the registration number he had provided and then radioed Ashfordly Control Room with a request that an immediate search be made for the old ambulance and the two men, whose descriptions I obtained from Joe. I reminded Control about the Starling brothers and suggested an immediate visit to their premises at Galtreford, albeit knowing it would be difficult to prove they were in possession of stolen property when we did not, at that stage, know what had been taken. We must also establish whether or not either of the brothers owned an old ambulance. While speaking to Ashfordly Police, I suggested the duty constable ring the secretary at Eltering Cattle Mart and make a tannoy appeal for Mr and Mrs Appleby. If they responded, the message was to return home immediately; I did not want the contents of the message to be made public. The kind of trauma generated by such a vague message was best left to the individuals to deal with.

Sergeant Blaketon and Alf Ventress arrived very quickly and I briefed them on my actions. After convincing himself that Joe was not in need of immediate medical attention, Blaketon had a chat with him about his role in these events, and then a message on my radio announced that the Applebys had been traced at Eltering market and would be home within half an hour. They arrived around the same time as the Scenes of Crime teams and suddenly the farmhouse was a whirl of activity as the unfortunate couple began to realize the full extent of what had happened in their home. It was then that Blaketon came over to me.

'I think you'd better take Mr Steel home,

Rhea,' he said. 'We can fetch his van along later. And I'd get a doctor to see him, just to give him a brief examination, we don't want any broken skulls or concussion to go unchecked. Better to be safe than sorry.'

Joe agreed. He was now feeling rather shaken as the shock of his experience began to intensify and so I placed him in my Mini-van and returned him to Aidensfield. As I pulled up outside the post office, his wife rushed out to meet us, looking harassed and distraught. During all the fuss, I'd forgotten to ring her to say what had happened or even to tell her I'd found Joe, but I did say that her husband had been a hero and he'd tell her all about his adventure. I suggested she called a doctor to give Joe an examination and she assured me she would do that. Having returned him to his beloved, I went back to the farm where Dick and Grace were doing their best to make an assessment of what had been stolen. Once their list was complete, my job would be to circulate details to all local police officers, neighbouring police forces, antique dealers and second-hand shops and any other outlet which might deal in stolen property.

I was there for a while as the couple made their tearful assessment of the loss and it seemed that most of the stolen property comprised antique furnishings like chairs and side tables, along with pottery and glassware, but some of Grace's jewellery had also been taken – a diamond ring, a pair of diamond ear-rings and six necklaces. The total value of the haul began to approach £1,000, an enormous loss in the 1960s.

But there was a happy outcome. Thanks to Joe's timely and spirited intervention with a bottle of tomato ketchup, a team of detectives visited the smallholding of the Starling brothers and there they found an old ambulance, albeit not bearing the registration number that had been noted by Joe at Aspen Hall. The Starling brothers denied being at Aspen Hall, and the number borne by the vehicle seen by Joe, we were to discover, had been allocated to a motor cycle in Lincolnshire. It began to look as if we'd be unable yet again to prove their involvement.

However, when our detectives examined the side of the ambulance, they found traces of tomato ketchup. Although the metalwork had been washed, traces were adhering to the rubber surrounds of the rear nearside window, and that residue was later found to match the control sample from Joe's well-aimed bottle. A tiny amount had oozed down between the glass and the rubber surround – and we found it. Thus we could prove that that particular vehicle had been at the scene of that crime and afterwards, when news of the raid hit the local papers, an anonymous tip-off came from someone who'd been angry at their treatment of Joe. That call revealed the whereabouts of an old barn used by the Starling brothers. And there, most of the stolen antiques were recovered – the thieves had not dared to dispose of them due to our intervention and the resultant publicity. The only objects we did not trace were Mrs Appleby's jewellery. Later, Joe identified the thieves during an identification parade. The Starlings were convicted of the Aspen Hall raid and several more, evidence of which was also recovered in the barn, and each was sentenced to three years in prison.

And it was all due to Joe's bottle of tomato sauce.

I was talking to him some time later and he said, 'You know, Nick, I'm not cut out for that kind of excitement. I've made my mind up – I'm definitely going to retire so if Sergeant Blaketon wants a post office to keep him busy until he's an old-age pensioner, ask him to give me a call.'

A couple of days after that chat with Joe, I met Sergeant Blaketon. He congratulated me yet again on my part in the conviction of the Starlings and said he was going to see Joe, too, to pass on the chief constable's gratitude for his actions.

'While you're there, Sergeant,' I said, 'Joe has something else to tell you.'

'Really, Rhea? What's that?'

'I think he should be the one to reveal it,' I smiled.

'You're being too mysterious for my liking, Rhea, but if it's anything to do with publicizing the forensic value of a bottle of tomato ketchup, I don't want to know...'

Apropos a sauce bottle being involved in the detection of a crime, there was another persistent and rather frustrating series of bottle-associated thefts in Aidensfield. It wasn't so much the bottles that were being stolen, however, it was their contents, although I must admit that we did not recover either the stolen bottles or their contents.

Late one autumn, I received reports that a thief was stealing bottles of milk from the doorsteps of the village houses during the early hours of the morning.

The crimes were by no means committed on a regular basis and in spite of keeping observations whenever I could, the bottles continued to disappear. Other officers who patrolled occasionally through Aidensfield also kept observations as did the villagers themselves, especially the victims. In addition, I received great co-operation from the milkman who delivered the bottles, but in spite of these joint efforts, the milk continued to disappear.

From my point of view, the difficulty was that the thefts did not follow any identifiable pattern. If the milk had been stolen, say, every Wednesday morning between 6 a.m. and 7 a.m., it would have been easy to arrange the necessary surveillance to catch the culprit red-handed, but I received one report of a bottle vanishing on a Monday, another on a Wednesday and another on a Friday. These were all within the same week. Then the following week there were no thefts. Two further weeks followed with no reported thefts and I thought the epidemic was over, then a bottle vanished one Tuesday. There were no more thefts that particular week and none the following week either and the erratic nature of the crimes made detection almost impossible. Even if I lurked in the main street every morning to watch for the culprit, it seemed only a slice of luck would bring him to justice. It was arguable whether the thefts were serious enough to justify the expense of maintaining police patrols in the main street every morning for weeks on end for the sake of one or two missing pints of milk, and, besides, even a permanent vigil could not guarantee supervision of the entire length of the street. There was no static position from which I could secretly observe everyone who used it at that time of day.

And, of course, my presence, however carefully I tried to conceal myself, could alert the thief and so he'd refrain from committing his crime that day. Whilst that would prevent the crime, it would not catch the thief. That eventuality was, of course, a possible option – the prevention of crime is an important part of our duty, but there is great job satisfaction in actually bringing a culprit to justice. That is what I wanted to do.

Our milkman, Harry Fletcher, began his deliveries at the western end of the village at 6 a.m. and worked his way along the entire length of the main street to conclude that section of his deliveries around 7 a.m. or just afterwards. During that time he did, of course, divert from the main street many times to deliver along narrow alleys and quiet lanes, or to hurry around to houses tucked away behind those which fronted the street. This routine meant he was not on the main street during the whole of that critical hour. In fact, when we worked out just how much time he actually spent on the main street each morning, it amounted to little more than half an hour during which, of course, he was fully occupied.

His frequent absences, however short, allowed sufficient time for the thief to zoom into Aidensfield, commit his crime and vanish without anyone seeing him. It took a matter of seconds to pick up a bottle of milk. It was clear to us that when Harry was in the street rattling his crates, the thief would be aware of the fact and would refrain from committing his crimes if he was within possible sight of the milkman. Another factor was that it was dark between 6 a.m. and 7 a.m. on those mornings.

Harry had no idea who the thief might be – several cars and vans passed through Aidensfield in those early hours but apart from the local people, he did not know any of them and none of the vehicles stopped when he was around. It might be that Harry was himself an unwitting deterrent because, in the darkness, his milk float was well illuminated and he made a good deal of recognizable and acceptable noise with his bottles. People certainly knew when he was around.

I was not sure how long this series of crimes had been running because, in the first few cases, the vanishing bottles were not regarded as thefts. Harry was accused of forgetting to leave the required milk and, in order not to antagonize his customers, he simply apologized and replaced the missing pints. At the outset, those early crimes were not reported to me and so they were not recorded even though Harry insisted he was not at fault.

Eventually, he came to see me and I suggested that every time he received a report of a missing bottle, he asked the loser to report it to me. From that point, most of them did report their losses although some did not want to make an official complaint about such a small matter. I suspected I did not have the complete picture. I was sure milk was being stolen without me knowing about it and that did not help me solve the

problem. However, I appreciated that someone was persistently stealing pints of milk
from the doorsteps of Aidensfield. Due to
other duties, it was impossible for me to
spend every morning on Aidensfield's main
street but I was determined to detect this
nuisance and bring the crimes to an end, if
only for my own satisfaction and, of course,
to maintain my professional image!

As autumn turned into winter, with Harry
and me maintaining our observations
whenever we could, the crimes continued at
unpredictable intervals and with frustrating
success. I decided to analyse the reports. I
had a record of every pint which had been
reported stolen and started work with a
large-scale map of Aidensfield. Every house
was marked upon it and I stuck a red paper
dot on every address from which milk had
been taken. Perhaps I ought to add here that
the pint bottles of the 1960s were shaped
differently from those we used in the 1990s
– they were taller with longer necks and not
so dumpy as the latter ones.

I wrote the day and date of the crime
beside each dot. One thing struck me immediately – some houses had suffered more
than one theft. Others had suffered none.
Next, I drew a chart on a piece of lined

paper; the down column on the left was the address of those houses already targeted, with ample space to add more when necessary. Across the top of the sheet, I incorporated other factors – the date and day of the week and the time at which the milk had been taken, the amount stolen, the number of bottles delivered to each address, sightings of suspects, any sounds of vehicles stopping or starting in the street and even the state of the weather. One thing we policemen kept in our pocket books was a brief note of the weather on every day of our duty, along with lighting-up times. Such a simple running record had proved immensely useful on many occasions, and this was one example.

As I was working on my analysis chart, the telephone rang. It was Sergeant Blaketon.

'Rhea,' he bellowed into the mouthpiece, 'I have just returned to duty after my holiday. I thought things would have ticked over nicely in my absence; I thought the explosion of crime in Aidensfield would have been brought to a satisfactory end, but what do I find? I find that crime is still soaring. There is a raging epidemic of crime on your beat and that means it affects Ashfordly section's statistics as well, and our divisional figures. Need I say more? It looks as if we are losing control, Rhea. Twelve crimes reported in the last month! That is a crime wave of great magnitude, Rhea. My quarterly return is due and our undetected crime rate is going to appear horrendous. It looks as if we are not doing our job. Headquarters will want to know what's going on in Aidensfield, Rhea. So might I ask what you are doing about it?'

'It's all pints of milk, Sergeant,' I explained. 'One crime per bottle. It's not such a serious crime wave as it appears.'

'When my returns arrive on the chief constable's desk at Force headquarters, Rhea, they will not differentiate between murders and stolen bottles of milk. They're all crimes, Rhea, all figures on a piece of official paper. That is what will concern him and, I might add, it will also concern the Home Office when they compile and analyse those figures. They – and he – will see that crimes in Aidensfield have rocketed and questions will be asked.'

'I do have the matter in hand, Sergeant. I am investigating the reports, trying to analyse the figures and the relevant factors involved...'

'Rhea, I don't know what you are talking

about. Analyse what figures? This is theft we are talking about, a series of thefts in fact, some villain nicking bottles of milk from under your very nose, Rhea. You don't need an analysis for that. You need to get your backside off that chair and get into the street at the crack of dawn and stay there until you've felt his collar. Wait until he's nicking the stuff and catch him red-handed. That's good real evidence for the courts, Rhea. That's how thieves are caught. You make the best use of good, positive, practical policing with a few collars being felt from time to time, not sitting in offices poring over statistics...'

'I'm doing this research in my own time, Sergeant,' I told him quietly.

There was a slight delay and I thought he'd rung off, then he said, 'Well, commendable though that is, it doesn't absolve you from getting your backside off that chair and into the street to do your duty, Rhea. Police work means plodding the beat and nicking thieves. I want this thief caught before our crime figures go through the roof.'

'Yes, Sergeant.' I knew better than to argue and equally I knew he would have no time for my theories. There were occasions I felt that some police officers worried more about their crime statistics than they did about the effect of crime on the public.

However, my efforts did produce something interesting. First, all the thefts had occurred during fine weather, albeit in autumn and winter conditions. Secondly, all the thefts had occurred towards the western end of the village. Indeed, it was possible to draw a line across the village street with a crime-free zone at one side –the east – and a crime-ridden area on the other – the west. I felt that was significant. Thirdly, no one had seen or heard any suspect person or vehicle, the only noises being that of the occasional motor vehicle passing through Aidensfield without stopping, and of course, the clink of Harry's bottles as he went about his deliveries. If a motorist stopped to steal a pint, someone would have heard the vehicle draw to a halt and drive away afterwards. No such noises had been heard. This made me wonder if the thief lived in Aidensfield to make his forays on foot, or of course, a pedal cycle could be involved. The other factors were that only one pint was stolen on every occasion; furthermore, and somewhat curiously, it was stolen only from an address where a single pint had been delivered. Addresses where two or more pints were delivered had not been targeted. I thought that was odd. And the stolen milk had always been taken between a Monday and a Friday, the five days of a normal working week. There had been no thefts on Saturdays or Sundays – milk was then delivered on Saturdays and Sundays. In my opinion, it suggested the thefts were committed by someone on his way to work – or on her way to work. An early-morning worker. No empty bottles had been found discarded and so it seemed the thief carried the bottle and contents to work – on a bicycle perhaps? I knew it was possible to carry milk bottles in the drinks containers that sporting cyclists attached to the down tube of their machines – these usually contained fruit juice and the rider would reach down while riding, haul the metal container from its resting place, sip the drink through a straw, and replace it without halting the cycle to dismount. I'd done so myself during my cycling days. Could a bottle of milk be carried like that? I felt sure it could.

I tried to think of anyone in the village who had a sporting cycle and who rode it to work at that time of day, but I did not know of anyone. There were, of course, many people in the village who did not go off to work and who might sneak out of the house in the early hours to help themselves to someone else's milk.

However, with these thoughts in my mind and armed with the information I had assembled, my first task was to walk the length of the village street to reappraise the site of each theft. I wanted to look at those places from which the milk had been stolen. My walk confirmed that all the victims' houses were facing the street – none of the stolen milk had been removed from houses tucked away up alleys or away from the front street. But, when looking critically at the victims' houses, another factor struck me. All the houses from which milk had been stolen had front doorsteps which led directly onto the footpath; many protruded onto the path and I'd had reports of people tripping over them in the darkness. Was this significant? I went to see Harry Fletcher and discussed my findings with him. It meant nothing to him, other than to confirm that he began his deliveries at the west end at 6 a.m. By 6.30, he'd be roughly halfway along the street ... I wondered if his 6.30 position was anywhere near my halfway mark. I then referred to the doorsteps.

'Do you put the bottles on the doorsteps, Harry, or down beside them?'

'Do you know, I can't rightly remember,' he grinned sheepishly. 'It's the sort of thing I do automatically. I usually place 'em where there's some empties waiting. But yes, I'd say I put the full bottles on the steps, not on the pavement or down beside the steps. That means I don't have to bend over more than necessary.'

'Right, Harry. Now, if it's fine tomorrow morning, can I come on your round with you?'

'Aye, 'course you can, Nick.'

'I want you to behave exactly as you normally do, putting the bottles in exactly the same places as you always do. Forget me, I'll lurk behind you, somewhere in the darkness.'

'It sounds like a bit of Sherlock Holmes to me, Nick, but yes, anything to catch this character. He's making my life hell, folks are saying I'm not leaving their orders and I have to give 'em another!'

'I have a theory,' I told him. 'I won't bore you with it now, but I'll bring my van into the village. I'll hide it out of sight before you begin your deliveries, but I want it close at hand in case I've got to chase our thief!'

'You think you might nab him, then?'

'With a bit of luck,' I said.

And so our plans were made. I was due to work an early turn tomorrow so I would normally be starting at 6 a.m. I warmed to my task, went to bed early and set the alarm for 5.15. By half-past five, I had driven into the village from my hilltop police house, parked my van out of sight and was hiding in the shadows at the western end of Aidensfield. I remained out of sight as Harry began his deliveries. At six o'clock he began popping some pints onto doorsteps, some into doorways, some onto window ledges and even some behind garden walls. I noted where every pint was placed, particularly in those cases where only a single bottle was delivered.

As Harry moved along the street with the chink of bottles and the lights of his van marking his progress, I made my way just behind him, albeit in the shadows. A few cars, vans and lorries passed along the street, but none stopped. I saw no pedestrians or cyclists and by half-past six, Harry had reached the point which I regarded as the halfway mark. Beyond that point, not a single bottle of milk had been stolen. It looked as if this was going to be another abortive observation exercise. I watched Harry move his van stage by stage further down the street, eventually parking on the garage forecourt as he delivered to a few houses in that vicinity, and I decided not to follow him any further. After all, no thefts had occurred from this point eastwards.

It was now time to walk back along the street and to check for the presence of every bottle that had been delivered. But when I reached Daleside Cottage, the pint was missing from its doorstep. I had seen Harry leave a pint there – the step jutted into the footpath which ran along the street – and now the milk had gone. And I'd not seen or heard a thing! There were no lights in the house – I tried the door and it was locked. I didn't think the residents had taken it in, but I did not want to rouse them this early; they were a pair of pensioners called Mr and Mrs Ingram – and I guessed what had happened. The thief had emerged as Harry had disappeared around the corner on his way to park on the garage forecourt; he'd nicked the milk from the Ingrams' doorstep and had headed west. That meant he would not pass Harry. I knew the thief had not used one of the incoming vehicles – I'd have heard it stop and pull away, so it had to be a pedal cyclist who was now heading west. I decided to drive westwards out of Aidensfield.

I hurried to my van and began my drive and there, on the road out to Maddleskirk, I found a pedal cyclist heading in the same direction. He was dressed in working clothes but his machine was a sports model with low-slung handlebars and it was bearing the correct lights. As I eased out to overtake him, I saw the bottle of milk in the wire drinks carrier on the downtube. I had found my thief. I halted ahead of him, switched on the blue light and caused him to stop. He did so without any trouble. After identifying myself and explaining the purpose of my action, I asked, 'So where did you get that bottle of milk?'

He looked at me steadily and knew there was no benefit in lying.

'I was going to pay,' he said. 'I was going to get some money from the bank today...'

'Get in the van!' I ordered him. 'And your bike – and I'll take care of that milk.'

'I have to start work at seven,' he said. 'At the bacon factory...'

'Not this morning,' I told him. 'You're

under arrest for larceny and we're going to Ashfordly Police Station.'

'Look, Constable, it's only a pint of milk for God's sake, I haven't broken into a bank or robbed an old lady...'

'You can tell that to the court,' I gave him the traditional answer. I drove to Ashfordly Police Station and arrived just after seven where everything was in darkness.

I hauled on the doorbell pull, knowing it would ring in Sergeant Blaketon's house which adjoined the station, and soon he appeared, bleary-eyed but having managed to drag on his uniform trousers and shirt.

'Rhea? What is it? It's seven o'clock in the morning...'

'I'm going to make your day, Sergeant. It's a wonderful start for you. I've a prisoner ... the milk thief.'

'You have? Well, you'd better bring him in and we'll see about charging him. You might put the kettle on as well, my mouth's as dry as a desert.'

The thief was a nineteen-year-old youth called Ben Marshall from York who had secured a job in the local bacon factory and who was using weekday lodgings with a distant cousin in Aidensfield. He had started his work only in September and had chosen to cycle to work when the weather was fine – if it was wet, he declined and used his old car so that he wouldn't arrive at work in something of a wet mess. There was nowhere at work to dry his clothes. When he cycled, however, he often found he had no time for breakfast before leaving and had developed the habit of stealing a pint of milk to drink *en route*. He rode his cycle along the footpath, grabbed a bottle as he passed a protruding doorstep, stuffed in into the metal carrier on his cycle frame to drink while riding. He had chosen solitary pints because if he tried to grab one bottle from a clutch of two or more while riding past, he might misjudge his actions and send the other bottles flying. He could cope with a single bottle in absolute silence. Because his digs were halfway along Aidensfield main street, behind the street's frontage, he emerged from an alley and turned west.

Harry had never seen the youth because he was always at the other end of the village when the lad made his appearance, but when we presented our records to Marshall, he admitted stealing every one of those missing pints. Harry was most relieved when I told him the outcome of that little operation – he said he could tell his customers his memory was not defective, and he was not inefficient.

'I'll tell you what, Rhea,' said Sergeant Blaketon, when the court hearing was over, 'by letting us take all his previous crimes into consideration, young Marshall has done wonders for our crime figures. Our detection rate has soared this month, Rhea. We've a wonderful clear-up rate to report. Well done.'

'I'm glad we caught him, Sergeant.'

'It just shows the value of good old-fashioned police work, Rhea,' beamed Blaketon. 'There's no substitute for bobbies on the beat when it comes to detecting crime. Backsides off chairs, feeling a few collars ... it works every time.'

'You're absolutely right, Sergeant,' I smiled.

'Now, Rhea,' he said, 'there is another rather personal matter and I would appreciate your absolute discretion here. What can you tell me about the post office in Aidensfield?'

4

One of the more puzzling aspects of the North York Moors is the reason for the large number of standing stones which dominate the bleak heather-covered landscape. These comprise waymarkers, religious crosses, parish boundary signs, the outer limits of large estates, disused gateposts, the remains of stone circles and other earthworks, memorials ancient and modern, relics of former buildings, natural outcrops of rock and a host of other edifices, the origins or purpose of which have sometimes been lost in time. It is a fact that these moors, in the north-east corner of Yorkshire, boast the largest known collection of standing stones for such a compact area – some 1,300 standing stones can be found within the 553 square miles (1,432 square kilometres) of the North York Moors National Park.

For many of the moorland farmers, particularly those who worked on these heights centuries ago, these stones helped to define the boundaries of their own farms.

On a bleak moorland landscape there was little else to serve as a boundary marker – there were no trees, no buildings and no rivers; in other words, there were few natural boundaries. Consequently, some landowners had to erect man-made features to mark the extent of their premises. Tall standing stones were ideal. They could be seen from a distance, they were durable and permanent and, if necessary, the names of the owners in question could be carved for ever in their stone faces.

Even so, the boundary line between any two distant standing stones was rather blurred and indistinct, often being determined by a small hollow in the landscape or perhaps a piece of rising ground.

The truth was that the smaller farmers did not appear to worry too greatly about their precise margins. A few yards of land within or beyond their boundaries was almost irrelevant. Many of them owned moorland sheep which roamed freely across the heights, cheerfully crossing unseen boundaries which did not exist in their sheepish minds, and it was the sheep which were marked with their owners' distinguishing colours, not the precise edge of their grazing ground. The sheep wandered, wherever they wanted, quite heedless of artificial boundaries, but they could be rounded up when necessary and allocated to their true owners irrespective of where they grazed. It seemed a free and easy method of following one's profession, one which relied on a lot of giving, taking and common courtesy.

The large estates, however, were more formalized and their boundaries did seem to be very well defined, even if they used something as primitive as massive boulders rather than the more conventional fences. One good example is the Three Lords Stone which stands at a height of 975 feet near Carlton Bank Top on the north-western tip of the North York Moors. This once marked the meeting point of three lords' estates – Duncombe of Helmsley, Marwood of Busby Hall and Aylesbury of Snilesworth.

In the depths of the more lush dales, however, boundaries were marked with greater ease – there were rivers and streams to create natural markers, with man-made barriers such as railway lines and roads to later aid the process. Thus the farms of the low-lying regions had well-defined boundaries, often comprising fences, hedges and dry-stone walls.

It was those on the wild and desolate

heights where such formalities seemed un-important. The truth was that some moorland farmers were not absolutely sure of the extent of their own boundaries, even when they owned (rather than rented) the land. This uncertainty probably arose because they had never bought their farms and thus had never experienced the legal complexities of such a transaction. This happened because the premises had been handed down from father to son over successive generations which meant that formalities like the precise boundaries were never very significant in the transfer arrangements. The son simply inherited what his father had owned without concerning himself too much with un-necessary detail. Precise boundaries became important only when there was a dispute of some land or perhaps when a piece of that land had to be either developed or sold or involved in some kind of legal process. As a policeman, of course, I was not involved in the legal aspects of such problems although, from time to time, I might be aware of them. These matters were within the realm of civil law and consequently of little official concern to the police although, from time to time, a farmer might approach a police officer for advice on civil legal matters of the more simple kind. If the officer was unable to help, then he would refer the fellow to the relevant authority or even to a solicitor.

Such a farmer was Don Yardley of Howeside Farm at Gelderslack. Situated not far from the renowned Surprise View at Gelderslack, the farm occupied a magnificent situation on the slopes of a valley.

The land behind the farm rose to become a heather-covered patch of moorland to the north while that below the farm house dipped into a lush and very fertile dale complete with a rippling stream and some beautiful woodland. In fact, some of the farm's land formed the panorama from Surprise View which meant that Don's cattle and his land often featured in tourists' photographs of the region.

Don could boast acres of moorland with a huge flock of sheep, but also herds of dairy cattle, arable fields and even a thriving poultry section. His family had farmed this patch of the moors for generations and he could trace the history of the farm to 1632 when it was owned by one of his ancestors. Like his ancestors, he was very successful without any sign of snobbery. Now in his late forties, he was a sturdy individual who radiated an aura of strength and reliability. With a round and cheerful face topped by thinning blond hair, he had a penchant for brogue shoes, heavy duty overcoats and colourful waistcoats. He was a well-liked and respected businessman who found himself sitting on all kinds of committees and panels.

Like most of the farms in this region, I had to call there regularly to examine the stock registers and it was on such an occasion that he invited me to stay for morning coffee because, as he put it, 'There's summat I'd like to talk to you about, Nick.'

Savouring the hot scone smothered with butter and strawberry jam, produced by his wife, Valerie, I invited him to explain his problem.

'Mebbe it's nowt to do with you fellers,' he began, 'but you know that old schoolroom at the crossroads down the dale?'

'I do,' I assured him. I knew the building well. It was a long, low, stone building covered with the blue slate tiles of the moorland region; it had a small paved playground behind it and stood at the crossroads which led variously to Brantsford, Ashfordly, Gelderslack and Rannockdale. The former schoolroom had not been used for years, except during a brief resurrection as the village hall for some eight or nine months while the actual hall in Gelderslack was undergoing some major repairs. From time to time, vandals targeted the building, throwing stones through its windows or endeavouring to enter the building for reasons best known to themselves. Due to that kind of unwelcome attention, the windows had been boarded up, the door reinforced and chained gates placed across the entrance to frustrate vehicle access to the former playground. Now, therefore, it was a sad and neglected building, even if it was sturdy and handsome.

'Who do you think owns yon school-room?' Don asked.

'I don't know,' I had to admit. 'I expect it will be the Education Department at County Hall – the county council in other words –unless it was leased to them under some arrangement. Finding the owner might be difficult, Don, it's been closed for years. Why? Is there a problem with it? Vandals again?'

'Nay, them window shutters keep such-like out of the place and its not in bad fettle. No, it's just that I was thinking of buying it, you see. It does border my land – that

123

bottom field of mine goes right up to the playground wall, Mr Rhea, and seeing the spot's never been used for years, and never likely to be used now that our local kids go to Ashfordly primary, well, I thought I might put an offer in.'

'I'm not sure how the system works, Don, but I think the county council has to put such places on the open market, rather than do deals with individuals.'

'Well, if it came to an auction or having to submit tenders or owt like that, I reckon I could outbid anybody else! What I'm thinking is that I could convert it into holiday cottages, you see. It would make a bit of income for the farm and we could sell the visitors eggs and things. But nobody round here seems to know who it belongs to. It's been shut for years and I was told by a bloke in the pub that the education people have said they want nowt to do with it any more. That's what they told me when I checked. Mebbe, way back, somebody bought it off the education people but the new owners have never got round to doing anything with it, so I just wondered how I went about finding out who it belongs to.'

'When did it close, Don? Have you any idea?'

'Well, I started school in 1925 and it was shut then. In those days, all of us from round here went to Rannockdale village school, then after the war, Rannockdale was closed and all the bairns were taken to Ashfordly primary.'

'So it must have been closed around the time of the First World War?'

'I think my grandfather went to school there, very handy really, being at the bottom of our fields, but I think my dad went to Rannockdale like me. So that old school might have closed about the turn of the century, Nick, some time before the 1914-18 Great War. Closed as a school that is. It's been used for other things since then, a reading room for example, for voting at elections, a temporary village hall like I mentioned and so on, but all very casual. Nowt permanent.'

'Who's the keyholder?' was my next question.

'Well, we have a key for it at our house,' he said. 'We've had one for as long as I can remember. Folks would come to the house for it whenever they had to get in for any reason.'

'And you've still got a key?'

'Aye, we have, hanging in our kitchen

cupboard. I've never known it not be there, Nick.'

'Possession is ninth tenths of the law!' I laughed, adding, 'But don't quote me on that! Have you contacted County Hall about it recently?'

'Yes I did, a few weeks ago. I thought I'd start things moving so I rang County Hall and got put through to the education people. Well, what a going on I had trying to find anybody that would talk to me; they kept putting me through to different departments and other offices and different folks and when I did get through to the right spot, there was nobody there knew owt about what I wanted. Anyway, I got talking to a chap and said all I wanted to know was who owned the old school in Gelderslack, so he said he'd check it out for me. He rang me back about two days later and said it wasn't shown in any of their records. He said he couldn't really help because all the old records had been removed but he reckoned the Education Department wasn't responsible for it. It didn't show up on any of their lists.'

'So when it was used as a temporary village hall, who authorized that to happen?'

'Nobody, so far as I can remember. It was

126

a few years ago, Nick, but I seem to think somebody rang the education people to ask for permission and a chap there said he had no objection so the parish council came to see me and because I knew no reason to stop 'em, I let 'em in.'

'Well, the Education Department wouldn't object if they didn't own it! That's the easy way to solve a problem – it would save that clerk having to check back in the files. You provided the key?'

'Aye, just like we've allus done. The same thing happened after it was vandalized. The parish council said summat should be done, the education lot said it was nowt to do with them, our rural district council wouldn't accept responsibility so Willie Bennison from Dale End had some bits of spare wood and he made them shutters that's still there, for nowt. A gift, he said. Nobody paid for them shutters or for that chain across the playground entrance, they were put there because it made sense to put 'em there. We've allus kept a key for the place so folks could get in and do bits of maintenance, and we've never raised objections to sensible things happening there.'

'So ever since it was closed all those years ago, it seems nobody has really taken responsibility for that old school, but you've let people in from time to time, so they could use it? Without paying anyone a fee of any kind?'

'Right, Nick. There's never been any charges since it stopped being a school. But if I started to convert it into cottages, you can bet your bottom dollar the owners would turn up and make a fuss.'

'That's a fair assumption!' I laughed.

'Well, it seems to me that so long as other folks take a bit of interest in looking after the spot, the owners are happy to keep their heads down and let 'em get on with it. It saves them money, doesn't it? Getting jobs done for nowt. Not a bad system if you can get away with it. But you'd think they would want to do something with the old spot.'

'It seems to me that you've done everything possible to trace the owners, but you can't just take it over, Don. Somewhere, there will be an owner or owners, especially if County Hall say it's not their responsibility. I think you should try the Registry of Deeds first, they keep records of sales of property and land, and if that fails, the County Archivist might have something on file.'

'Those places are like foreign countries to

me, Nick. It's easier learning to speak Chinese than finding somebody sensible in those places. I wondered if you knew anybody who works there? A name for me to contact. You did work over there for a while, didn't you?'

'I worked in the offices of Police Head-quarters,' I told him. 'They're next door to County Hall, in Racecourse Lane. But yes, a former colleague of mine works in the Registry of Deeds. A retired inspector. I could have a word with him, if you like.'

'I'd be very grateful,' he said. 'All I want is a starting point, some name to contact with my offer.'

'I'll see what I can do,' I promised.

'Not a word to anyone else, though, please. I wouldn't want other folks getting the same idea as me and nipping in before me with a better bid...'

'Scout's honour!' I laughed, giving him the Boy Scout salute.

The former inspector of my acquaintance was called Bob Hollowood; he'd been a senior constable on the beat at Strensford when I was stationed there, and had subsequently been promoted to sergeant and then into a headquarters' post as inspector. Soon afterwards, he'd retired with ill-health

– a heart problem – but had taken a modest clerical job in the Registry of Deeds as a means of providing an interest in his declining years. I rang him from home.

I gave him precise details of the old school building in Gelderslack, along with a map reference and an account of its history as explained to me by Don Yardley and he promised he would check his records. As it might take some time to locate the relevant files, he said he would contact me later, probably within a couple of days or so.

He rang me late one Friday afternoon. I was at home, enjoying a day off as a prelude to a long weekend – a Friday/Saturday/Sunday weekend off came around once every month or so, consequently they were cherished, but I was happy to take this call. After all, it was not really a police matter.

'Bob Hollowood,' the voice said. 'I've traced that old school, Nick. It meant going back to 1907, but it's all here on paper.'

'Great!' I was delighted.

'It stopped being a school in 1907,' he told me. 'There were insufficient children to justify it, so it closed and the children went to Rannockdale instead. The old school at Gelderslack had been opened in 1807, a century earlier, and the original building was thatched with heather. It was erected by voluntary subscription from the local people on land given by a local farmer and there were no title deeds in those days, although we have correspondence relating to the founding of that school. In those early days, the parents paid for the education of their children, but by the time it closed, the school came under the auspices of the county council.'

'So they did own it?' I put to him.

'Not quite,' he laughed into the phone. 'The farmer at the time managed to engineer an unusual deal – although the farmer had donated the land in the first place, he, being an astute Yorkshireman, had given it specifically so that a school could be built on the site. His condition was that if the building ever ceased to be a school, the land *and any building upon* it would revert to his ownership.'

'So in 1907, that old agreement had to be honoured?'

'Yes, even though there were no deeds for the original school, the conditions agreed in the letters were quite specific and legally binding. So the land and the old school building – all of it – reverted to the local farmer. By then, of course, the original

131

farmer had died, but his family still owned the farm, and so he found himself with a school building quite free of charge.'

'Yardley is the name,' I said. 'Howeside Farm, Gelderslack.'

'Yes, Leonard Yardley was the farmer in 1907.'

'He was grandfather of the man who asked me to ring you – so I now have a farmer who owns a school and knows nothing about it! He thinks someone else owns it, he's been trying to find out who it belonged to!'

'It looks as though grandad never told anyone.'

'Right, Bob. Anyway, so long as the school doesn't belong to the County Council...'

'No, it doesn't, and never really did! Not entirely – they had an interest in it because it was a school but the land was never theirs. According to this file, it reverted to the Yardleys of Howeside Farm and I've nothing to say it was ever transferred to anyone else.'

'That's good enough for me,' I thanked him.

It was the following Monday morning when I resumed my duties after an enjoyable weekend off and I decided to visit Don

Yardley before any other matters called for my attention. As before, he settled me in his kitchen with a mug of coffee and a slice of cake, this time a fruit cake made by Val.

'So what have you discovered, Nick?' he asked, after I had explained the reason for this visit on a Monday morning.

'Did you contact your solicitor about the old school?' I asked him, just to wind him up a little!

'No, of course not, Nick. It's not on our land, so he's got no interest in it.'

'It is on your land,' I said. 'Your family gave the land for the school on condition that if it ever ceased to be a school, the land and the buildings on it would revert to your family. That's what happened in 1907, Don. It's been yours since then!'

'Ours?'

'I think it would be your grandfather, Leonard Yardley, who would have received back the land and school when it closed.'

'Well, he wasn't one for putting pen to paper, Nick, and my dad never said anything about it. Mebbe he never knew? But nobody told me the land had been ours...'

'You'd better have words with your solicitor,' I suggested. 'It should all be in your deeds, all the conditions attached in the first place, dates of transfer back to Howeside Farm, the lot.'

'I don't know what to say!' He looked slightly embarrassed. 'I once heard it described as our family school, but thought it meant some of my ancestors had gone there. I think it meant more than that, eh?'

'Well, it's your family school now, Don. just make sure everything's in the deeds, though, before you start knocking it to pieces. And record it all for the future, of course, so your descendants will know all about it!'

'Well, I'll be damned,' he muttered. 'If I'd seen my solicitor in the first place...'

'You'd have been making money from it instead of letting it lie fallow, eh?' I smiled.

'I might have done just that. But fancy owning a school and not knowing about it! But there's always security in stones and mortar, Nick. But I don't know what to say, except thanks.'

'That'll do,' I said, draining my coffee and preparing to continue my rounds.

If Don Yardley was somewhat vague about the precise extent of his moorland empire, then the problems that befell a befuddled

134

lady who rejoiced in the name of Tabitha Gumlock – Miss Tabitha Gumlock – made him appear to be in complete control of his life. Tabitha, of an indeterminate age somewhere in the 45-60-year bracket and with a moderate income that did not involve working, lived alone in a lovely old cottage on the main street of Aidensfield.

Her house was always a picture because it was smothered by a variety of colourful climbing plants which bloomed throughout the year from spring until autumn. At times, the front doorway seemed to disappear beneath a canopy of hanging vegetation and then Tabitha would go berserk with her cutting shears and clear the whole front of the house so that it looked obscenely bare.

She always dressed in black – long, flowing black dresses or matching skirts and tops, often covered with shawls of deepest funereal black; she wore black shoes and a black scarf and black gloves, all complemented by gleaming black Whitby jet jewellery. She'd even appear like this during her time at home, but went off to her many social engagements in the same outfits.

All this complemented her black hair, black eyes and rather white face, and there is little wonder the village children thought she was a witch.

I never did know where her money came from, but she seemed to have a useful private income, and although she was not wealthy, she was by no means poor. She owned her house, she ran a Morris Minor car, her clothes always looked clean and neat and she enjoyed a drink of wine at home surrounded by her beautiful antique furniture. The general view was that some rich relation had died to leave her financially secure, although no one knew who that might have been.

Tabitha's most evident weakness was that she never knew what time it was, and she never knew what day of the week it was. How on earth she struggled through her life in such a fog of bewilderment can only be guessed because she had a continuing habit of turning up at events on the wrong day or at the wrong time. It was widely known that if she got the day right, usually with a little help from her friends, then she'd get the time wrong. She'd turn up on Wednesday for Tuesday events, and would arrive at 1 a.m. for something due to begin at 3 p.m. or, much worse, she would turn up for important meetings many hours after they had finished. She never got it right and it was generally said of Tabitha that she would even contrive to miss her own funeral.

Those of us living in Aidensfield knew about these foibles because she provided lots of examples on a very regular basis – she'd turn up at the parish church for morning service on a Saturday instead of a Sunday, she'd arrive at the shop just after it had closed, or she'd book a hair appointment and turn up a day early. She'd book a tradesman to call and fix something in the house, then disappear on a shopping expedition the very day he was due. She'd arrange nice lunches and dinners at home for her friends and acquaintances, and then forget to prepare the meals, thinking her guests were coming tomorrow. Whenever we could, those of us who knew Tabitha would make an extra effort to ensure she got the day and time right and it was Joe Steel at the Aidensfield shop who suggested she had a daily paper delivered.

He suggested that if she destroyed each newspaper on the evening of the day it was delivered, it would ensure she never saw it after the day of publication, consequently she would no longer confuse her days and dates. She should then place the new morning's newspaper in her kitchen where it would remain throughout the day to remind her of both the day and the date. She'd not have to worry about precisely what day it was – all she had to do was look at the date on the newspaper. The system might have worked if Tabitha had thrown out the old papers on a regular daily basis, but she tended to hoard them in the kitchen while forgetting to collect the present day's paper from the letter box. Thus she accumulated several days' papers and this led her to think that a Wednesday was a Tuesday and she'd forget to attend any function or event she might have planned for the Wednesday. Once she realized it really was Wednesday, she'd start preparing for an event on Thursday which she would later forget about because she'd be thinking ahead to Friday's engagements, eventually believing that Thursday was in fact Friday and that she really should be thinking of preparing her wardrobe for Saturday's outings.

Sometimes, I thought her confusion was the reason she always wore black – whatever the event or occasion, she always turned up in black which meant she didn't really have to distinguish between weddings and funerals, or lunch parties and baptisms –

that is provided she got the day and time right, which in fact rarely happened. By wearing black all the time, however, she never had to worry about what to wear for any intended destination or predicament in which she found herself.

It might be thought that such vagaries in the personal behaviour of a villager were of little concern to the local constable but, as any competent constable will confirm, it is important that the rural policeman is aware of such peculiarities among the people living on his patch. One never knows when such knowledge will prove useful.

In Tabitha's case, a problem developed when she drove her little car into the city of Leeds for a shopping expedition. She found a most convenient parking place on a side street very close to the shops, observed that the sign announced 'Free Parking Permitted this side – Mondays, Wednesdays and Fridays' and left her car neatly positioned there for most of the day. When she returned to it with her purchases, she was dismayed to find a ticket under the windscreen wiper. It was a very formal printed note signed by a patrolling constable of Leeds City Police and it said she had infringed the parking conditions by parking there on a forbidden day and, because this was prior to the days of fixed penalty tickets, it added that she must visit a named police station in Leeds to explain herself and to produce her driving licence and car insurance.

Off she went as directed; she did her best to explain to the desk constable that she had fulfilled the necessary parking conditions. Tabitha was rather upset when the constable pointed out that it was Tuesday, not Wednesday, and that she would have been all right to park all day at the other side of the street. He said she would be reported for the offence of unauthorized parking, and would have to appear at Leeds Magistrates' Court in due course. She would receive a summons to that effect.

The whole episode did really upset Tabitha and she came to see me about it. I explained that, in some cases, it was possible for a court to deal with such a minor matter in the absence of the accused but if a summons arrived she would have to obey whatever conditions it imposed, if any. Ignorance of the law is no excuse, I had to tell her; the fact that she had once again got her days confused was no defence. Sorry though I was for her, I had to explain that the due processes of English law would have to take their course and if the summons insisted on her presence before the magistrates, then she would have to obey. Some courts did insist upon the personal attendance of defendants even in minor cases, usually when a new law had come into effect; the personal attendance of offenders tended to generate useful publicity in the early stages and helped to establish the new provisions in the minds of the public. I told Tabitha that she might have infringed a very new parking restriction in Leeds, one which the authorities were anxious to publicize. She went away looking rather glum, but I warned her that if she received a summons, she must be sure to attend the named court – and on the right day!

The summons did come; I served it personally upon Tabitha and took great pains to warn her that she must attend in two weeks' time on Tuesday at 1 a.m. I told her not to forget. But she did. She turned up on the Wednesday, a day late, by which time her case had been deferred and new process issued. Even though a court was sitting, her case was not scheduled for that day and so, full of apologies, she wrote to the Clerk of the Magistrates. He accepted her apology but warned her that a summons must be obeyed – on this occasion, however, she would be given a second opportunity to attend. A new summons would be issued. She said she was most grateful for his consideration and eventually, the second summons arrived. It stipulated she must attend on another Tuesday, in a further two weeks' time.

Unfortunately, Tabitha got her days confused on that occasion too. She arrived at the court-house on the Wednesday, thinking it was Tuesday. On two successive occasions, therefore, she had failed to obey a summons and it was perfectly under-standable that the officials of that court felt she had no intention of responding. When she rang the clerk to tender her most sincere apologies, he said she would be given one final opportunity – the hearing would be scheduled for a further two weeks ahead, this time on a Wednesday. Fortunately, due to the volume of work, the court sat on most weekdays and the clerk seemed to think that if she had turned up twice on a Wednesday, then she would do so again.

She didn't. She arrived the following Thursday. By this stage, the hitherto patient officials had decided that they *would* get this reluctant female defendant to court.

Using their powers under the fairly new Criminal Procedure (Attendance of Witnesses) Act of 1965, the magistrates issued a warrant for Tabitha's arrest. Such warrants could be issued when a witness (and a defendant was a witness) had persistently refused to attend court and if the court felt that such witness had no intention of attending.

And so it was that I received the warrant for execution. It ordered me to arrest Tabitha Gumlock of Aidensfield and convey her to Leeds City Magistrates' Court on Tuesday next at 1 a.m. where she would be dealt with for the outstanding parking offence. Being arrested is a most humiliating experience but I had no choice. I tried to soften the blow by calling on Tabitha in advance and saying that I would come to her house on Tuesday to take her to Leeds for her court appearance – she apologized for being such a nuisance and said I had no need to worry; she would make absolutely sure she appeared on the date in question. I knew she could not be relied upon to do that. I had then to say that things had gone a stage or two further. I had to personally take her to court, I stressed, and would come for her on Tuesday morning.

'Oh,' she said. 'I do hope those people at Leeds don't think I am trying to evade justice. Really, Mr Rhea, I am a most diligent person and have no desire to avoid my responsibilities. So, thank you, I understand how much they want to see me there, so I will be ready for you on Tuesday. What time?'

'I will pick you up at nine o'clock in the morning,' I said.

I must admit that afterwards I wondered if I had done the right thing because I feared that Tabitha would not know which day was Tuesday. However, it was a risk I had to take, there was no alternative short of locking her up straight away, but I rang her the night before, just to remind her. She assured me she would be ready and dressed for court at nine o'clock tomorrow morning.

As an added form of security, I decided to arrive at her house rather earlier than the appointed hour. I had the warrant in my possession as I hammered on her door at half-past eight. I was in uniform and my little van was full of fuel ready for its trip to Leeds. Tabitha came to the door in one of her finest black outfits; I thought she looked splendid, then she smiled and said, 'Oh, Mr Rhea. I am so sorry, I am just dashing off to Newcastle, it's my niece's wedding, you know...'

'Tabitha,' I said firmly, 'it's Tuesday, it is your day for going to court in Leeds.'

'Oh no, Mr Rhea,' she said. 'It is Wednesday. I know because I checked in my diary, the wedding is today, you see, and I must dash because I have to be at the church before eleven o'clock...'

'Tabitha, I am here to arrest you.' I had to shock her into recalling the purpose of my visit. 'We are due in court at Leeds at eleven o'clock,' and I showed her the warrant. 'It's my job to get you there.'

'Is it really Tuesday?' She looked deflated as the possibility dawned upon her.

'Yes, it is,' I smiled. 'And tomorrow is Wednesday. Tomorrow, you can go to the wedding – if you'd gone to Newcastle today, the church would have been deserted, wouldn't it? You'd have got there on the wrong day and might have missed all the fun.'

'Yes, I would, wouldn't I? What a blessing you came for I was just about to leave, you know. In another ten minutes, I'd have been chugging up the Great North Road in my little car. So things have worked out well, haven't they? For a change.'

'I suppose they have,' I said.

'Then I shall plead guilty, Mr Rhea. I wasn't guilty, you know, not really. I did park in Leeds that Wednesday.'

'Tuesday,' I reminded her.

'No, it's Tuesday today, you've just told me so, haven't you?'

'I meant it was Tuesday when you parked on that restricted area...'

'Was it really? I don't like Tuesdays, Mr Rhea, they always cause such problems.'

'Come along,' I said, ushering her into my van. 'Let's have a day out in Leeds.'

Tabitha was fined £5 and I wondered if it was worth all the fuss, then on the way home she asked, 'Mr Rhea, is it this Wednesday that I must attend that wedding, or next Wednesday? It's Wednesday now, you see, and I am rather confused...'

'No, it's Tuesday today,' I reminded her.

'Ah, yes, Tuesday's child is full of woe,' she sighed.

'No,' I said. 'Wednesday's child is full of woe. Tuesday's child is full of grace.'

'I am a Tuesday child,' she smiled at me.

'I can see that,' I told her, thinking she had

conducted herself with extreme grace in the formal atmosphere of Leeds Magistrates' Court. I did hope she would remember to go to Newcastle tomorrow – I decided I would call upon her early tomorrow morning, just to remind her. The wedding would not be the same without her.

5

'Is that the policeman?'

'Speaking.' It took me a while to answer the shrilling telephone because it was only half-past six in the morning and I had to clamber out of bed, find my slippers, gather my wits and then work my way downstairs to the office without falling over the cat or disturbing my wife and children. On a cold and dark winter morning, answering the phone in my chilly office was not the most pleasant of experiences. One of these days, I thought to myself, the Force will decide to install bedside extensions for country constables even if such things were then regarded as a luxury rather than a necessity.

'I thought you'd gone out,' said the deep voice at the other end of the line. 'I thought I'd mebbe missed you.'

'It's only half-past six...' I yawned and tried to wipe the sleep from my eyes. 'I was in bed...'

'Bed? At this time of day? I've been up two hours; I've got milked, had my breakfast and got mucked out and now I'm wanting to start hedging in my front garden and somebody's pinched my trimmer.'

'I was working late,' I tried to excuse myself, but he wasn't listening.

'Late? What's that? I never stop work, there's no such thing as late in our house,' was his response.

'Who's calling?' was my next question.

'Who's calling? Well it's me; you know me well enough, you've been up here plenty of times.'

'Sorry, I can't recognize the voice,' I had to admit.

'Well, you've heard it plenty of times and I never go far away from here. It's not often folks mix me up with somebody else.'

'Sorry, that doesn't help.' I was now responding to the new day, with my intellect improving almost by the minute and I had even managed to find a ballpoint and a note pad while holding the phone to my ear. 'So, who's calling?'

'You're having me on, aren't you, Mr Rhea? You know very well who it is all the time but you want to know if it really is me ... well, it is. It's me, Jack Shawcross from Broadgate ... there you are, you knew all the time, didn't you? Nobody mistakes me, Mr

Rhea, not a bloke of my size.'

'Right,' I said, writing down his name. 'I realize who it is now, Jack. So you've lost your hedge trimmer?'

'Not lost it, Mr Rhea, its been nicked.'

'Stolen,' I wrote on the pad. 'How?'

'How? Well, some light-fingered bugger has been in my outbuildings and cleared off with it. Without asking, I might add.'

'Anything else gone?'

'No, nowt else.'

'Was it locked in? Was the shed broken into?'

'Broken into? It hasn't a door – you know the spot as well as me. It's that lean-to behind our cowshed, where I keep my lawnmower and other gardening things.'

'So when did it go? Yesterday? When did you last use it?'

'Last year, when I did my garden hedges.'

I groaned. If the thief had had a whole year's start, it was highly unlikely I would be able to trace him or the stolen property, but I had to go through the motions of investigating the crime and entering it in our records. I decided there was no urgency, not if the property might have vanished at any time during the past twelve months.

'I'll come along to see you, Jack,' I

promised. 'Will you be in all morning?'

'Well, I'll not be cutting my hedge, that's for sure,' he grunted. 'But I'll be around. Ten minutes then?'

'More like half past ten,' I said, replacing the phone.

I struggled back upstairs and, having decided not to climb back into bed tempting though the idea was, shaved quietly with a wet razor, washed and donned my uniform. Most surprisingly, Mary and the children were not disturbed by all this activity – perhaps there was an argument for not having a bedside telephone. At least when it rang in the office, it did not sound in the bedrooms to raise the whole household – luckily, I was a light sleeper and usually managed to hear it if it rang during the night. I made myself some breakfast – cereals, toast and coffee – and then found myself wondering what to do to fill the time. I was not scheduled to start duty until nine o'clock, but it was not yet 7.30.

I decided to surprise Sergeant Blaketon and everyone in Ashfordly Police Office by booking on duty earlier than expected. Few of us ever volunteered to work early – there were more than enough organized duties of the early kind to get us out of bed at the crack of dawn. I rang the office and told the office duty constable that I was reporting on duty earlier than expected because I'd had a crime reported and was going to visit the scene. I provided brief details along with my intended destination. And so it was that, by quarter to eight and now feeling wide awake, I was *en route* to Broadgate Farm, Briggsby, to investigate the matter.

Jack Shawcross was a huge man; he must have been six feet seven inches tall with a chest like a barrel. He had a shock of very dark brown hair with no sign of balding even if he was in his late fifties, and this was enhanced by a thick bushy beard of the same colour and intensity. Powerful in every sense of the word, he ran a large and very successful mixed farm, but he was always in a rush in spite of getting out of bed at the crack of dawn and working until the end of every day. When I arrived, he was carrying a hay fork while clad in denim overalls and wellington boots.

'You took your time!' grumbled Jack as I walked across the farmyard to meet him. 'It could be anywhere by now.'

I ignored him and asked him to show me the shed from which his hedge trimmer had been stolen. It was completely open and full of other tools and implements, mainly those used in domestic gardening. Some were in fairly new condition and others were rusting badly. I noticed a very smart steel spade among the tools.

Their home was one of several lean-to shelters which backed onto a high brick wall. The other sheds contained barrels and cans of fuel, sacks of potatoes, cattle feed, small pieces of farming equipment, milk churns, rat traps and snares, a couple of ploughs, three harrows, a pair of seed planters, a trailer with rubber-tyred wheels, disused cartwheels, various lengths of rope and much more, the uses of which were unknown to me. I wondered if he really knew what was here.

'What else has gone?' I asked, gazing in bewilderment at the conglomeration of equipment.

'Nowt,' said Jack. 'I told you that.'

'Are you sure?' I asked.

'As sure as I'm standing here.' He folded his arms across his chest as if daring me to find his missing property somewhere on the farm.

'You've searched all these buildings for it, have you?' was my next question. So often, things reported stolen turned up on the owner's premises, having been mislaid and forgotten, or moved by someone. This could be especially true in this case – there was so much stuff lying around the place. Really, I should have undertaken my own careful search, but I did not want to antagonize this fellow by suggesting he was incapable of doing that. Clearly, he had searched everywhere.

'By gum, Mr Rhea, you're asking a lot of unnecessary questions. I thought you'd have been getting round all them other farms and gardens hereabouts and looking for it there, not here. But yes, I have looked everywhere. It's nowhere on this farm and it's not in our garden, I can tell you that.'

'There are certain procedures I must follow,' I said. 'And one of them is making sure the stolen property has in fact been stolen and is not elsewhere on the premises. One person can move an object without another knowing about it, you see, with the result it's thought to have been stolen. It happens a lot.'

'Well, I can tell you that neither my wife nor my daughter nor that feller of hers or the wife's mother would have shifted that hedge trimmer, not without telling me. If I say it's been stolen, Mr Rhea, then that's exactly what's happened to it. And it's your job to find it, if I'm not mistaken.'

'I'll need a description of it,' I said.

'I can do better than that, I have a picture of it, a catalogue photograph in colour,' and he turned away and hurried towards the farmhouse with me galloping at his heels. He took me into the kitchen, pointed to the table and said, 'Sit down there while I go into my office.'

Then he went to the kitchen door and shouted, 'Elsie! The constable's here and if I know him, he'll not say no to a cup of tea and a slice or two of cake.'

Over the meal, which was more like a second breakfast than a snack, I completed the necessary statement forms and description of the missing hedge trimmer – a two-stroke fuelled chain-saw type of machine which could be held by hand and used by one person. It was for domestic use rather than cutting the tall, thick hawthorn edges which enclosed his fields. It was a Crowne make with green engine casing bearing white lettering, a twenty-four inch blade with cutting edges on a moving chain and it was about four years old, being worth around twenty pounds according to Jack.

I explained the procedures to him, advising him to notify his insurance company while I circulated the missing trimmer through our various channels. I'd also keep my eyes open and ask questions as I patrolled my patch, just in case the thief had sold it to someone else, and Jack said he would do likewise. I quizzed him about unexpected strangers who might have called on his farm, but he said there'd been no one whom he did not know, and none of the people he did know could be considered a suspect. Either he, or other members of his family were around the farm all day and every day, including his mother-in-law who lived there permanently. I got him to sign a statement to the effect that he had not given anyone permission to remove it. He thought the guilty person might be some itinerant thief passing in the night, someone who'd perhaps seen the trimmer and had stolen it during an opportunist moment while looking for somewhere to shelter from the weather. The trimmer was portable, of course, that was its very purpose; it was for use by hand and no vehicle would be needed to transport it from the farm, and its very portability meant it could be miles away.

'What am I going to do about getting my hedge cut, then?' he asked as he accompanied me back to my van.

'Ring your insurance man,' I suggested. 'Your policy might allow you to hire one or pay someone to come in and do it. You do hire workers don't you?'

'I do; I hire them by the day, Mr Rhea, generally for farmwork like ditching, harvesting, hoeing turnips, that sort of thing. And I pay 'em in cash, on the day.'

'Could any of them have taken the trimmer?'

'I hope you're not suggesting I pay good money to untrustworthy blokes,' he said. 'The chaps I bring onto my land are all reliable types – I do let 'em borrow my stuff if they want and they allus fetch it back, and besides, some of 'em even leave their own stuff behind. Like that smart spade in that shed of mine, where the trimmer went from. The lad I had in to turn my garden over ready for winter left it, he said he'd be back.'

'Who was that?' I asked.

'I don't know his real name, everybody calls him Sandy because of the colour of his hair. You'll have seen him around, he has a motor bike with a trailer behind it for his tools; he hires himself out for gardening jobs. He hasn't been doing it long; I think he got laid off somewhere so he set up on his own. He's very busy, he seems to be rushing about these days, trying to cope with the demand.'

'Where does he live?' I asked. I couldn't recall seeing this lad and wondered about the legality of towing a trailer with a motor bike. So far as I was aware, it was not permissible to tow a trailer with a two-wheeled motor bike.

'Nay, I've no idea. He just turned up one day looking for jobs so I gave him a couple of hours work and he made a good job of it, so I said he could come again. He comes every week now. Very reliable lad. Good worker.'

'I'll look out for him,' I said. 'He might have seen somebody snooping about the area. Right, I must go – and don't forget to contact your insurance people.'

'And that'll mean driving into Ashfordly. I could do without that, seeing how busy I am.'

I left Jack to his problem and drove to Ashfordly Police Station where I entered details of the theft in the necessary registers and typed the formal crime report. As I worked, Alf Ventress came into the office

159

and as we discussed the theft, he said, 'I wonder if it's got anything to do with that wheelbarrow theft at Pattington?'

'Wheelbarrow?' I asked.

'It's off your patch so you might not have heard about it, but someone went into the local market garden and disappeared with a wheelbarrow. A good one, fairly new. It was about a month ago, Nick. It was never traced.'

'Any suspects?'

'Not to my knowledge. The crime was never cleared up.'

'I'd better check the details,' I said. 'Have we anything on file?'

'Only the weekly crime circular,' he said. 'It's not in Ashfordly section so we won't have much information here, as you know. You could always have a ride out there, have words with the loser and local constable.'

It seemed a good idea, but it meant obtaining the necessary permission from Sergeant Blaketon. If I was to conduct these enquiries off my own beat and in another sergeant's section, there was local politics to consider. Blaketon understood the reason and gave his approval, so I rang PC Derek Warner, the local constable, and explained things to him. He invited me to visit him immediately and so I drove across the hills to Pattington, a journey of around fifteen minutes. This is a pretty place away from the moors and it boasts handsome brick houses, a pond, a fine church, garage and popular market garden.

Derek had suggested I meet him at the market garden where I could get details of the wheelbarrow mystery at first hand in an attempt to compare it with the trimmer theft. I arrived to find a well-tended plot surrounded by a high wire fence with two stout gates. The owner was a woman called Liz Bolam, a slender blonde in her mid-forties who had taken over the garden when her husband died. In her green overalls, she greeted us with a cheerful smile and led us into the premises where Derek explained my wish to discuss the missing barrow.

'It wasn't a new one by any means, but it wasn't the value that mattered.' She was almost apologetic at this intense police interest in her barrow. 'It was the nuisance of having to cope without it until I could get into York or Ashfordly to get another.'

'I see you're well protected with a high fence,' I observed. 'So how did the thief get in?'

'I don't know,' she admitted. 'That

puzzled me and Derek...'

'The gates are locked each night, Nick, and yet I'm fairly sure the barrow disappeared overnight. I think chummy must have got over the fence somehow – it's not impossible to scramble over it and it's not impossible to lift something over either – like a domestic barrow.'

'So where was it taken from?' I asked.

'Well, I can't be absolutely sure,' she said. 'I keep it among my other gardening equipment, rakes, spades and so on, in a shed at the far end. Come on, I'll show you.'

She led us to a long shelter with a corrugated iron roof; it was open on three sides and, rather like Farmer Jack's sheds, was built against a high brick wall. The roof was supported along its length by pillars of brick and it was here that Liz Bolam kept her gardening tools and equipment. In one part of this long building I noticed an assortment of barrows, some with four wheels and handles at each end, others of the more conventional type and one specially made for carrying lengths of timber. She had arranged her equipment sensibly, with all the barrows in one place, all her spades and forks in another, the rakes and hoes in another, pruning shears and cuttings tools in another, trowels and hand forks on wall hooks in one place, plant pots arranged in sizes and shapes, and so on. All very orderly and neat.

'It went from here.' Liz pointed to the remaining barrows. 'I don't lock my stuff in because the surrounding outer fence is most adequate, and this is the first time anything's been stolen. Mind you, somebody's left me something – that watering can's not mine, I've no idea where it came from. It's huge, far bigger than a normal domestic one. I'm leaving it there in case the owner returns.'

'Where could that have come from?' In the back of my mind was an image of the spade left at Jack Shawcross's farm.

'Oh, I get all sorts left here,' Liz shrugged. 'Customers come in their cars to pick up their purchases, take things out of the boot to make room as they rearrange the space, then drive off and leave their belongings. You've no idea how many boxes of groceries I've had left here! One Saturday somebody left a box of new shoes and another time I found myself with a box of kittens.'

'But not many ten gallon watering cans?' I smiled.

'No, you'd wonder why somebody would

want to bring a watering can of any kind to a market garden, but there's no accounting for people's peculiarities. They'll come back for it one of these days.'

As I looked around the market garden with Derek Warner and Liz, I realized it was quite possible for the barrow to have been removed while Liz was working out of sight and some distance away in one of the other areas – the office or one of the greenhouses for example – but she was adamant that it had not been removed while she was on the premises. Just as it was a puzzle how Jack's trimmer had vanished from his outbuildings, so the disappearance of Liz's barrow was equally baffling.

As I prepared to leave, thinking I had not learned a great deal from this visit, I said to Liz, 'It's a fine place you've got, clearly you must have help to cope with all this?'

'Oh yes,' she nodded. 'I use a lot of casual labour, people from the village and surrounding area who want to earn a few pounds. Some are pensioners, others are youngsters who can't get regular work.'

'Have you come across a youngster called Sandy? He's got a motor bike and tows a trailer with it,' I said.

'Oh yes, Sandy's one of my regulars. A real

good worker, I give him as much work as he can cope with, but he does have a lot of customers.'

'He works occasionally for Jack Shawcross over at Briggsby,' I said. 'Jack has lost a hedge trimmer.'

'Well I would trust Sandy with anything,' she said. 'He's always in a rush, but he's honest enough.'

'So he wouldn't have taken your barrow?'

'No, but I have said he could borrow anything whenever he wants,' she said. 'With him just starting his business, he's sometimes short of tools or equipment. I don't mind him borrowing my things, and he knows that.'

'Where does he live?' I asked. 'And what's his surname? Any idea?'

'I think he comes from Slemmington,' she told me, 'but I don't know his surname. He'll be in his twenties, I expect, and he mentioned his parents once. He said something about his dad managing a shop in Eltering but I've no idea which one.'

'Right, thanks,' I said, making up my mind to interview Sandy if I could trace him – even if the lad could not help with my enquiries, I must admit I was intrigued by the idea of a motor bike towing a trailer. I would have to check on the legality of that.

I returned home, reported the rather unhelpful outcome to Sergeant Blaketon and then rang Jack Shawcross to say, 'Jack, if that lad Sandy comes to work on your place again, can you give me a call? I'd like words with him.'

'Well, I've no idea when he's due, he just turns up when he's got some spare time but you don't think he's nicked my trimmer, do you?'

'No, but I am interested in his motor bike.' I decided not to suggest that Sandy was a suspect – but he was the common factor between the two recent crimes.

But before Jack rang me, there was another theft. This time, a Flymo had vanished from a splendid house overlooking the moors at Thackerston. The house was a sixteenth-century mansion with beautiful terraced gardens, lawns like billiard tables, immaculately trimmed hedges and realistic topiary, superb borders and famous roseries. Owned by a self-made businessman who owned properties for rental throughout Yorkshire, the gardens were occasionally open to the public to raise money for the Red Cross and other charities. It was called Thackerston Lodge and the owners were Mr and Mrs Fellowes – Philip and Josephine, a dog-loving couple in their mid fifties.

'It's Philip Fellowes,' he introduced himself when he rang me that Friday. 'I have to report a theft, Mr Rhea, from my garden store. Can you pop in when you're passing?'

'I'll come immediately,' I said. 'What's been stolen?'

'My Flymo,' he said. 'Wonderful machines you know, they float on a cushion of air and produce lawns like bowling greens ... I love using mine.'

'When did it vanish?' I asked.

'Sometime during the past week,' he said. 'I used it myself last Saturday; I like to cut my own front lawns. I leave the other grassed areas to my staff, but I enjoy caring for the two lawns directly in front of the house.'

'I'll be there in fifteen minutes,' I assured him.

Mr Fellowes kept his gardening equipment in an outbuilding behind his mansion and although the door was always closed, it was never locked.

The Flymo was kept hanging on a hook on the wall, the recommended storage method. It was a fairly new machine with a red hood and two-stroke engine, and it was in good condition. It was worth around thirty-five pounds, according to Mr Fellowes. He could not be too specific about the time of the theft because he'd not been in the shed since last Saturday – and now it was Friday. I obtained a full description and asked if I might make a search of all the likely places on his small estate – he assured me he had looked everywhere, but with good grace, said he would accompany me upon a search of all his outbuildings, stables, garages and greenhouses. And there, in one of the loose boxes used to store garden tools, I found a hedge trimmer. It was a Crowne make and appeared identical to the one lost by Jack Shawcross.

'Is this yours?' I asked Fellowes.

'No, I do have one, but that's not mine. Mine's a Qualcast, bigger than that one. I think that one was left by one of my part-time staff. He used it to trim my hedges last week, it's been there ever since.'

'What's his name?' I asked.

'Sandy,' said Fellowes. 'He comes to me once or twice a month and does casual work around the place. A good worker he is too.'

As I quizzed Fellowes about Sandy, it appeared that the young man turned up on a motor bike and sidecar, sometimes with an additional trailer and sometimes without, and he did work by the hour, generally attending to the domestic garden. As Liz Bolam had said, Fellowes assured me that Sandy was a very good worker and totally honest, but no one seemed to know his surname or where he lived.

Rather like window cleaners turn up unexpectedly to complete their chores, so Sandy turned up unannounced to provide an hour or two's work in the gardens he serviced, invariably on his motor bike with its sidecar in which he carried his tools. For big jobs, it seemed, he attached a small trailer which carried his additional equipment – and I knew that a motor bike with a sidecar attached was permitted in law to tow a trailer, provided the trailer did not exceed five hundredweight unladen and was not more than five feet wide. A two-wheeled motor bike on its own could not do so.

Having dealt officially with Mr Fellowes' larceny, I told him I wanted to take the hedge trimmer to Briggsby for inspection by Jack Shawcross, and Fellowes agreed, albeit with a proviso that I did not accuse him of stealing it! I explained about the other crimes which had come to my knowledge, adding that one factor appeared to be that when an object was stolen, another of a different sort appeared at the scene and Sandy with his motor bike was always in the background.

'I have told him he could borrow my equipment from time to time,' said Fellowes. 'I said he need not ask permission on every occasion, provided he gets the items back to me when I need them ... he's never let me down, Mr Rhea.'

'Nonetheless, I would like to talk to him,' I said. 'I have no idea where to find him at the moment so if he turns up, can you call me? I'm not going to accuse him of stealing your property – it's just that he must be interviewed, for elimination purposes really.'

'I'll give you a call,' he assured me.

Jack Shawcross identified the hedge trimmer as his property – he had an invoice bearing the serial number and it corresponded to the machine I had recovered from Thackerston Hall. As I chatted to Jack, a theory developed in my mind because he was sure the mysterious Sandy was no thief – but without speaking to Sandy, I could not write off the incident as 'no crime'. Sandy had to be found and an explanation had to be obtained from him. It meant I had to retain the trimmer for the time being, just in case it had to be used as evidence in court.

Finally, I made contact with Sandy some three days later. As I was driving towards Ashfordly one afternoon, I saw a motor bike and sidecar, complete with little trailer, heading in the opposite direction. I executed a rapid about-turn and gave chase, eventually overtaking the combination near Briggsby lane end. The rider, a young, sandy-haired man in his mid-twenties, looked shocked at being ordered to a halt by a police vehicle complete with flashing blue light, but he stood near his now silent machine and awaited my interrogation. As I approached, I noted that the trailer was full of gardening tools – spades, forks, rakes, trowels, hedge clippers, some sacks for waste, plant pots and other assorted bits and pieces.

'Is your name Sandy?' I asked him, noting that he appeared to be extremely worried by the predicament in which he found himself even though I had not yet explained the reason for halting him.

'Yes. People call me that.'

'And your real name and address?' I asked. 'And your driving licence and insurance, please.'

His real name was Alec Longman, he was twenty-six years old and he lived with his parents at Slemmington; his father managed a shoe shop in Eltering. His driving licence and insurance were in order. I checked with particular reference to the trailer and he was covered for its use for agricultural and horticultural purposes. Satisfied with his identity and documents and noting that he was polite and well-spoken, I said, 'Did you leave a Crowne hedge trimmer at Thackerston Grange?'

'Yes, I took it back. I've been using it, Mr Rhea, with permission I might add. I always get permission before I borrow anything.'

'I see,' with my formulated opinion in my mind, I began to quiz this lad. 'And what about the Flymo, Sandy? You had permission to borrow that?'

'Yes, when I used it, I said how good it was and how useful it would be for another job I had to do, and so Mr Frankland said I could take it anytime ... so I borrowed it last week.'

'And you took it back?'

'Oh, yes, Mr Rhea. The minute I've finished with a piece of machinery or a tool, I make sure I return it, just in case I have to borrow it again.'

'So where did you return it?'

Well, to Mr Frankland at Stovensby. Mile House is where he lives.'

'And do you borrow a lot of things?'

'Yes, I'm just setting up on my own you see, freelance gardening, but I haven't been able to afford all the machinery and equipment I need, so my customers let me borrow things, like that Flymo and hedge trimmer, until I get myself fully equipped...'

'And big watering cans?'

He frowned as I said that, and asked, 'Is there something wrong, Mr Rhea?'

'Sandy,' I said, 'you did not borrow the hedge trimmer from Mr Fellowes.'

'Didn't I?' I could see the frown on his face. 'But I took it back to him...'

'Yes, you did. You borrowed the Flymo from him, didn't you?'

'Did I? Well ... oh crumbs ... I've taken that back to Mrs Pendleton over at Ashley House...'

'The hedge trimmer came from Jack Shawcross and he's found a spade among his stuff, a lovely stainless steel one...'

'Oh dear, I borrowed that from old Mr Baker at Elsinby ... he'll think I've stolen it, won't he?'

'And there was the question of a wheel-barrow missing from Liz Bolam's garden centre where a whopping watering can was returned...'

'Well, I think I got most of the things back to where they'd come from, Mr Rhea, but it does look as if I've made a few mistakes. That's the problem with doing so many odd jobs, I forget where I've been and where I got things from and folks are so helpful, you know, letting me borrow things until I get myself fully equipped. I hope I haven't upset any of my regular customers, that's the last thing I want to do!'

'We've had several reports of thefts of gardening tools,' I told him. 'They've all occurred at places where you've worked and in all cases, something's been left behind, some other item of garden machinery or equipment.'

'Maybe I should keep a diary or a list of places I go to and where I borrow things and where they've got to go back to.'

'I think that would be a good idea. Now, the snag is that I have to convince my bosses that you are not a thief, Sandy. So, let's think about that hedge trimmer, the one that you borrowed from Jack Shawcross at Broadgate Farm, Briggsby, if you remember.'

'Did I?'

'Yes you did. Now, did Jack give you permission?'

'He said I could borrow it any time I wanted, Mr Rhea, so long as I got it back to him the minute I'd finished with it. But you say I took it somewhere else?'

'You took it back to Philip Fellowes at Thackerston. So was Jack around when you borrowed it?'

'No, it was daytime, Mr Rhea. I was passing one day and knew I wanted a lightweight hedge trimmer for another job, so I just went into his farm. I knocked on his door and shouted around, but neither he nor his missus were there so I just took it, like he said I could. But the snag is I took it back somewhere else, so he'd think it had been stolen, wouldn't he? I was there, you see, working on his garden the week after I'd taken it, so he'd see me there and know I would have taken it back, like I said I would. So what did I leave there, Mr Rhea?'

'A very nice stainless steel spade...'

'Oh dear...'

'Look, what are you doing now?'

Well, I'm on my way to a job at Maddleskirk.'

'Right, well you almost pass Briggsby so I

reckon you and I should pop in to see Jack Shawcross and you'd better explain things, then I'll get him to say you did have permission to take the trimmer. That means I can write it off as "no crime" and you won't get yourself arrested!'

As things transpired once I got delving into his movements, Sandy had borrowed lots of items from several other places whose owners had not missed their property or who had not troubled to report its absence to the police. In all those cases where we had reports of larceny, the owners were revisited and without exception, all said they had given Sandy permission to borrow their equipment whenever he wanted. In those cases where the losses were reported as theft, however, he'd returned to the premises to remove the items while the owners happened to be elsewhere and, of course, had not returned them. When we examined Liz Bolam's timetable in more detail, she'd popped out of the market garden to have her hair done, leaving it in the temporary care of another part-timer who'd forgotten to mention Sandy's flying visit to acquire the wheelbarrow.

Happily, Sergeant Blaketon accepted Sandy's explanations and in all cases, the

176

reports were written off as 'no crime'. All the missing objects were recovered and Sandy got himself a small notebook in which he recorded all his visits, with particular emphasis upon those occasions he borrowed equipment. As time went by, however, he managed to buy his own gardening equipment and graduated to a small van with his name along the sides.

One morning the following spring, he arrived at my police house. It had a very well-tended hawthorn hedge along the front, the result of hours of careful cutting by me and my predecessors. I'd been absent on a course of three weeks' duration and in that short time, the hedge had begun to look rather unkempt – and its state had attracted the attention of Sandy as he was driving past.

'I owe you an apology for all that time you put in, Mr Rhea,' he said as he called. 'You remember, when you were looking for thieves when I'd got the stuff ... so shall I cut your hedge for you? As a way of saying thanks. It's the least I can do, I could have got arrested and locked up ... and I've got my own trimmer now.'

I smiled. 'Yes,' I said, 'that would be very helpful – but on one condition.'

'What's that?' he asked.

'That you don't leave anyone else's garden tools behind!'

Two other people caused minor headaches among the people of Aidensfield while I was village constable. They were Geoffrey and Joyce Rudd of Three Howes Farm who spent their time fighting with one another. Their never-ending battles were part of local folklore, and yet they remained married.

Theirs was a very remote holding tucked away at the end of a long, narrow lane which led to a cleft in the moors. The road ended at Three Howes – there was nowhere to go once one reached the house, but Geoffrey and Joyce owned the farm and, in spite of their stormy relationship, had successfully worked it all their married life.

Their main income was from sheep-rearing, but they also kept poultry, cattle and a few pigs. The house enjoyed a spectacular and very beautiful setting on heather-covered slopes and even if it looked slightly unkempt and in need of paint, it was secure, dry and very comfortable. The couple were in their late fifties when I first encountered them. Geoffrey, with his fair hair now turning grey and thinning, had a ruddy face full of character. He was a stocky moorland farmer who habitually wore overalls; he never looked entirely clean and many of us wondered if he ever had a bath. Joyce, heavily built with long grey hair tied behind in a pony tail, and legs like tree trunks, was equally unkempt and she gave the impression of being as strong as any man. Certainly, she could heave sacks of meal around as if they were domestic bags of sugar. Each had a loud and powerful voice, each could use bad language to its fullest extent, especially to each other, and each drove the farm tractor as if it was a racing car showing its paces at Brands Hatch.

Not surprisingly, the pair had no children and it was inevitable that, as the Rudds grew older, people began to wonder about the fate of the farm. Would it be sold, or was there someone who might inherit the place? There were fairly persistent rumours of nieces and nephews living in the Teesside area and it was generally thought they would benefit from the eventual death of the couple. In spite of that, some local speculators had their eyes on the farm – some thought it ideal for conversion into a small hotel, others saw it as a place of retreat from a hectic city life and one or two local farmers thought it might complement their own spreads if they could acquire the land and perhaps sell the house as a separate unit.

One constant source of surprise was that the Rudds continued to live and work, together. Their everlasting warfare continued outside the home too; they'd continue their antagonistic behaviour in the village, in the streets, in the shops and even in the church. One could only imagine what life might be like within that remote farmstead but few, if any, had ever witnessed the daily confrontations between the Rudds in their own home.

It seemed that neither of them was shy about their behaviour because whenever Geoffrey and Joyce came into the village, they would tell us in graphic detail about their most recent row. Inevitably it was about something trivial, like not bringing in the bucket of coal for the fire, or failing to have a meal ready on time, or listening to the radio with its sound turned to the highest volume, or losing the toothpaste, or leaving the hot water tap running to drain the supply, or lighting the fire with today's newspapers instead of yesterday's.

The real problem, however, was that Geoffrey and Joyce hated one other – at least, that's what they wanted everyone to believe. Although they remained married and lived in the same house, they claimed to utterly detest one another. They slept apart, although Joyce – being married to Geoffrey – did do his washing and his ironing, and she prepared his meals which he ate alone in his own part of the large house, while Geoffrey continued to provide financial support for his wife. Their famous rows would be broadcast about the village shop or pub and, sometimes, they would both arrive at the same time, one by tractor and the other by car, when their row would be openly continued in the shop to the astonishment of all.

Some sensitive folks did not approve of their choice use of ripe language, but in spite of their angry exchanges, the Rudds never came to blows – at least, no one thought they did. I had no reason to think that either of them was beating the other – each was strong enough and powerful enough to do lasting damage to the other if they so wished, which is perhaps why they never started. It seemed that their arguments were all powerfully verbal.

In the pub, after such a battle, Geoffrey would say, 'By, I really do hate that woman of mine ... I'd rather have a dog as a friend any day, dogs are such good pals, faithful and biddable and they don't lose the lids off marmalade jars neither...'

And at the WI meetings, Joyce would grumble, 'I've never come across such a difficult man as my Geoffrey. You try getting him to change his socks more than once a month, or asking him to put the lid on the toothpaste or wash his own pots ... and he always belches after my Yorkshire puddings. Manners? He has none. He doesn't know the meaning of the word...'

The question that people who were new to their acquaintance always asked was, 'Geoffrey, if you hate your wife as much as you say you do, and if she hates you just as much, and if you both spend your life arguing and fighting with each other, then why remain married? Why not get a divorce, or even live apart?'

'I can't do that!' he would retort. 'She's my wife, even if I do hate her guts, and remember, when I got married I promised to keep her for better or for worse. I think the Good Lord knew what He was doing

182

when He wanted me to promise that, He must have known what she was like all along. I've certainly got the worse end of it all, but divorce? Live separated from her? You don't do that sort of thing if you're married! She's my wife and that's it ... just because I'm married to her doesn't mean to say I've got to like her.'

People who spoke to Joyce received a similar kind of response – they had married and made promises to the effect they would support one another, so that was that. The idea of divorce or separation never entered Joyce's head either.

Then one day when I called at the farm for my usual quarterly check of their stock register, I found Joyce in the kitchen all alone. It seemed Geoffrey had a dental appointment in Ashfordly and when I arrived, she was sitting with a pile of official-looking papers spread around her on the table.

'Sit there, Mr Rhea.' After finding the books for me, she pointed to the clear end of the kitchen table. 'I'll fettle a cup of coffee and I know you'd like a bit of home-made apple pie and Wensleydale cheese.'

As she busied herself preparing my snack, I checked his register and it was up to date;

I signed and dated it, and pushed them aside as she settled in her chair.

'You look busy,' I said. 'All that paperwork! I've got to cope with more and more of it and I know you farmers have mountains of forms to deal with.'

'This isn't farm accounts or monthly returns, Mr Rhea, I'm checking Geoffrey's papers to see if he's made a Will but I can't find one.'

'Your solicitors will know,' I said.

'Aye, but I don't want to trouble them, not just yet. Word might get back to our Geoffrey. Now you're here, though, you might be able to help with a small matter. I'm not sure whether I should see the vicar about it, or my solicitor, or who. So you're a likely starting point.'

'Well, I'll help if I can.' Country police officers were regularly asked for help and advice by people on their beats. 'So what can I do?'

'You might know that us Rudds have a sort of family grave in Aidensfield churchyard, the Anglican church that is. Generations have been buried there, all in one corner, not far from those yew trees.'

'I didn't know,' I had to admit, 'but I know that some families occupy the same general area of a churchyard generation after generation.'

'Well, me and our Geoffrey are the last in the line, you see. When we go, there'll be no more Rudds of Aidensfield. We shan't be having a family at our age, and our nephews and nieces live away from here; besides they're not called Rudd. They're my sister's bairns, separated from the Rudds by my family blood – thank God! So they'll never be buried in our plot.'

'Right,' I said. 'That's a pity, isn't it? When a family name dies out.'

'In some cases yes, but so far as the Rudds are concerned, it's not a minute too soon. They ought to be exterminated with our Geoffrey being first in the queue and I for one shan't be sorry to be known as the last ... anyway, Mr Rhea, it's always been the custom for a Rudd man and his wife to be buried side by side in the family plot.'

'Oh, I see. How nice.'

'No it isn't. It's not nice at all! I have no intention of being buried side by side with our Geoffrey. I want my own space. I don't mind being laid to rest in the Rudd plot – after all, my name is Rudd, but I've no wish to spend the rest of eternity lying beside a chap like him. No way, Mr Rhea, not the way he snores and besides, he never changes his socks from one month end to another and some of his personal habits aren't the sort you'd expect in polite society. Have you ever seen him scratch himself? And do you know when was the last time he washed his hair? Well, I shan't tell you but it's a few Christmases ago. So I intend to alter my Will, you see, to make sure I don't get stuck next to him in that grave, and, I wondered if he'd made a Will saying summat else. If he has, I don't know what he's said, but it's always been understood, without having to say so, that a Rudd will always lie beside his wife in the burial ground.'

'It would be a grave departure to alter that...' I said, and then groaned at my unintended joke.

'There's a first time for everything,' she said without commenting on my *faux pas*. 'The way I see it is that if I don't say so in a Will of my own, then I'm going to finish up beside him for the rest of my life ... well, afterwards, I mean. For ever. Eternity, however long that is. So that's what I wanted to ask: do I have to go to the trouble of making a Will for something as simple as that?'

'I would say yes,' I expressed my own

opinion. 'If it's something as radical as changing a long-established family custom, then you'd be better making a Will which makes your own wishes absolutely clear, especially as you are a member of the Rudd family. If you don't express your own wishes, you'll finish up beside him. You'll have to see a solicitor about it, Joyce. It'll only take an hour or so and you could then rest assured your wishes would be carried out.'

'I couldn't just have words with the vicar or undertaker?'

'They might change several times before your time comes,' I warned her. 'No, Joyce. A Will is the only sure way to ensure any special wishes are carried out after your death.'

'Right, well, that's put it very clearly. I'll book an appointment right away, but I don't want our Geoffrey to hear about it. So say nowt to him, will you?'

'Not a word,' I promised.

A week later, Geoffrey spotted me in the village and asked if he could have a confidential chat. I said he could, anywhere at any time, and he suggested an immediate conversation in his car. To prevent anyone overhearing, he drove out of the village and parked on a deserted verge overlooking the moors.

'So what is it, Geoffrey?' I asked.

'I wasn't sure who to turn to for advice,' he said. 'Then I saw you and thought you were just the chap.'

'If I can help, then I will,' I promised.

'You know about the Rudd family graves in Aidensfield churchyard?' he asked.

'I had heard there's a family plot there, yes,' I said cautiously.

'Well, it's been the custom for generations of Rudds to be buried there, with the wife always lying beside the husband,' he said. 'For a few months though, our Joyce has been saying she doesn't want me buried next to her, Mr Rhea. Now I'm the first to admit we've had our differences down the years and we hate each other but we are man and wife, Mr Rhea. In my mind, that's very important. She's as much a Rudd as I am, whether she likes it or not. That means, in my book anyway, that she should be buried next to me like all them past generations of Rudds.'

'I see,' I nodded. 'So how can I help?'

'Well, I wonder how I can make sure she is buried there, Mr Rhea. It's always been the custom, you see, without anybody having put anything in writing. All our family knew about it; the family custom was passed down from father to son and no vicar ever said we couldn't have it done. But me and Joyce are the last Rudds; I've no son or daughter to make sure we're buried side by side and I must admit I'm a bit bothered about it all. You're a man of the world, Mr Rhea, you're impartial, you're not a family solicitor who'll try to talk me into one thing or another ... so how do I make sure I am buried next to her when there's nobody to look after things?'

'You could put it in your Will,' I suggested.

I could see that he fully expected to die after Joyce but I did not venture any opinions about the problems which might arise if he died first. At least, I thought, if Geoffrey made his Will and died first, he would die happy in the knowledge that the Rudd family practice would be followed – even if it wasn't. He would die a happy man.

I reasoned that if Joyce remarried after his death, she would no longer be a Rudd and thus would not qualify for a space in the family plot. So it was an academic argument ... wasn't it?

'Right, I thought that might be the only sure way,' he said. 'But I wanted a second

189

opinion. Not a word to Joyce, though. I'll make damned sure she's buried next to me whether she likes it or not. I'll see my solicitor first thing tomorrow.'

'I'll not say a word to anybody,' I assured him.

Having said farewell to Geoffrey, I was relieved that I would not be involved in executing the provisions of those conflicting Wills, although I realized that a lot would depend upon who was first to leave this world. In some ways, I was surprised they had seen fit to incorporate their wishes in a Will – not many Yorkshire folk bothered to make Wills because there was an old belief that it was unlucky to make a Will. The persisting belief was that it hastened the death of the person making it. Lots of country folk would avoid any discussion about their final wishes, always hoping there would be time just before they passed away. Invariably, of course, they died without making a Will. But Geoffrey and Joyce had felt compelled to express their wishes in this very formal manner.

And then, within six months of making her Will, Joyce died very suddenly. It was a heart attack which had been brought about through lifting heavy sacks of corn. The funeral was arranged with Geoffrey over-seeing the arrangements.

I was notified by Bernie Scripps, our new garage proprietor, who had managed to persuade the planning authorities to allow him to conduct his undertaking business from behind the garage.

'It's next Saturday morning, Nick,' he told me. 'Eleven o'clock. Will you be there to look after the traffic outside the church gate?'

'I will,' I promised him. Whenever possible, I endeavoured to be present during weddings and funerals, a small way of helping those involved to avoid unseemly traffic congestion on our narrow country roads. 'Is she being buried in the Rudd plot?' I asked almost as an afterthought.

'Oh yes,' Bernie nodded. 'I've had Geoffrey in to see me and he was most insistent about that. A Rudd is a Rudd, he told me, and she has to be laid to rest in the family area. She didn't object to that – her solicitor's been on to me about her wishes – but she doesn't want Geoffrey beside her when he passes on. I don't know what I'm going to do when Geoffrey passes on but he says it's in his Will that he must be buried beside her when his time comes. Mebbe

191

somebody else will arrange his funeral?'

'You might not have to do it,' I told him. 'Geoffrey looks fit enough for a few more years.'

'Well, I've known folks like this go very soon after one partner has died...'

'But they fought and argued and never got close,' I said. 'There was no love lost between them.'

'Don't you kid yourself, Nick. Geoffrey was in tears when he came to see me about the funeral; I think he loved that woman, you know, deep down, in spite of everything. He wants the very best for her now she's gone, a splendid pine coffin with silver handles and a white satin interior, lots of hymns, and organ music, a sherry reception in the pub with a ham lunch to follow and the best headstone I can find with her Rudd name carved in big capital letters. No expense spared, he told me. And he doesn't know how he'll cope without her, that's what he said to me.'

It was on the Friday evening before the funeral that I was patrolling Aidensfield on foot and heard noises in the churchyard. Always wary of vandals causing damage to tombstones or tramps sleeping rough beneath the yew trees, I walked through the lychgate and headed in the direction of the sounds. It was Claude Jeremiah Greengrass and he was digging a grave very close to the wall near a clump of yew trees.

'Evening, Claude,' I said. 'That looks like hard work.'

'It's them ruddy Rudds,' he grunted, as the perspiration ran down his whiskery face. 'Wanting their family graves among all these tree roots. But I've found a good spot with soft ground.'

'It's a bit close to the wall, isn't it?' I observed. 'There's no room for Geoffrey when it's time for him to join her.'

'She doesn't want him beside her, she told me that, Constable. It's in her Will an' all, she told me but she has no objection to being buried in the Rudd plot because that's her name. So this grave is in just the right place. They can't put Geoffrey beside her, can they? There's no room for him.'

'His Will says he wants to be buried beside her, Claude. He told me that – and he is paying for this funeral, and his own when the time comes.'

'Well, that's not my problem, is it? I was just told to dig a single grave on the edge of the Rudd plot, and that's what I've done.'

'Can I suggest you dig it a bit deeper than

usual?' I grinned.

'Deeper? How much deeper?' he frowned at me.

'Deep enough to take an extra coffin,' I said. 'A couple of feet deeper.'

'So Geoffrey can rest in peace on top of her?' Claude laughed.

'Right,' I said. 'That will conform to her wishes Geoffrey won't be buried beside her – but they'll both be in the same grave and that'll please Geoffrey when his time comes.'

'It'll cost extra,' Claude reminded me. 'Digging a double depth grave.'

'I'll talk it over with Geoffrey,' I said. 'I have to see him later this evening about car-parking.'

And so it was done. I told Geoffrey that wide spaces in the Rudd plot were scarce due to the spreading of the tree roots and he agreed to the digging of a deeper grave. He told me that he missed Joyce dreadfully and had no idea how he would cope; he even said he was looking forward to joining her in the family grave.

Six months later, he did so.

6

No one could understand why Claude Jeremiah Greengrass suddenly bought himself a traction engine. He'd never mentioned the idea to any of his cronies nor had he ever openly praised the merits of these impressive machines, but one bright and sunny afternoon in early May, he arrived on the outskirts of the village while battling with the steering wheel of just such a locomotive. He was driving the smoking, hissing giant slowly along the narrow lane into Aidensfield and there was a queue of furious motorists behind him. I reckon some two-dozen cars were queuing to his rear, many of which were smothered in soot and wreathed in smoke, but Claude had no intention of easing into the side of the road to allow them past, even though he was chugging along at a mere five miles an hour. It so happened that I was driving in the opposite direction because I had an engagement in Eltering and found myself confronted by a monstrous and advancing cloud of black smoke and the sound of clanking machinery.

Fortunately, I was in a police vehicle which meant I could do something about the advancing dreadnought, although not immediately recognizing the black-faced character at the helm. I halted my van at the side of the road, climbed out and raised my hand in the best tradition of a constable on traffic duty. My hand indicated 'stop'. The snag is that traction engines can't stop as quickly as a car – they have to be allowed to gradually come to a halt among a cacophany of sounds rather like thousands of kettles coming to the boil with their lids bouncing up and down in anything but unison.

I must say that I was somewhat relieved when the beautiful green-bellied steam-driven colossus managed to pull up a few yards from me. It was a very impressive sight, one to delight the enthusiasts. Then, as the overall-clad driver clambered down and the relieved car drivers squeezed past, I recognized Greengrass.

'Don't tell me! Don't tell you've bought this thing!' I cried.

'Beautiful, don't you think, Constable? Moves with the grace of a gazelle, she does. Tessa the traction engine, that's her name.

Did you know that all traction engines are females, like ships? I think it's because they're big around the back end, make a lot of noise and take a lot of money to maintain. And look at all that brasswork, all polished and gleaming ... anyway, what do want? Why stop me in the middle of nowhere just when I've got up a nice head of steam?'

'First things first. Where did you get it from?' I asked.

'Eltering,' he said. 'I bought it off a chap I know. It's all legal and above board and it's paid for. None of these overdrafts and bank loans for me, you know. I'm a cash man always have been. Anyway he's had this one for years and his wife can't stand the smoke and noise it makes, and she needs the space for her new lawn mower and washing line, so he's had to sell it. She's called Tessa, funnily enough. His wife, I mean. Anyway, I happened to be there when he was getting it ready for sale and snapped it up. A real bargain, Constable. A real bargain.'

'What are you going to do with it?' was my next question.

'Do with it? What does anyone do with a traction engine?' he put to me. 'What would you do with a traction engine?'

'How should I know?' I retorted. 'I haven't

197

got one and have no intention of getting one. The only time I see them nowadays is at steam shows ... once, you'd see them powering threshing-machines or wood-cutting equipment or working in fair-grounds. They're working machines, Claude, not for fun, not toys.'

'I've enough work to keep her busy,' he chuckled. 'But I'll show you that later.'

'You'll have a licence for it, have you?' I asked, partially serious and partially tongue in cheek. 'You realize it is classified as a mechanically propelled vehicle even though it is steam driven. Bear that in mind whenever you take it on the road. All the rules of the road apply. A light locomotive, that will be its classification, I would think, judging by its weight – that's over seven and a quarter tons but less than eleven tons. It means you need a road fund licence, insurance and a driving licence which allows you to drive this class of vehicle...'

'I know,' he muttered. 'And I've got all those! You don't think I'd risk bringing Tessa into Blaketon country without the right papers, do you? I'm fully covered, Con-stable. Everything's legal. Now, if you don't mind and if you're satisfied I've done nowt wrong, I have to finish my journey because it's getting on for tea-time and my Alfred wants summat to eat.'

'You've got to avoid excessive noise, Claude, with this kind of machine. I don't want complaints from the villagers. And you've got to ensure ashes and sparks aren't emitted, we don't want moor fires, and there must be a tray to prevent deposits of ash and cinders from falling onto the road and you've got to stop if you need to attend to the fire ... you can't keep driving it while stoking up...'

'Look, I've gone into all that,' he said. 'I had a long chat before I bought it and I know the rules of the road so far as these engines are concerned.'

'Sergeant Blaketon might want to make sure you do,' I warned him. 'All right Claude, on your way – but when you're on the road, will you stop regularly to let other drivers through? Your Tessa takes up a lot of room and she's not the most speedy of ladies. If you don't, there could be complaints from motorists, they're not all as patient as those behind you today. You might find yourself at Eltering Magistrates' Court charged with obstructing the highway.'

'This doesn't obstruct highways any more than caravans do or big parties of ramblers,

Constable. At least I know how to drive this thing which is more than can be said about some caravanners.'

'All right, point taken. But when you are out on the Queen's highway with Tessa, you are highly conspicuous. Just remember that.'

'Aye, well, I won't be doing much travelling on Her Majesty's roads, Constable, more on my own land, I'd say,' and he went back to his hissing locomotive chuckling to himself as I boarded my van and resumed my journey. It was clear that he had plans for his new acquisition, but he was being very secretive about them.

A few weeks later, one Friday afternoon just after lunch, I drove past the track which leads down to the Greengrass ranch and noticed the traction engine standing beside Claude's house. It was puffing out great clouds of smoke and steam and looking quite handsome in its smart green paint and polished brass livery. It was not mobile, however, being merely stationary as if awaiting some particular task.

To my knowledge, there was no event in the locality which might tempt Claude and his new love to leave home and I thought he might be putting Tessa through her paces as part of her maintenance programme. When I returned to the village a couple of hours later, the traction engine was still parked on Claude's land and still belching forth smoke and steam, but now I noticed three caravans parked on the moorland behind his house. Their presence registered in my mind, making me wonder, albeit fleetingly, whether Claude had established a site to accommodate holidaymakers' touring caravans, or whether these visitors might be a party of steam enthusiasts who just happened to call in for a look at Tessa while passing. If Claude had obtained planning permission for a caravan site, then I thought I would have been informed, but there had been no such notification. With only three caravans parked there, however, I thought they must be casual visitors and went home to book off duty without worrying too much about Claude and his dubious enterprises.

Saturday was the first of my two-day weekend break from duty which meant I had no routine patrols to perform either that day or Sunday. Around half-past ten that Saturday morning, I decided I needed a book of stamps from the post office. In addition, Mary needed a few items of shopping and so I walked down the village, taking two of my children with me, with the intention of undertaking that small domestic chore.

In the post office, Joe Steel served me and then said, in almost conspiratorial tones, 'Your Sergeant Blaketon has been here, Nick, he asked for a look around and now he's arranging to look at my books and past accounts. I think he's serious, you know, about taking over the post office and shop.'

'Well, I know he wants this kind of place when he retires ... well, Joe, I hope everything works out for you but I'm not sure what it will be like, having my former sergeant living in the village!'

'You'll just have to let him know who's boss!' he grinned. 'And have you seen what's going on at the Greengrass place?'

'No?' I had momentarily forgotten about the caravans.

'There's about a dozen caravans parked behind his house, Nick, and an old traction engine steaming away. I saw them when I went past early this morning. Is there something happening in the village that we don't know about?'

'Not to my knowledge.' I shook my head. 'I saw some caravans there last night, only three, and he's just bought the traction engine. I saw him bringing it home yesterday afternoon. I wondered if the caravans belonged to steam enthusiasts, stopping by to examine his new pride and joy.'

'Well, they've multiplied since then. I've no idea what he's up to, Nick, but if he's accepting caravans on his land, it won't please Ken Murray.'

Ken Murray had a thriving and officially approved caravan site on his land in a former quarry above Aidensfield. He had applied for the necessary permission and had been told to conform with the prevailing regulations; this meant having toilets, a shower-block and water standpipes installed. Vehicular access to the site had been improved, a small shop had opened and Ken was running a very popular and well-maintained site.

The only grumbles came from village motorists and business people who were held up by the constant procession of cumbersome and slow-moving caravans, but once these mobile homes were on site, they caused no further trouble. But it was a living for Ken and unsightly though it was on the edge of the moor when full of white box-shaped vans, the site provided some part-time summer work for students and villagers.

'Has Ken complained?' I asked.

'Not to my knowledge,' Joe said. 'But I don't suppose he knows yet, they only appeared at Claude's place overnight.'

Well, it's not a police matter!' I told him. 'It's for the National Park authority or the planning committee or even the parish council to sort out if Claude's doing anything wrong. But I must admit I am rather curious to know what precisely he's up to.'

By Sunday morning that same weekend, more than twenty caravans had congregated on the open moorland behind Claude's ramshackle house and his traction engine chuffed and puffed throughout that morning. As Sunday passed, however, its fire was allowed to die out after Claude had removed it to his old barn for storage. And then, as Sunday morning turned into late Sunday afternoon, most of the caravans began to move away. Some remained, however – only three in fact – and I noticed they stayed for the whole week. And then, the following Friday, I noticed that the traction engine had once again appeared in full steam on Claude's land.

Clearly, the old rogue was up to something of a devious nature and my suspicions were confirmed when Ken Murray knocked on my office door. I could sense that he was angry as I invited him in. It was six o'clock on the Friday evening and Mary had just made a pot of tea; I poured Ken a cup.

'What's the problem, Ken?' I asked. He was a decent man, a former farmer whose health had deteriorated due to arthritis, and so he had given up active farming, turning instead to catering for leisure-seekers such as caravanners. He had a few holiday cottages as well, some having been created from former barns and other farm buildings. He had also purchased some in the locality.

'Greengrass!' he spat the name. 'He's the problem!'

'What he up to now?' I asked.

'Have you seen that patch of moor behind his house?' Ken put to me. 'It's full of caravans ... well, it was last weekend and now he's at it again!'

'Doing what, precisely?' I asked.

'Stealing my customers,' Ken said. 'He hasn't got an approved site, Nick, there's no facilities there and the planning authority haven't given him permission yet there he is, as large as life, poaching my customers!'

'So how does he do that?' I was intrigued at the Greengrass ingenuity.

'Well, to get to my site as you know, the vans have got to climb Brant Hill and that seems to defeat most caravan drivers. They're not the world's best drivers, as you must know, Nick, and lots of them get stuck on the hill. Some of them are downright clowns when it comes to negotiating country roads, they haven't a clue. But even with a good driver, all it needs is a sheep to wander into the road and the vans have to stop – and if they do that, they can't pull away again, the hill's too steep. Lots of them do get stuck, Nick, it's one of the hazards of caravanning life. If they get stuck, they usually come to me for help and I've a tractor which I use to drag them up the hill top.'

'I've seen you in action, Ken. You provide a good service!'

'But Greengrass is undercutting me, Nick. He's waiting on a Friday and Saturday, as the caravanners arrive, and I'm sure he's driving sheep onto the hill to force them to stop, and then he offers to tow them up the hill with that traction engine of his, for a fee, of course. At the same time he offers them a pitch for the night or weekend, as part of the deal. He does a package which is cheaper than I can do – I've got to cover my costs with staff and so on, but all he does is tow them onto that patch of moor which doesn't even belong to him. He's making a fair bit of cash.'

'Don't the caravanners book in advance for your site?' I asked.

'Not all of them; they're the ones he's poaching, casual passing trade. Valuable trade, I might add. Those who've booked ahead will come here, even if he does tow them up the hill with his traction engine ... they love it, Nick, being towed like that, out come the cameras. He's hit on a wonderful scheme. But he's losing me a lot of customers, Nick, and I wondered if there is anything you can do about it.'

'It's hardly a police matter, it's more for the planners to deal with, Ken,' I had to tell him. 'They're the ones to prevent Greengrass running an unauthorized site. They'll give him notice to stop.'

'That'll take ages, Nick. By the time I get the council to do something, we'll be well into the summer and I'll have lost hundreds of customers, some for long stays. I can't afford to wait that long.'

'You've had a word with Claude, have you?'

'Yes I have – because his lot are using my

facilities, would you believe! They come into my site and use my toilets and showers. Those are for my customers, not all and sundry, they're not open to the public. But all I got from Claude was his opinion that there was nowt wrong in helping folks in distress, and besides, that bit of moor didn't belong to him so he couldn't stop caravanners from using it if they wanted to. He claimed that if they pitch their vans there, it's nothing to do with him. It's open moor, common land. And he also said it was nowt to do with him if those caravanners used my facilities.'

'There must be something other than an absence of planning permission to stop caravans from using the open moor like that,' I said. 'Look, Ken, leave it with me for a few hours. I'll get my books out and see what I can do.'

'Right,' he said. 'Thanks.'

'And it might pay you to hire a man to sit with your tractor engine running on Brant Hill ... to get in first, I mean, and undercut Greengrass. I reckon a tractor is faster and more manoeuvrable than Claude's traction engine!'

'I might just try that!' smiled Ken Murray. 'See you.'

If Claude was taking those caravans onto the open moor rather than parking them on his own property, then it could rightly be argued that they were not his responsibility. All he did was to haul them to the top of the hill for a suitable fee and if he completed that journey by towing them off the road and onto the moor, then he could say he was doing so for reasons of road safety.

His argument would be that he pulled the caravan off the highway and onto a safe traffic-free place so that it could be unhitched without becoming a traffic hazard. Knowing Greengrass as I did, I could see that could form at least part of his argument. A plausible explanation from Claude might defeat rule-bound officials, but I felt sure there was some law, ancient or modern, which could be applied to this situation. But first, in fairness to Claude, I should tell him that I had received a complaint about his activities.

I went to see him that same evening and mentioned Ken's complaint. Exactly as I had anticipated, he said, 'They're parking on the moor, Constable, it's not my pro-perty. It's common land, so far as I know, which means it's nowt to do with me. Yes, I do go to their rescue, being the Good

Samaritan that I am, just as folks with traction engines rescue cars from boggy agricultural show fields or race meetings.'

'So you're not going to prevent those people parking there?' I put to him.

'I am not! How can I? It's not my land; it's nowt to do with me even if it does adjoin my premises.'

'Do you tell them that when you levy your charge for towing them up Brant Hill and hauling them onto the moor?'

He blinked now and twisted his head from side to side, saying, 'Well, I tell 'em there's a good pitch or two on that bit of moor and they pay me extra for towing them there ... that's business, Constable, there's nowt illegal in that.'

'And I suppose you tell them they can use Ken's toilets and showers?'

'No, I never say that, Constable. I just tell them there's toilets over there on Ken's site, and a shop and showers and things. But I never say they have to use them. I just point out the fact they're very convenient!'

'Claude, you are being at your most devious. So, you are telling me you have no intention of ending this practice?'

'Ending it? Why should folks have to pay through the nose for parking a caravan when I can render a recovery service *and* direct them to a parking site cheaper than my rival? That's even bearing in mind he recovers them for nowt, with his tractor. That's on condition they use his site, you understand. It costs a fortune to park there overnight, Constable. If the caravan isn't heading for Murray's site, then he charges more than me for towing them up the hill. I'm doing folks a favour, really I am ... they love my Tessa, you know, they take happy snappy photos of her in action, in all her glory.'

It was precisely the kind of response that I expected and it was clear that he planned his exercise with more than his customary attention to detail. I returned home to find there had been a telephone call from County Councillor Maureen Coupland who lived in Aidensfield. Mary had told the councillor that I would return her call.

'Ah, PC Rhea,' she oozed into the phone as I returned her call. 'You are aware of the unwelcome development on the Greengrass property, are you?'

'I've just come from there,' I told her. 'I've been to interview Mr Greengrass but in fact the caravans are not on his property. He is not responsible for where they park. They're

211

on common land.'

'Well, I have received two complaints already, PC Rhea – both from independent and rather influential members of the public, I might add, not from Ken Murray. Not yet, that is. I anticipate a complaint from him in due course. I can see that if we can't dissuade Mr Greengrass from hauling them onto that land, we shall have a *cause célèbre* in Aidensfield.'

'It's not a police matter.' I felt I had to state my own responsibilities at this early stage. 'However,' I added, 'I shall do some research into the legal situation from my point of view, just to see if there are any regulations that might apply, and if I find anything that could be used to solve the matter, then I shall do so – and I shall inform you.'

'Well done,' she said. 'And I shall do likewise.'

Clearly, a session with my law books was required. I was already aware of one provision under the Road Traffic Act of 1960, section 18, which created the offence of driving a motor vehicle more than fifteen yards onto any common land or moorland which did not form part of a road, or upon footpaths or bridleways, unless it was done with lawful authority or for emergency purposes, but a caravan was not a motor vehicle. Thus that useful piece of legislation did not apply.

If Claude towed the units to their positions, the car drivers had not 'driven' motor vehicles onto common land, and caravans themselves were not motor vehicles. Indeed, Claude's Tessa was not a motor vehicle either, even if it was a mechanically propelled vehicle. All this was a play on words, but that's how the law functions. It all depends on the precise meaning of a word.

The Highways Act of 1835 was still in force at that time and section 77 created a wonderful range of offences relating to carts, wagons and carriages. This old act contained an early offence of obstructing the highway with a carriage, another of failing to keep to the left of the highway, another of one person driving more than two carts at the same time and perhaps the most wonderful of all – the offence committed by a carriage or cart driver who 'quitted the carriage and went to the other side of the highway fence'. That was a polite way of reminding drivers that they should attend to the needs of nature before embarking on a long trip.

I did find a provision under the Caravan Sites and Control of Development Act of 1960, section 16, which said that a rural district council may make an order with respect to named commons in their area, prohibiting the stationing on the land of caravans used for human habitation, but Ashfordly Rural District Council had not seen fit to make such an order.

None of the old offences created by the Highways Acts and other statutes of similar nature could be directed towards caravans, which were a modern invention. And no offence involving a motor vehicle could be directed towards a caravan either unless, of course, the caravan had an engine like some motorized mobile homes.

In traffic law, a caravan was a trailer and none of the regulations governing trailers could be associated with parking caravans on common land. The more I searched, the more it seemed that Claude's caravan swindle was annoyingly beyond the scope of police duty or criminal law. And then I had a brainwave.

I knew that some traffic cases involving certain modern vehicles had been determined by declaring that they were 'carriages'. As long ago as 1879, the case of *Taylor v Goodwin* had established that a bicycle was a carriage. I knew that a motor car could be regarded as a carriage for traffic law purposes, thus making it possible to use some old statutes against offending motor vehicles, like being drunk in charge of a carriage. But could a caravan ever be regarded as a 'carriage'?

Carts, wagons and stage coaches were all classified as carriages, and all were driven by drivers and drawn by various means, such as horses or motor vehicles. But a caravan was classified as a trailer; perhaps that ruled out any claim that it was a carriage? I had set myself a small problem – and then I found what I wanted.

In the Interpretation portion of the Road Traffic Act, 1960, section 256 said, 'A motor vehicle or *trailer* shall be deemed to be a carriage within the meaning of any Act of Parliament, whether a public general Act or a local Act, and of any rule, regulation or by-law made under any Act of Parliament...'

That was enough for my purpose. A caravan was a trailer which meant it could also be regarded as a carriage. This Act said so which meant that the laws applicable to 'carriages' also applied to caravans. Furthermore, if I could not find any useful piece of legislation in current statutes, then I would search the by-laws.

It took a long time but eventually I came across the very thing I sought. In fact, I found two quite separate by-laws and one of them, made in 1932, relates specifically to caravans. It said that 'no person dwelling in a tent, booth, shed or similar structure, or in a van, caravan or similar vehicle, shall occupy land within 300 yards of any dwelling house so as to cause injury, disturbance or annoyance to the inmates of such house after being required to depart by any inmate of the house, or by his servant or by any constable on his behalf.' This by-law was applicable to the whole of the county of the North Riding of Yorkshire.

I was not sure whether the caravans in question were parked within 300 yards of Ken Murray's house or any other dwelling, but I felt I could find someone who had been annoyed by their presence – and that meant I could require them to depart. The penalty for infringement of this by-law was a fine of five pounds.

The second by-law applied specifically to the Rural District of Ashfordly in the County of the North Riding of Yorkshire. It had been passed in 1887 to regulate the use of 'any waggon, wain, cart or carriage' and among the provisions was one which said, 'No person shall drive or cause to be driven or draw any waggon, wain, cart or carriage onto any open moorland, common land, heath or other such land not forming part of a road except for agricultural purposes or for fire fighting and other emergencies.' The penalty for infringing this by-law was also five pounds for every person and every offending waggon, wain, cart or carriage.

This was what I wanted.

It meant I could report Claude for drawing the caravans onto the moor, and I could also report the owners or occupiers of the caravans for *causing* them to be driven, i.e. paying Claude a sum of money to haul them from the road onto the open moor. I thought this would solve the nagging problem and rang Councillor Coupland to explain my intentions. She fully agreed, suggesting that a warning should be issued first and if no one heeded that warning, then proceedings should be taken. That appeared to be an amicable way of dealing with the matter. Armed with a copy of the by-laws, therefore, I sallied forth to the Greengrass residence first thing on Saturday morning and found him stoking up Tessa for another day's caravan hauling.

'Now what do you want?' he demanded, as he noticed my approach.

'Just a word of friendly advice, Claude,' I smiled, making sure he noticed the file I was carrying.

'If it's about them caravans, we've been through all that and they're nowt to do with me.'

'But they are, Claude. I am sure I could interview some of the occupants right now, as they're preparing for a happy breakfast and a carefree day in the countryside, and I am sure they would confirm that you towed them with Tessa to their present position on that stretch of open moor.'

'I'm not disputing that,' he said. 'It's not my land, that's the important thing, it's not my responsibility.'

I then played my trump card; I showed him the by-law, explained his culpability and said he was liable to a five-pound fine for every caravan which he towed onto the moor – and that the occupants were also liable to a five-pound fine.

'I don't believe this!' he exclaimed. 'How can you rely on an old law like that, this is the 1960s, Constable, in case you hadn't noticed, not the 1860s.'

'This law is still in force, Claude. You've got until two o'clock to get all those caravans shifted.'

'But where to ... I mean, how can I get 'em to move when they're happily settled in and buy eggs off me and milk and things...'

'You can always tow them away, free of charge,' I said. 'And take them over to Ken's site, or pack them off home with their cars and caravans ... it's up to you. Just get them away – or it'll cost you – and them – a fiver for every one that remains.'

'That's all my profit gone! But what about my traction engine, how's it going to earn its keep? I mean, I'm doing a service...'

'You can still do a service by hauling them up the hill when they're stuck,' I said. 'But when it comes to hauling them onto common land or the open moor to set up their pitches, you're breaking the law. And so are they,' I said, as I walked away from him.

Fortunately, the moor was cleared of all the caravans by two o'clock and eventually a 'For Sale' notice appeared on the traction engine. But Ken Murray did allow Claude to sell eggs to his caravanning customers.

There was another occasion when the interpretation of an Act of Parliament came into question through the activities of Claude Jeremiah Greengrass. Bernie Scripps from Aidensfield Garage had been offered a derelict car which had been stored unused in a remote farm shed for about thirty years. It was a red sports car, an old MG built in 1925 with a bull-nose type of radiator, wire spoked wheels with the spare wheel fastened to the offside bodywork, half eliptic springs front and rear, drum brakes but no roof or windscreen.

The car was complete, but the engine was not in working condition, and it had not been operated since the car was laid up around 1934. Although the vehicle was in such a state that it could never propel itself without major restoration, Bernie felt that, with some loving care and attention from himself, he could make the car roadworthy and even display it at classic vehicle rallies in the district. Beyond doubt, it was a spectacular car and there might be scope for hiring it out on special occasions like weddings or even as an extra in films and television programmes. Such was Bernie's enthusiasm that he agreed to buy the car for ten pounds and remove it without further ado to his garage in the village.

Bernie did have a breakdown vehicle, an old lorry cab unit and a compatible trailer with which he towed or sometimes carried broken-down cars or accident casualties into his premises for his personal attention, but on this occasion his trailer had broken its axle and he was awaiting a replacement. Thus he could not haul the old MG on his trailer, but he could tow it by making use of his trade plates.

Not having a rigid tow bar, however, he had to make use of a length of thick rope or a chain but that meant the towed MG required someone to sit in it during the towing process, that person's job being to steer it and operate the brakes. These did work – a spot of grease inserted under pressure and some muscle force had ensured that, and so the idea was to tow the MG from Low Hagg Farm, Elsinby to Aidensfield, a distance of about four miles. As his co-driver on this enterprise, Bernie selected Claude Jeremiah Greengrass; for insurance purposes, Bernie would drive the breakdown vehicle and Claude would control the MG at the end of the tow rope.

On the face of things, this seemed a very simple operation. However, Low Hagg

Farm was tucked into a deep hollow behind Elsinby with access down a very steep, winding hill. The hill – Low Hagg Bank – had three gradients. They were 1-in-3, 1-in-4 and a further 1-in-3, with each slope being marked by a sharp corner. It was like a miniature Alpine pass with steep drops beyond the verges, but it led to Low Hagg and then passed the farm on its route through the dale where it emerged eventually on to the moors above Ploatby. As the name of the farm suggests, it was situated in a marshy area, but a very beautiful and peaceful place.

At the agreed time, therefore, Bernie and Claude arrived at the farm, made their presence known to Tony Hirst, the former owner of the old car, and set about removing it. Bernie reversed his breakdown truck into the shed where the car was stored and it was not difficult for him to attach a thick rope to one of the front cross members of the car's frame.

It had no bumper bar and lacked any other attachment for towing from the front, and so that front member, which protected the starting handle and spanned the front of the car between its front wheels, seemed ideal. In fact, it was the only place to which a tow rope could be attached. When every-thing was done, Bernie mounted his truck, started the engine and shouted, 'Right, Claude?'

'Right,' said Claude, as he sat majestically in the cockpit of this beautiful old car, looking almost like a racing driver in his bucket seat. 'I've tried the steering and it works, and the brake pedal's pumping up and down OK.'

Gently, Bernie began to ease his truck forwards, and for the first time in years, the old MG began to move. Bernie shouted to Claude to try the brakes when the car was moving and he did; surprisingly, they worked, as did the steering. No other function was required and so Bernie's little procession began its journey back to Aidensfield.

There were no problems until they reached Low Hagg Bank. Bernie slowed down so that he could engage bottom gear for the long ascent – almost three-quarters of a mile – and so the truck and its splendid trailer began the climb. Claude sat in splendour, steering the wonderful old car as it moved slowly behind the truck, and they surmounted the first severe climb and navigated the first severe bend without a scrap of trouble. Bernie's skilful driving revealed a hidden talent – he could cope with the gradients, the bends and the weight behind him and even Claude later expressed his admiration of Bernie's driving.

But as they began the slow ascent up the second incline, disaster happened. The front metal member to which the tow rope was attached snapped and separated from its anchorage points; one of the retaining nuts, rusted and rotten after all those years of inactivity, had fractured. The member, now loose at one end, moved and the tow rope slid off the unattached end. Claude shouted in alarm but, in those initial moments, Bernie did not hear him and within a split second, Claude was careering backwards down the hill. I am assured that he released several loud and panic-stricken yells before Bernie realized what was happening, but in the meantime, the old car was gathering speed on its free run backwards down Low Hagg Bank.

Claude, alternatively looking over his shoulders and over the sides of the rushing car, pumped at the brake pedal, but nothing happened. For some reason, the brakes did not work efficiently as the car was racing backwards. Claude tried to find the gears, but they were rusted and impossible to engage. In fact, he did a wonderful job guiding the old car at speed down that steep hill and it is believed he might have reached the bottom successfully had not a pair of tourist cars been ascending.

They were driving slowly up the hill some distance behind Bernie and Claude and the drivers of both cars – friends and holiday partners – had been able to observe the small procession ascending ahead of them. They saw what happened, they saw Claude suddenly begin his backwards rush. Each of them stopped in the vain hope that the uncontrollable old car would pass them by, but it didn't.

Rushing backwards down the hill with the wind whistling through his hair and his voice being lost in the vacuum of his descent, it was all Claude could do to keep the old car on the road. He collided with the first car which by this time had stopped; it was a glancing blow, but it was sufficient to demolish the front wing of the smart, modern car, knock out the headlights, and detach its bumper bar before hurtling backwards towards the next victim. This time, it collided midships with the halted car, hitting it fair and square in the middle of the front bumper to crumple the entire front and bonnet area, smash the headlights, radiator and bonnet, and then come to a halt resting against the car as its bewildered driver praised the Lord for saving his life.

'Sorry about all that,' said Claude somewhat unnecessarily. 'But it ran away with me...'

To cut short a long story, the holidaymakers reported the matter to the police by ringing from a nearby cottage and I had to interview Claude and Bernie about the escapade. Having listened to both, and having taken statements from the two angry holidaymakers, I submitted my accident report to Sergeant Blaketon who sent it along to the superintendent at divisional headquarters. He recommended that Claude be prosecuted for dangerous driving.

I must admit I was unhappy about this because, in my view, Claude was not actually driving the old car. He could not be regarded as 'driving' because the engine was not working and could never be made to work without a major overhaul. You can't *drive* a car which does not have a working engine.

Furthermore, it had not worked for more than thirty years and at that stage, it was incapable of functioning as an engine. Thus, I reasoned, the vehicle was not a motor vehicle – it was trailer, and there is no offence of dangerous driving of a trailer. When the time came for me to serve the summons on Claude, therefore, I thought it only fair I should express my personal opinion to Claude before the case.

'You need a good solicitor,' I put to him after explaining my belief.

'I can't afford a solicitor!' he snapped. 'How can I afford to pay their fees?'

'There's always legal aid,' I said. 'And if you have to pay, then surely Bernie will share the costs – and if you're found not guilty, the court could order that you be paid costs.'

'Are you on the level with me?' he asked.

'Yes, I am,' I said. 'There was a case in 1946, known as *Wallace v. Major* which established that a person who is merely steering a broken-down vehicle which is being towed is not a driver. And if he's not a driver, he can't be convicted of careless, dangerous or reckless driving.'

'So I don't have to go to court?'

'Yes, you do,' I said. 'You have to go and

plead your innocence – but even if you are found not guilty of dangerous driving, it means the two owners of the damaged cars can claim through the civil courts. They won't lose by the decision but you'll be the winner because you won't have a dangerous driving conviction recorded against you.'

'I thought you coppers always presented the case against mere mortals like us?'

'Then you're wrong, Claude. Our job is to present the facts, not to prejudge a case. I'm telling you the facts of this one so you can take advantage of them.'

When the case came to court, Claude was represented by a fiery young woman solicitor, a recent addition to a practice in Ashfordly. Her name was Jackie Lambert and she quoted two cases – *Wallace v. Major* (1946) and a more recent one, *Regina v. Arnold* of 1964, both of which had decided that the mere steering of a broken-down vehicle did not constitute 'driving'. And so Claude was found not guilty.

He bought me a pint of beer next time he saw me in the pub.

7

It was during the 1960s that farmers began to consider alternative means of using their land and premises to greater financial advantage. In some instances on the moorland near Aidensfield, farms had several acres of derelict land which was impossible to cultivate due to its rocky nature, heathery roughness or inaccessibility, either because it was on a steep slope or surrounded by marshland or potholes. Most moorland farmers managed to use some of these rough acres for sheep-rearing, but the land could rarely be used for anything else, nor was it capable of being cultivated for any worthwhile commercial plant-producing purpose. Preparing such rough land for the growth of conventional crops was extremely expensive and practically impossible because these rocky pastures defied the use of sophisticated modern machinery; hand tools used by past generations such as scythes, spades or hay rakes were the only means of cultivating these small rough pastures, but such laborious methods were no longer viable. Combine harvesters, tractor-drawn ploughs and other modern machinery was needed if farming was to be commercially successful, but such equipment couldn't cope with this kind of tough terrain.

Furthermore, there were other instances where land, for a variety of reasons, had become uneconomic, but this was generally due to the small size or barren nature of the pastures. The days of family-sized harvests were coming to an end – modern farming demanded larger fields, larger crops, more financial investment, greater production for large commercial outlets, speedier and more effective harvesting methods and it all had to be done with greater efficiency.

For some moorland farmers, this was a sheer impossibility – they had neither the cash nor the available land for such grandiose agricultural schemes and they began to consider other means of producing an income from their property.

Caravan sites and holiday cottages were probably the most popular example and several farmers in the North York Moors had converted surplus buildings and developed previously barren land for this purpose. One man operated a zoo on his former farm; another began to collect ancient equipment and machinery to create a local museum of farming; some turned to breeding exotic or rare animals and birds; one built a herd of milk-producing goats; another began to specialize in heavy horses, and another decided to breed racehorses. One grew lavender as a commercial crop; some turned to the growth of strawberries and raspberries on a pick-them-yourself basis; one converted some derelict buildings into a mushroom farm; one turned a barren corner of his land into a forest of conifers, and I did know that one was considering the development of a vineyard. Other enterprises included turning one farm into an ice-cream production centre, while another cow-byre became a noted art gallery.

In some ways, it was an exciting time for rural development even if it meant that the landscape was being altered, often irrevocably, but most rural dwellers, be they country people or incomers, realized that the countryside could not be allowed to remain unchanged if society was to develop and flourish, and if the best use was to be made of our vast and wonderful natural assets. Many of them did appreciate that

231

change was inevitable.

But even if the 1960s produced an era where inhibitions were cast aside along with a conscious and determined effort to break with the past, there was one farmer whose ideas for an alternative use of his land could have caused a furore.

He decided to develop a nudist camp.

His name was Tim Greaves and he lived on a splendidly situated spread near the outskirts of Waindale. It rejoiced in the wonderful name of Elves Hollow Farm and the surrounding area was rich in folklore about the little people. They were said to live in caves in the nearby woods, or in holes along the riverbanks. For centuries, elves had been associated with this remote dip in the hills and it was said that the local people believed in elves well into the last century. Even now, the most down-to-earth Yorkshire people admit the place exudes a curious and attractive aura of magic and mystery. The approach to Elves Hollow is through Waindale, a quiet hamlet with neither a shop nor a church, and then, just past the ruined abbey on the edge of the hamlet, there is a narrow lane which leads behind the ruins before heading through a densely wooded hillside area. Once past the wood – a distance of about a mile and a half – the road dips suddenly to reveal the wide spread of Elves Hollow reclining deep in the lush green dale. The panorama of rich farmland extends on both sides of a slowmoving stream and in spring the banks of this stream are alive with wild daffodils and bluebells.

This road leads nowhere else; a sturdy wooden gate and large signs announcing 'Private – No Through Road' signify the end of the public highway and the beginning of Greaves' extensive property.

During my time as the constable of Aidensfield, the farmhouse was almost concealed behind a further lush growth of deciduous trees but one or two outbuildings were evident when approaching it even if they did merge with the leafy background. Tim Greaves ran a large dairy herd of Friesians and indulged in some noteworthy breeding of prize-winning large white pigs, consequently the farm was one of those places at which I called every three months to sign his stock registers. I found the whole place magical – it was so remote and isolated that it seemed to exist in a different world and even in a different time. I could understand why the local people had long believed this place to be the haunt of the little people. It was the sort of place that could hold secrets, and it was the sort of place where those secrets may never be revealed to ordinary mortals. And that is precisely what happened.

A tall, handsome man in his mid forties, Tim Greaves had inherited the farm from his father and maintained it in an immaculate condition; his house was always welcoming and his wife, Greta, was always cheerful and immaculately dressed. She dressed beautifully, even on an ordinary working day, and was the sort of woman who could muck out the hens or cows and finish the job without getting a speck of dirt on her clothing. In spite of the busy lives and evident success of this couple and their farm, there was always an air of welcoming calm and peace around Elves Hollow.

It was during one of my routine visits to the farm that Tim mentioned his controversial plans. I was enjoying a coffee and a bun in the kitchen, having signed his registers, and for a while we chatted about nothing in particular. Eventually, though, he said, 'What I'm going to say to you now, Nick, might shock this village if it became public knowledge.'

'Sounds interesting!' I had to admit.

'It's a scheme for part of my land. It's not that I'm setting out deliberately to upset the village – I'm not, because I hope I can maintain complete secrecy about the whole thing, but I reckon I've identified a gap in the market.'

'You're not going to stage pop concerts, are you?' I put to him as the potential horror of that idea struck me.

'Not me!' he said. 'I'm going for something much more discreet and much quieter – and with less potential for trouble – all the necessary ingredients if I'm not to let the locals know what's going on.'

'A campsite, you mean?' I could see that he wanted me to attempt a guess.

'Of a sort, yes,' he smiled. 'But for folks who don't like wearing clothes!'

'A nudist camp?' My voice must have registered the depth of my surprise.

'There is a demand for such places,' he said. 'Not that I'm into nudism or new-age experiences or drugs or flower power or anything like that myself, but I am well-read and I'm always open to new ideas. I think of myself as being enterprising and rather adventurous in business. However, I saw an article in one of the national papers which said that nudists have a constant problem in finding suitable places to spend their holidays or weekends. There's a few nudist beaches around the country, but they're often located at the end of ordinary beaches with the risk of oglers, pimpers and intruders always there.'

'That's quite true,' I said, thinking of one such beach on the Yorkshire coast.

'I see nothing wrong in folks cavorting around in the nude if they want to, so long as they're on private property and they don't interfere with other folks or cause embarrassment, and I've got the ideal place at the far end of my land; it's well off the beaten track; and totally secluded; it can't be seen from anywhere.'

I wasn't quite sure how to react to this but his basic arguments appeared to be perfectly logical. I realized he would have to apply for planning permission and felt sure that that would generate a spirited public response, but from my point of view, I could not see any objection from a police aspect. There might be personal objections, even from police officers, but I couldn't see any scope for official police antagonism. And that was his next question.

'What do you think the police attitude will

be? I thought I'd ask while you're here. It's something I have to consider.'

'It's hardly a police matter,' I said. 'It sounds more like something for the planning authorities or the parish council, but there are some laws which would have to be respected.'

I then told him that some Victorian laws remained effective, with prosecutions being regularly brought to court even now when their provisions were breached. One such law dealt with the indecent exposure of what the legislators politely called 'the person' and it seemed the Victorians did not even contemplate that a woman could be guilty of this offence. The wording which created one of the offences of indecent exposure came from the Vagrancy Act of 1824.

It said it was an offence for any person to wilfully, openly, lewdly and obscenely expose *his* person with intent to insult a female. There was no corresponding offence directed at women. There is no doubt that some sad and unfortunate men, known far and wide as flashers, were compelled to reveal their private parts to their victims but whether this behaviour insulted all the women witnesses in question is open to some doubt. Some worldly ladies just laughed at the display although I'm sure some might have been impressed as well. However, if this statute was to be enforced, it had to be borne in mind that it catered only for male offenders and that the offence could be committed anywhere; it was not restricted to public places.

Thus a man flashing from a bedroom window which overlooked the garden of his neighbour – both private places – could be prosecuted, but there were two more indecent exposure offences which could be committed only in public places, or in places where the display could be seen by members of the public. And women could be guilty of these other offences. A swimming pool open to the public, albeit upon payment, was deemed to be a public place for these purposes, but the ingredients of all these offences, whether committed in public places or elsewhere, involved more than merely wandering around with no clothes on. There had to be some other activity, such as visible male excitement or overt lewdness of behaviour, particularly if a woman was prosecuted. Accidental and unintentional exposure of bare flesh did not constitute an offence.

238

These aspects of the law did not affect nudists who were all of like mind and who would not be insulted by the unadorned nakedness of another, whether of the opposite sex or not, but the very nature of the nudists' form of recreation meant they had to follow their whims in places which were not accessible to the public. The simple way to overcome the 'public' aspect was for the nudists to form a club which was available only to members and to which the public did not have access.

I explained all this to Tim and he understood what I was saying, adding, 'I've read up about the notion of forming a club,' he said. 'The way I see it is that I can form a club based on my property and then open up my premises to *bona fide* nudists who are members of other clubs to which mine will be affiliated.'

'That deals with one aspect of public concern. Club members only, that's the rule. Now for another – your proposed site,' I asked. 'Is it completely away from public view? I know it's well off the road, but is it away from public footpaths or rights of way? Or can it be overlooked from anywhere?'

'It's totally secluded, well off the pro-verbial beaten track and with no access from

239

elsewhere, that's why it's so ideal,' he assured me. 'Would you like to see it?'

'Yes,' I said, thinking it would be sensible to examine the proposed site so that I could speak with some authority should I ever have to.

'Right, come on, we'll take the Landrover.'

He drove along a well-surfaced but narrow lane which led east from the rear of the farmhouse and soon we were crossing a meadow bordered by the stream; our drive took us through a gateway in the hedge and then down a further dip in the landscape. And there, nestling deep in a fold in the hills, was an L-shaped building, which appeared to be very old. It was roofed and appeared to be divided into small cells with a covered walkway running along its full length; in my opinion, it looked like cloister running the full length of the L shape.

'There we are.' Tim indicated the building as we made our approach. 'It's got a cobbled forecourt in front of it, and it's hidden from the world on all sides. I'll have to extend it and bring it up to date so far as conveniences and comfort are concerned, but I'll do so in keeping with the architecture; there's a dozen cells there now. I reckon I'll need upwards of fifty.'

What is it?' I was fascinated by the sight. 'It's in the middle of nowhere!'

'Nobody's sure what it is, or what it was,' he said. 'The general opinion is that it's a former part of the old abbey, and that when the abbey was knocked down, Henry VIII's Commissioners didn't know about this part of it. As you can see, it's quite a long way from the main building and it seems it was overlooked. It survived the Reformation and I think it was used secretly by the local Catholics for mass when their religion was forbidden during the Penal Times. There was a statue in that forecourt at that time, a life-size carving of the Virgin and Child, but later the Puritans got to know about it and demolished it, saying it was an example of popish idolatory. They actually thought Catholics worshipped statues, somehow being incapable of understanding they served only as reminders of the real thing. Anyway, when I did some deeper research, I discovered the child of the statue was naked so they might have been objecting to that. It shows what dirty minds the Puritans had!'

'So this is a fitting place for modern naked people then? Let's hope the modern Puritans don't find out and take the law into their own hands.'

'Oh, I think most people have more brains than that these days. After all, we are living in the twentieth century.'

As we pulled up in front of the strange building, I realized it did have all the appearances of a cloister even if it was separated by distance from the original abbey.

Tim was saying, 'These rooms might have been for the nuns who formed part of Waindale Abbey's community or they might have accommodated travellers or pilgrims. I favour the latter – centuries ago, this road – little more than a footpath at that time – extended over those hills towards the south and, as you know, Nick, the monasteries of old did cater for travellers and pilgrims. Lots of them came to Waindale in those days, it was an important abbey. Abbeys were the hotels and motels of the past. Anyway, thanks to an accident of history, that former building is on my land and it belongs to me now. I've decided it would be better if it was used although I expect I'll find some restrictions when I come to converting it.'

'You couldn't find a more secluded place though, could you?' I said.

'No, it's ideal. It's all on private land, the

public never strays down here and I've got PRIVATE notices all around my property, especially at the entrances.'

'There are public footpaths in the vicinity, though, aren't there?' I was still unsure whether the public might stray onto Tim's land and receive a shock while looking for willow warblers or rare orchids.

'They're all over those hills and far away,' he smiled. 'Several miles away in fact. You'd never stray from one of them and find your way here – to get here on foot, you'd have to make very determined effort, Nick.'

He then escorted me around the old accommodation block and it was a fascinating place, as dry inside as it had been the day it was built, although lacking windows and doors. But the potential was enormous. I thanked him for showing me around and on the return trip said that, in my personal opinion, I could see no reason why this place should not harbour a nudist camp. Quite literally, no one would know they were there. Tim asked me not to mention this to anyone at this stage. He wanted all his preparatory work to be secret, to prevent any undue antagonism from the beginning. Meanwhile, he had arranged to visit his adviser and his architect early next week, and would then submit his proposals to the next planning committee meeting.

He asked that I make no prior hint of the surprise awaiting them and I assured him I would respect his confidentiality. 'I'll keep your secret!' I promised.

I returned home wondering what kind of reception Tim would receive at the forth-coming planning meeting, and likewise I wondered how the Press would deal with the inevitable outcry. In the days that followed, there was a rumpus in the national Press on at least three occasions, each case involving proposals to create areas for exclusive use by nudists. One was in a woodland glade, one was a private beach and the third was a private riverside area somewhere along the banks of the upper reaches of the Thames. But Tim's project was not mentioned.

'I don't know what the world is coming to,' grumbled Sergeant Blaketon during one of my subsequent visits to Ashfordly Police Station. 'Why on earth do people want to wander about with no clothes on? Especially in England! And especially in places full of nettles and briars, and with hosts of hungry midges ganging up to eat you raw. Did you see that case in the paper this week? Some chap wanting to form a nudists' club on the banks of the Thames of all places? Not only is it likely to frighten the fish, it's indecent, Rhea, unnatural if I'm not mistaken, people seeing each other naked and frolicking in the all-together and not being married to each other or members of the same family ... it's exhibitionism, Rhea. Indecent exposure legitimized, that's how I see it. It's beyond me, I must admit, I just fail to understand what prompts someone to take all their clothes off in front of other people, strangers into the bargain, and then behave as if nothing is different ... I'm sure very few of them can be regarded as a pretty sight, so it's nothing to do with beauty. Some folks are positively ugly when they're starkers. It's all lust, Rhea, undisguised lust, if I'm not mistaken...'

I let him air his prejudices and when he'd finished, I asked, tongue in cheek, 'So if someone wanted to start a nudist club in this area, you'd object?'

'I would not be happy about it, Rhea, that's for sure, but being a police officer means I must be careful about making my views known outside these four walls. As police officers we are supposed to be impartial in our dealings with such things,

Rhea. Our job is to uphold the law of the land and not have opinions about what is right and what is wrong, but, no, I would not be pleased. I would not be pleased at all. I might make my views known to the councillor of the ward in which I reside in the hope he or she would bring them to the notice of the planning committee or whatever authority was involved, but, as a private individual, I could express my views. The trouble is Rhea, as I am the police officer in charge of Ashfordly section, any views I express will inevitably be seen as official police policy, so I have to be very careful. Very careful indeed. Why do you ask? You're not telling me that there is going to be a nudist camp hereabouts, are you?'

'No, I just wondered where you and I stood in such matters, I think you've answered that.'

'Always be careful about expressing personal opinions or taking sides in matters of likely dispute, Rhea; the public cannot distinguish between what is official police policy and what is a personal opinion when we police officers make pronunciations. But nudist camps are not within our province, Rhea, so long as the criminal law is not broken.'

It was a few weeks later that I saw a snippet in the local paper to say that Timothy Greaves of Elves Hollow Farm, Waindale, had been granted permission to convert some outbuildings into holiday chalets. His application had been approved subject to certain conditions relevant to the age, appearance and history of the buildings in question. There was no mention of nudism in the note. That, it seemed, was Tim's opening move – he'd get this first application approved before his final intentions were made known. Work on the necessary conversion began immediately.

The normally very quiet Elves Hollow dell became full of noise and activity as workmen began their task. Tim took me to have a look as the work was in progress and when it was almost complete. In the latter stages, I must admit the outside appearance of the former cloister did not look greatly different, but the internal parts had been transformed into cosy apartments, each with a kitchen, lounge, one bedroom, a bathroom/shower-room, a separate toilet and small lobby. Some apartments were for two persons, others for singles, and all were tastefully furnished. In each case, the front doors emerged onto the forecourt where each unit had its own parking area for one motor vehicle and Tim told me he was going to plant fast-growing conifers as one means of obstructing the views of possible pimpers.

After a year or so, the work was complete. At this stage, there hadn't been the tiniest hint of nudism coming to Waindale, but when I was invited to inspect the finished site, I thought it looked rather like a Red Indian reservation or even an open prison. It was surrounded by high wooden walls with a gate marked 'Private – No Admittance', the walls being a temporary measure until the conifers had grown sufficiently tall. But inside there were seats and gardens, private rooms for saunas and a gymnasium, a frontage to the bubbling stream, suitably shielded, and a larger room for use as a community centre – for dances, social gatherings, parties or such.

'So when do you open?' I asked Tim.

'This coming spring,' he said. 'I'll be placing my first advertisements very soon.'

'Well, I must admit it's the best kept secret hereabouts,' I said. 'I've not heard one whisper about it being used by nudists.'

'I've never mentioned that in any of my negotiations,' he smiled. 'If I had, I'd have been turned down from the start. But my idea is to get the people to come here for holidays or weekends, without saying anything about their special activities, and then to see how the locals accept the idea. So, Nick, it's a case of keeping mum for a little longer!'

I could well imagine that no one would have any idea of the true role played by this holiday centre in the moors – the residents wouldn't parade their nakedness beyond the limits of their special place, no one would enter it without authority and it could not be seen from anywhere else. Whenever the holidaymakers left the premises, they'd be fully dressed and no one would consider they were nudists if they went into a local pub or for a walk on the moors. Thus it was a secret place – and for that reason, it was remarkable. More remarkable, I think, was that no one else ever knew the secret of Elves Hollow. Somehow, Tim and his family, as well as his guests, had maintained their secret.

I continued to visit Elves Hollow during the ensuing months and was told that the first customers had arrived and were very happy with their specially developed site deep in the moors. Eventually, Ted formed the Elves Hollow Holiday Club but he did not apply for a registered club liquor licence for his club-rooms because he had decided not to sell liquor on the premises. Thus, the police did not become involved with his enterprise.

They were not involved due to any problems either – there were no fights, thefts, damage or trouble of any kind with the result that the local police officers – either me or those from Ashfordly – were never called to the site.

And really, there is nothing more to say, except that Elves Hollow Holiday Club with its full complement of nudist members continues to run quietly from its beautiful setting beside the stream in the lost reaches of Waindale. Tim's son now runs the farm but apart from the select few, no one knows it is the haunt of nudists.

If the Elves Hollow Holiday Club is one of the locality's best kept secrets, then the many moorland farms which belonged to Lord Knowscott-Hawke stuck out like the proverbial sore thumbs. It was almost impossible to overlook them because each one boasted a bright red front door.

The Knowscott-Hawke family was a

product of the industrial revolution; the family was not descended from the ancient nobility of this land but from the new money generated by the vast incomes enjoyed by people who, in the industrial turmoil of the last century, founded mills, built railways, mined coal, manufactured cotton, created department stores and helped give life to the iron and steel industry of north-east England. In my time at Aidensfield, the incumbent of Whemmelby Hall was Lord Ralph Knowscott-Hawke; he was in his middle twenties and had inherited the estate and the title from his father who had died early. I had never met him but knew he was a member of a family which had helped create the local iron and steel industry.

His business empire also included the manufacture of bricks and he was involved in several building booms over the years. In addition, the family were shareholders in a huge range of other companies and enterprises. On the female side, however, the family claimed descent from minor members of the nobility, although no one was quite sure of the precise details. Thus Young Lordy, as he was known, could claim some blue blood in his otherwise rich rust-red veins.

While creating their wealth, members of the family had begun to purchase local farms, inns and cottages when they became vacant and by the end of the Second World War, the Whemmelby Estate owned several pubs, more than fifty moorland farms spread across a huge area, a couple of complete hamlets (of which Whemmelby was one) and countless small cottages which were let either to tenants or to others who required them. In accumulating this wealth and, it has to be said, the power that went with it, the Knowscott-Hawkes did not endear themselves to the local population. The people claimed they lacked the breeding and style of the old aristocracy; they used bullying tactics and power and threats to achieve compliance from their subordinates, tenants and workforce alike. It seemed that as each new generation of Knowscott-Hawkes came along, so their lack of breeding, their bad manners and their sheer rudeness became more evident. The tiny quantity of blue blood which flowed in their veins was not able to counter the effects of a more common background. Lots of local people said that Young Lord Ralph behaved like an inner city lout rather than a sophisticated Yorkshire landowner.

When I was the constable at Aidensfield, I did encounter his relations and staff from time to time; lots of distant family members came to spend week-ends or holidays at the hall. On occasions, Young Lordy tried to use my services for car-parking at his social functions, asking his estate manager to make the necessary arrangements, but always I managed to avoid being hired as their lackey for the night. I explained that I was an officer of the Crown, and that I was not for hire as a servant of the local gentry. I undertook my duties seriously, however, and responded whenever the hall and its occupants required the professional services of the police which, happily, happened on very few occasions.

One lunchtime, though, I found myself caught in the middle of an embarrassing saga involving Young Lord Ralph and Jessie Skinner, the wife of a moorland farmer. Jessie was the no-nonsense wife and business partner of Jack Skinner who very successfully farmed Lingberry Farm on the moors above Whemmelby. In their mid-fifties, the couple were renowned for their black-faced sheep, their Border collie dogs and their Herefordshire bulls, winning prizes at shows all over the north of England

and further afield.

Jessie was a very kind woman, the sort who would give food to the elderly and poorly without wanting anything in return. She'd drive into Ashfordly or Malton or York with a passenger who had a dental appointment or needed to visit the optician and who could not find a suitable bus or could not afford a taxi; she'd give money to the needy, she'd go shopping for the elderly, she supported all the local charities and gave Christmas presents for the annual school party.

But Jessie could not tolerate fools – she remonstrated with vague and unworldly tourists, swore at townsfolk who let their dogs loose on her land, remonstrated with caravanners and campers who left litter behind, wrote letters to the Press about ramblers leaving gates open and damaging fences, criticized politicians in the Press and lambasted local councillors who fell short of her vision of professional competence. And yet she could be utterly charming when necessary.

In other words, Jessie was a formidable opponent who could make use of her innate cunning and her feminine charm. A short, stout woman, she had a head of thick grey hair, a round and surprisingly jolly face with red cheeks and smiling, almost mischievous eyes and she wore horn-rimmed spectacles which gave her an owlish appearance. Without any formal education, she was a very intelligent woman, a voracious reader and regular speaker at local women's clubs and organizations. She never wore any kind of make-up and always dressed in very simple country clothes, things which were practical rather than fashionable such as brown shoes with low heels, aprons which covered everything and woollen jumpers. In short, she looked like a typical plain and rather simple countrywoman – which most definitely she was not.

Whenever I called during my regular rounds to sign the stock register or renew a firearms certificate, she would produce the inevitable slab of fruit cake, piece of Wensleydale cheese and mug of hot coffee made with fresh full-cream milk from her dairy.

Sometimes, we would chat about inconsequential things, with Jessie telling me about her latest battle with authority or a visiting fool and I would respond with matching tales from my own experience. On other occasions, she would reveal a remarkable knowledge of English literature, or a total understanding of the world situation or British politics which she'd gleaned from reading newspapers. We got on well, in spite of our age difference and the wide gaps in our professions.

Then, one hot September day, I found myself heading for Lingberry Farm just before lunchtime. I was running slightly later than intended due to having to deal with a reported theft of some garden gnomes in Elsinby, but I reckoned I could visit Lingberry Farm and complete my examination of the books before breaking for my own lunch. But by the time I arrived at Lingberry Farm, I was almost an hour behind schedule.

'Why don't you stay for dinner, Mr Rhea?' she invited. Dinner was the name given to the midday meal in this part of Yorkshire. 'It's nearly ready; Jack will be in from the fields in ten minutes or so, so you might as well wait till he gets here and then eat with us. There's more than enough for the three of us.'

This kind of spontaneous invitation was quite normal on moorland farms and so I accepted – it would have been churlish not to – and made a radio call from my van to

Ashfordly Police Station, asking Alf Ventress to ring Mary to say I would not be home for lunch. Jessie's husband, Jack, a big powerful man with a lovely sense of humour, arrived from his work in the fields as expected, removed his boots, changed out of his working clothes and washed his hands, then joined me.

We chatted as I signed the necessary books and then we adjourned to his spacious lounge as Jessie busied herself laying the table and serving the meal. As we talked, I heard a commotion outside. I looked out of the window and saw that several expensive cars and some Landrovers had arrived. They had parked outside the front of the farmhouse, some of their vehicles blocking the view from the lounge window. There was a lot of raucous laughter followed by the slamming of car doors and then what appeared to be a small army of men in shooting tweeds heading for Jack's kitchen door. I estimated there would be a dozen or so, all laughing and making loud and raucous remarks.

'Are you expecting company?' I asked, thinking that if he was, then I would be intruding. I would make an excuse and leave; I had no wish to be a gate-crasher at a farmhouse lunch.

'I am not,' he said with jutting jaw. 'I've no idea who this lot is ... come with me ... I might need your uniform...'

As he rushed along the corridor to the kitchen, I followed almost at a trot and we arrived in the large, stone-floored kitchen just as Jessie was answering the door. As she opened it, a tall, thin man with a black moustache and very dark hair pushed his way rather brusquely past her and stood in the centre of the kitchen with his hands on his hips and his chin in the air. Although he was in his late twenties, his demeanour was that of a man who owned the farm. I recognized him – it was the Young Lord Ralph, but I said nothing at this stage. I was merely a guest.

'And who are you?' he asked Jessie, as his cronies crowded into the kitchen and stood around him, some grinning and some looking rather puzzled or even embarrassed. They were all about his age, all clad in shooting tweeds and all of the same or similar class as their spokesman.

'Jessie Skinner,' she said quietly. I could see she was speedily weighing up the rather baffling situation. 'I'm Jack Skinner's wife. This is my husband coming in now, with PC

Rhea, the constable from Aidensfield.'

'Of course, PC Rhea. A farm with the backing of the law...'

'And who are you?' she smiled. 'And your friends?'

'You do not know?' He sounded mortified and displayed mock anguish at her lack of ability to recognize him.

'I haven't the faintest idea,' she said, without any show of anger or submissiveness. She was staging one of her charming acts.

'I am Ralph Knowscott-Hawke.' He displayed a mock smile. 'Lord Knowscott-Hawke to be precise, the owner of Whemmelby Hall and estate. And these are my friends. Guests is perhaps the more accurate word, shooting guests to be even more precise.' And he chortled.

'And how can we help you, sir?' she smiled.

'We want you to provide us with lunch,' he said. 'There are fourteen of us.'

'Lunch for fourteen?' She looked puzzled. Jack was about to say something but Jessie caught his eye and silenced him with a quick shake of her head. I noticed her reaction; the crowd of hooray-henrys did not.

I knew she was about to teach these men a

quiet lesson in good manners.

'Yes, fourteen. A slap-up Yorkshire lunch please. How long would you say it will take to prepare it? It is ten minutes to twelve by my reckoning....'

'It takes at least an hour to prepare a lunch of that kind – and that would be rushing things. It would be a hasty meal, but I have the experience to cope with such demands at short notice,' she smiled at them. 'I have already prepared lunch for my husband and PC Rhea, so while they are enjoying their meal, perhaps you could wait in our lounge. I do not have any good quality sherry in the house, I'm sorry, but you are welcome to what drinks we do have.'

'We have our own pre-lunch drinks in the cars. We know that working farms are not acquainted with the best drinks or fine wines. We have our own sherry, wine, malt whisky, champagne ... do you mind if we bring it in? I know that farmers do not go in for this kind of liquid hospitality, but their meals are renowned.... My friends and I will bring in our own aperitifs, so would you be so kind as to call us when you are ready?'

'Please use our lounge for your drinks,' she said sweetly. 'Now, I shall show you the way, there are sufficient chairs for all and you can use the front door to reach your vehicles.'

Beaming like a welcoming hostess, Jessie led the way along the corridor and they followed like a herd of noisy young bullocks, chortling and laughing as they headed for the lounge. I heard Lordy say, 'There you are, it's as simple as that ... these people know their place...'

When she had directed them to the room, Jessie unlocked the front door and allowed it to stand open so they could fetch and carry their own drinks with the minimum of trouble. Then she closed the interior doors and returned to the kitchen.

'What's all that about?' Jack asked when she smiled at him.

'They expect me to provide lunch,' she said.

'I can see that, but why?' He spread his hands in a gesture of bafflement. 'Why you? And why such short notice? You weren't told in advance, were you?'

'No, but Young Lordy obviously thinks this farm belongs to Knowscott-Hawke's Whemmelby Estate,' she smiled. 'He thinks we are his tenants.'

'And you're not?' I smiled.

'No, we are not. I own this place, lock, stock and barrel,' said Jack. 'I owe His Lordship nothing and he doesn't own me.'

'So I thought it was time to teach Lordy a modest lesson in front of his guests,' said Jessie. 'That is what I am doing. You'll note that I did not say I would prepare a lunch for them.'

Jack grinned at this response, but I must admit I did not know what was going on. Jack recognized my ignorance of local customs and decided to enlighten me as he pointed to a chair at the table. 'Sit down, Nick, and I'll tell you.'

He told me that it was a condition of the tenancy of all Whemmelby Estate's moorland farms that, should the estate owner so decide, the tenant farmer and his wife should prepare, quite free of charge, a meal for him and his guests provided the farmer's wife in question was given reasonable notice.

The definition of 'reasonable' was open to question, but invariably when such a lunch was required, those guests were members of a shooting party out on the moors for a whole day's sport when a trek back to the mansion for lunch might take hours. To cope with such eventualities, the organizer of the shooting party selected a convenient farm on the moors and demanded lunch from the tenant's wife.

Jessie then said, 'Judging by their dress and vehicles, these people are a shooting party out on the moors for a day's sport, and Young Lordy has decided to impress his friends by showing how he can dictate to us while expecting hospitality from the farmers of the North York Moors. I'll bet he's been boasting of the power he exerts over the rustic natives.'

'So you're not going to prepare lunch for them?' I asked.

'No, of course not,' she smiled. 'I'm going to let them wait in there for an hour while we have our lunch, and at one o'clock, I shall break the bad news to him.'

'Will you need police protection?' I smiled.

'I doubt it. But by then, of course, it will be too late to go anywhere else....'

'But there will be some unfortunate tenant farmer's wife somewhere nearby, won't there?' I suggested. 'Won't he go and bully the wife into doing lunch, even if it won't be ready until the middle of the afternoon?'

'He's new to this idea, Nick. In fact, it wouldn't surprise me if this was his first attempt to follow in these particular footsteps of his ancestors. His father didn't often demand this kind of service from his tenants – if he wanted a lunch for his shooting parties, he would contact a farmer's wife well in advance – a week or more – and he would pay for the meals as well. He was a nice old man – even though the tenancy agreements said he could have a free meal, he never abused the privilege. Anyway, the farmers' wives hereabouts are well aware of the lack of consideration by Young Lordy – even when he was in his teens he would take his pals out for a day on the moors and try to get a free meal.'

'The agreement extended to all the family then, not just the Lord of the Manor?' I said.

'Yes, but the ladies of the moorland farms around here are not stupid, Nick. We all get together you know, from time to time, and I can tell you that when Young Lordy has guests for a day's shooting, the ladies get to know about it in advance and all of them contrive to be out of the house over the lunch period. Now he's the lord, though, it seems he's going to continue the custom and there's no doubt he thinks he has scored today...'

'You'd think he would learn a lesson if he's been greeted by lots of empty houses!' I said.

'His sort never learn, Nick. But today, he will go hungry. Now, you enjoy your meal before the fun begins!'

We did enjoy our lunch and although it began shortly after twelve, it was almost one o'clock by the time we finished. Jack said he had to get back to his work in the fields, I said I had to resume my patrol and Jessie said she had to deal with the fourteen shooting men in her lounge.

Even as the grandfather clock in her hall was striking one, she marched along to the lounge and opened the door to be greeted by a huge cheer from the assembled men. Jack and I waited in the kitchen; we could hear everything that was said and the braying voice of Lordy sounded above the babble of chatter.

'Ah, Mrs Skinner. How nice to see you. Lunch is served, is it?'

'No,' she said. 'Lunch is not served, Your Lordship. And it will not be served in this house. Not to you or your party. You will recall that I did not promise to make lunch for you.'

Her strong voice carried above the incessant chatter and everyone became silent as the full import of her words penetrated their minds. There was, quite literally, a stunned silence as the audacity of this woman made its impact upon them; they all looked at Lord Ralph in anticipation of his reaction.

'This is intolerable, Mrs Skinner!' he shouted. 'You know as well as I that it is a condition of your tenancy that you shall provide lunch to me and my guests given reasonable notice...'

'I am very aware of that condition, sir, but it does not apply to me.'

'And why are you exempt, might I ask?'

'Because I am not one of your tenants, Lord Knowscott-Hawke. This farm belongs to me and my husband, it is our property: it is not part of your estate.'

Behind him, someone chuckled, but Ralph spluttered, 'But ... but ... you allowed us in to have our aperitifs and led us to believe we were to have lunch...'

'You thought you were going to have lunch. I did not make any such offer but I am very happy to have guests in my house, even if they are uninvited and rude at times. Your friends were not to know of your mistake, Lord Ralph, and I have no wish to be rude to them. So yes, you were welcome to drink your aperitifs in the comfort of my home. But you cannot and should not demand a meal from me.'

'You silly buffer!' Someone from the crowd turned on their host. 'Ralph, you've done it again ... God, when will you get things right! Come along, gentlemen, it looks as if we shall have to go hungry today.'

They filed out of the Lingberry Farmhouse, now all silent; they had not had too much to drink because it would have spoiled their aim, and one of them halted in front of Jessie.

'I am sorry about this, Mrs Skinner. Ralph can be such a bloody fool at times ... thank you for dealing with him in such an effective way.'

'I hope he won't go around demanding meals from his tenants,' she responded. 'Most of them are much more hard-working than him, and he's got more money than they have. He needs to be taught a lesson.'

'We'll make sure he learns from this experience,' said the fellow. 'But, sadly, he's not the sort who learns easily!'

'I hope you get something to eat,' she smiled.

'I have sandwiches in my car,' he laughed. 'But it would have been nice to have had a full farmhouse lunch!'

'Perhaps another time,' she said.

And so the lunchtime drama of Lingberry Farm was over. Later that month, however, a team of painters from Whemmelby Estate began to tour all the farms owned by Lord Knowscott-Hawke. They had orders to paint every front door bright red – so that His Lordship would, in the future, be able to recognize his own property. Even so, I now knew that the ladies living on those farms would always contrive to be away for the day whenever one of Lord Ralph's shooting parties was in the vicinity

This was one ancient custom that was destined to become obsolete.

8

Having been brought up in a village deep inside the North York Moors and having spent a good deal of my childhood playing around my grandfather's farm, I was accustomed to the sights, smells and experiences that only a busy working farm can produce. Much of that general experience involved animals, large and small, wild and domestic.

In my formative years, I helped to milk and feed the cows, watched as the sheep were shorn and lambs were born; I fed the pigs and stood by in wonder as the horses were shod, wondering why they never protested as the nails were driven (apparently) into their feet; I helped in the dairy where cheese and cream were produced and the milk was bottled; I helped in the hayfields and cornfields, the potato fields, turnip fields and the orchard; I fed the hens and ducks, collected eggs and cleaned out their houses. I was around when rats were trapped, foxes were hunted and rabbits and hares caught for meals. I helped feed the ferrets, calves and lambs, attended shoots of pheasants, partridges and pigeons and picked apples in the autumn. There were cats and kittens galore, most of whom lived around the buildings without ever being allowed into the house, and there were dogs too – dogs for herding the cows, driving the sheep, gun dogs for retrieving shot game or dogs merely acting as companions for the resident family members.

When I grew up and moved away to begin my police career, my varied duties took me to farms where there were no animals – huge enterprises serving only to grow cereals for example, or massive spreads growing nothing else but potatoes.

As a consequence, it was difficult to visualize a real farm without animals; farms and animals were, in my mind, inseparable, like eggs and bacon, fish and chips, Abbot and Costello, cock and bull, horse and cart, hook and crook and topsy and turvy. Most of the farmers I knew loved their animals, even if it meant having them butchered. I've seen farmers weep as a favourite cow or pig went to market, I've seen farmers' wives become highly emotional at the thought of having their favourite sow sent to the bacon factory and I've known tough, unemotional moorland farmers grow very weepy at the thought of their favourite sheepdog having to be put to sleep due to old age or disease.

In the world of the farmer, an animal is often thought by outsiders to be a mere commodity but few farmers can totally detach themselves from the emotions which can sometimes surge to the surface after years of working with, and depending upon, a range of animals. Farmers would rear pheasants for shooting, but never be cruel to them; they would hunt foxes because they killed their livestock but respected the fox for his good looks and cunning, and they regarded badgers as our most ancient of Britons. Farmers, accustomed to death among animals in their daily routine, would never be cruel to an animal.

One animal-loving farmer was a hardened old Yorkshireman called Irwin Dowson. Irwin was a sheepbreeder whose spread at Merlin Crags Farm, Shelvingby, included hundreds of acres of open heather-covered moorland. Upon this he ran thousands of black-faced moorland sheep, buying and selling them as the markets dictated his moves, and producing lambs galore in the spring.

If ever there was a specialist in sheep-rearing on the moors, it was Awd Irwin, as he was affectionately known to all. And if ever there was a specialist in the training of sheepdogs, it was the same Awd Irwin. Generations of Border collies had passed through his skilled hands over the years; he would even take semi-trained dogs from other sheep-farmers and run them with his own dogs and flocks to complete their training.

A dog trained by Awd Irwin was regarded as a golden asset to any sheep-farmer – with immense skill and speed, those dogs could gather sheep from their moorland grazing grounds often without detailed instructions from their masters, and they would bring them off the moors for shearing or lambing or dipping. It was even said that an Irwin-trained dog could separate one owner's flock from another, recognizing the animals by the coloured dye on their fleece, and some went so far as to suggest that an Irwin-dog could even count up to ten. Fact and fiction mingled a good deal in the sheep lore of the moors but it was beyond any doubt that Irwin was the finest sheep-man on the moors. He worked well past the normal retiring age and as he passed the seventy-five years of age milestone, people began to ask, 'When is Awd Irwin going to call it a day?'

He did retire, but not until he was eighty years old, and he went to live with his seventy-six-year-old sister, Alice, in her cottage in Aidensfield. Aidensfield was about nine miles from Merlin Crags Farm – a world away in the opinion of poor old Irwin.

In all his life, he'd never been so far away from his farm for such an extended period of time – his biggest trek away from the place was visit to the Great Yorkshire Show but then he'd return the same day.

Irwin's wife had died some years earlier which is probably one reason why he continued to spend all this time on the farm; he needed something to occupy him in his widowerhood. By tradition, however, upon Irwin's retirement the farm was due to be handed over to his son, Martin. Poor Martin had had to wait a long time but men of his calibre were very patient. As one said to me, 'Everything comes to them that waits – so long as they wait long enough!' I do know that, as the years went by, Martin wondered whether he would ever be able to regard the place as his very own and all the hints dropped by him and his wife that

Irwin should retire in time to enjoy his remaining good health were met with a terse 'I'll go when I want to and not before.'

But Irwin, with his old legs growing increasingly painful due to arthritis and a distinct shortage of breath beginning to manifest itself, did eventually decide to retire. It was not something he wanted to do – the last thing he wanted was to leave his beloved farm and all the animals he had cherished during his long life, but his doctor recommended a few years of easier living. After all, Irwin was still in remarkably good health and with a bit of care, could have many happy years ahead of him. Clearly, he had thought it over and concluded that it was really time to leave the hard task of running the farm.

By the time he had reached that momentous decision, however, Martin was fifty-five, his wife was fifty-two and their sons were rapidly maturing with the eldest already wondering when he would inherit Merlin Crags. Every one of them was pleased to see the end of Irwin's long reign, but in departing from the premises, one extremely important question loomed.

'What's going to happen to Awd Shep?' asked Irwin.

'Well, he'll have to stay here,' Martin was adamant about that. 'He's our best dog; we can't run a moorland sheep farm without a good dog, and he's the best. We've no up-and-coming pup to take his place either. He's part of the farm, Dad, just like all the sheep and cows and pigs.'

'Aye, I realize that...' said Irwin.

'So what's the problem, Dad, you weren't thinking of retiring him or having him put down, were you?'

'Having him put down? No, I was not thinking of that!' snapped the old man. 'It's just, well, he's my best pal ... we've been together now for twelve years, man and dog, in all weathers, in all conditions on those moors, fog and sunshine alike, snow and gales, the lot. We work well, me and Shep, we've never been apart, Martin. So, well, what I thought was – he might like to retire with me. Then we could be together for our final years, me and him, just like it's always been.'

'Dad, don't be so sentimental. Shep's only a dog, and a working dog at that. He's no poodle or pet dog; he likes work; he's good at his work and we need him here. He's a farm dog, Dad. He's part of the business, a vital part of the farm's livestock.'

'He's nothing of the sort!' snapped Irwin. 'Dogs aren't like other livestock!'

'Why not?' questioned Martin. 'How about the cats then?'

'Cats are different, cats don't have loyalty like dogs ... cats warm to anybody who'll feed them. Dogs are personal, and Awd Shep's my dog, Martin.'

'He's not your dog, Dad, he's the farm dog. And there's a few more years in him yet. Besides, if we got another one, we'd need Shep to bring him on, to work beside him, to teach him his job. You know that as well as I do. Sorry, Dad, Shep stays to work here. It's you that's retiring, not him.'

I was given the gist of this exchange a couple of weeks after Irwin retired because I saw him sitting on the seat near Aidensfield's war memorial. I went to join him for a few minutes' chat because I thought he looked rather miserable.

'Now then, Irwin,' I greeted him as I settled at his side. 'How's retirement suiting you?'

'Oh, it's not too bad, Nick.' He knew me from my official visits to his farm. 'Better than I thought, to be honest. I'm meeting up with some of my old mates who've packed in work like I have. I get into the pub

276

on a night for a couple of pints and one of my grandsons comes down from the farm to take me up there for my Sunday dinner. My sister looks after me, does my meals and washing, things like that. So, yes, things aren't too bad even if they are a bit on the quiet side.'

'I thought you looked a bit unhappy,' I said. 'Looking at you from the other side of the green, you didn't look too cheerful.'

'Mebbe you're right, so can I ask you a question?' he put to me.

'Of course,' I smiled.

'When one of your police dog-handlers retires, what happens to his dog?'

'Well,' I said, not at that stage knowing the saga of Awd Shep, 'it depends on the age of the dog. If it's a young dog or one with a lot of work left in it, it will be allocated to a new handler.'

'And if it's getting on a bit? With not much work left in it?'

'That will be a matter for both the handler and the chief constable to decide. Sometimes, a dog will be retired with its handler and the handler will keep it. It becomes his dog, but that's only if the handler wants to have the dog. It's never forced on him.'

'But he can have his dog then, if he wants?'

'Well, sometimes, but he might have to pay a fair price for it.'

'Pay for it?'

'Well, police dogs don't belong to their handlers,' I informed him. 'They belong to the police authority. They're official police property, like our uniforms, motor vehicles, houses and so on. The chief constable can't go around giving them away as presents! They never belong to the handler, even if man and dog have always been together in their working lives, and even if the dog lives at home with its handler. Police dogs are always police property,'

'And is it the same with police horses?'

'Yes, it is. They've got longer working lives than police dogs, so the chances are they'll have several different handlers or riders during their working lives. They do retire eventually, of course, and are usually bought by people who can care for them rather than those who want hard work out of them. But they're sold as well, not given away.'

'Oh, I see. You never think of that, do you?' He was talking to himself. 'It's like farm animals then? When my lad took over Merlin Crags, he took over the animals as well. They're farm property, just like police dogs are police property.'

'Right,' I said. 'Exactly the same idea.'

'But if an ordinary chap retires and moves house, he takes his dog. with him, doesn't he? He doesn't leave it behind with the house, like he might leave curtains or carpets behind?'

'If it's his own dog, yes, he'll take it with him. But domestic dogs are not the same as working dogs, Irwin; they're pets. They belong to their owners. But working dogs are different, like guard dogs. If a security guard retired, he'd have to leave his dog behind for someone else to take over. Why are you asking this, Irwin?'

'Well,' and I could now see the sorrow on his face. 'I had to leave Awd Shep at the farm when I retired. I miss him, Nick, but our Martin said they couldn't do without him and he was the farm dog, not my own dog. He's the only one they've got fully trained for driving sheep, you see. They can't manage without him.'

'Well, in that case, Martin was right. But surely, they'll want a replacement before too long and once the new dog is fully trained, you might be able to have Shep here to spend his retirement with you?'

'Aye, that's more or less what Martin said. But it's useful to know similar things happen with police dogs. That's sort of straightened things out in my mind, knowing Shep is a working dog with responsibilities. Not like poodles and pets.'

As Irwin told me the full story, I felt a twinge of sorrow for him but could fully understand his son's requirement to have the dog on the farm. A farm such as Merlin Crags could not function without a fully-trained, completely reliable working sheepdog. It was a few days later that I had to visit the farm during the course of my duties, and this time I had to deal with Martin rather than Irwin. I could see that the farm's new boss was firmly in control and that he was making his own impression on the place. There was some new machinery in the implement shed, for example; Irwin had been prone to keeping his equipment until it fell apart.

We attended to our official business and as I left the house, I saw old Shep lying on the concrete area in front of the cow byre. He was stretched out along the ground with his chin resting on his front paws and his ears registered a slight movement at my presence. He wasn't the bouncy, lively dog

I'd noticed on previous visits.

'He's missing your dad, is he?' I asked.

'I think he must be; he's gone all listless and it's one hell of a job to get him to work,' Martin told me. 'All his sparkle's gone.'

'Pining, is he?'

'He could be. I'm not sure how to tackle this, Nick. We can't do without old Shep and I am looking at pups for a replacement. It takes time to find the right one; it's not the sort of thing that can be rushed along. But I worry about Shep – mebbe the old lad's past it?'

'Your dad does come to see him, doesn't he?'

'Oh yes, every Sunday and other times in between. Shep perks up then, so he's not ill. He was Dad's dog, I think that sums it up.'

I then told Martin about his father's questions concerning police dogs and said I thought he had accepted, perhaps with some reluctance, that Shep was a vital part of the farm rather than a pet dog, and that he would have to remain here to work. And then I said, almost jokingly, 'What you need is for Shep to spend part of his time with your dad and part of his time here. He likes your dad and he likes his work – perhaps he needs both to keep him happy?'

'Travel to work, you mean?' he laughed. 'Spend his nights with Dad and his working days with us!'

'Now that's an idea!' I laughed. 'It might work.'

'Aye, but Dad's living nine miles from here and he's not got a car and we can't spare the time to do that run every day, twice a day, there and back.'

'There's always the bus,' I said, almost jokingly. 'It leaves Aidensfield and comes past your gate every morning just after eight, and comes back again at tea-time, half-past five or so. I've often seen it.'

'Dad would never stand the journey, not now...'

'I was thinking of the dog,' I said. 'He could go to Aidensfield on the bus to spend the night with your dad, and come back next morning!'

He looked at me, unsmiling for a moment, and then his face broke into a happy grin. 'You're serious, aren't you?'

'I knew one man who put his dog into a taxi every morning and sent it off to his daughter's house where it spent the day. The taxi took it back home at six o'clock every evening. The dog got into the habit of sitting and waiting for the taxi, all by itself...'

'I'll have words with Dad and see what he thinks. But he must realize we need that dog here for work!'

Only two days later, I saw Awd Irwin waiting at the bus stop in Aidensfield as I performed an early patrol. Shep was sitting at his side. I pulled up in my van and climbed out for a chat.

"Morning, Irwin. Going for a day out?'

'Nay, but Shep's going to work,' and Shep thumped his tail on the ground at the sound of his name. 'He's a proper working dog now, he commutes by bus and he'll come back at tea-time to spend the night here with me. I reckon he likes it, and I like it ... we can go for walks and he loves sniffing in the hedges and chasing rabbits.'

It was a few weeks later that I saw Martin in Shelvingby village and he hailed me. 'Shep's a changed dog, Nick. It hasn't taken him long to get used to his new routine. I used to put him on the Aidensfield bus, but he goes to our lane end and gets on all by himself now and takes himself off to visit Dad on an evening. He knows he has to get off in Aidensfield and knows his way to Dad's house. And next morning, he does the same thing in reverse, all by himself. He comes to work on the bus, just like people do, and I settle up with the conductor once a week. Mind you, I never thought I'd see a dog catching a bus to work, but our Shep does. And he loves it. He works really well now, full of enthusiasm. And we've found a suitable pup, by the way, another Border collie. I know his background and he's learning fast. Shep's a very good teacher, and the young 'un's really keen on his work. Mebbe Dad can have Shep at home full time before too long, but to be honest, I don't think Shep would like to be stuck in a little cottage all day with nothing to do, he loves his work too much. I don't think he wants to retire just yet.'

'Well, Shep's got the best of both worlds at the moment,' I laughed. 'A happy place to work in, and a happy home to go back to at night. He sounds like a very contented and lucky dog to me. I'd leave things as they are for the time being.'

'We'll do that, Nick. Shep'll let us know when it's time to retire.'

I could easily understand that a dog of his calibre would dictate his own terms and make his wishes fully known, and then I wondered if Shep would teach his under-study how to catch buses.

From time to time, the police had rather unpleasant dealings with farm animals, such as when outbreaks of contagious diseases occurred or when some owners displayed cruelty to their beasts.

But I think the worst was when police marksmen had to shoot bullocks or cows which somehow managed to escape while being delivered to the slaughterhouse. Although these escapes could not be regarded as frequent, they were not unusual because several occurred during the course of a year in most towns where a slaughterhouse was located. The pattern was surprisingly similar in all cases. Just as the animal was being persuaded to leave the cattle truck within the grounds of the slaughterhouse to which it had been taken, it seemed to realize what was about to happen and made a spirited bid for freedom. With a series of hefty kicks of their hind legs, accompanied by head butts and general leaping up and down, they managed to break free from their handlers to make a dash for the nearest open space. Inevitably, this was done with one or more slaughter-house staff in hot pursuit, an action which often served only to make the escapee run faster and further. As many deliveries to the local slaughterhouses occurred in the morning hours, it was usually the case that a fleeing bullock or cow was on the run just as the nearby towns were coming to life and the morning traffic was building up.

We had reports of cows galloping along main roads, through shopping centres, into crowded railway stations and bus stations and even into the bewildering maze of deepest suburbia where their hooves wreaked havoc on lawns and gardens. In most cases, the bewildered and terrified animals were rounded up very quickly by the slaughterhouse staff with some help from the public or police. From time to time, however, an animal would evade its hunters with amazing skill and speed and somehow get itself into the town centre where it created spectacular mayhem among the traffic and shoppers. Much of this was due to sheer terror in the unfortunate animal – bullocks are accustomed to fields and the presence of other farm animals, not streets, cars and alarmed people waving arms and shouting at them. On one memorable occasion, a fleeing bullock galloped into the centre of Ashfordly and went straight into a department store whose doors were standing wide open.

The resultant devastation of crockery, china, kitchenware and cut glass had to be seen to be believed – to say nothing of the gigantic cow pats which appeared on the lush carpets.

Once the animal was cornered, it was allowed to calm down and then, in most cases, driven on foot back to the slaughter-house, or perhaps led with a halter. From time to time, however, a bullock or cow would escape in circumstances which made its live capture impossible. Such beasts seemed to go mad and would attack humans, dogs, other animals and even their own reflections in shop windows or in a car's polished paintwork – and the only way to stop them was to call out police marksmen. These would stalk the animal and shoot it – a sad end but a necessary one when the public was in danger from a mad, rampaging bull, bullock or cow.

In witnessing some of these dramatic chases and recoveries, I wondered whether the fleeing animals escaped because they knew they were doomed to be executed within a very short time, perhaps recognizing the scent of blood from afar?

But Seamus Mulligan's cow differed from those unhappy creatures in several ways.

For one thing, she was a truly beautiful animal who was the sole cow kept by Seamus, a man who hailed from Ireland and who had settled on a smallholding in Elsinby many years ago.

Seamus kept just the one cow – Amelinda – and she lived in a lush paddock beside his cottage. It was well equipped with fresh spring water which flowed into a stone trough, and she had a stone-built barn in which to take shelter from the elements. Seamus kept her for her milk – she produced enough for himself and his family, with a little extra for sale. The pub liked to buy her jersey milk to add to meals organized for special occasions and the villagers would do likewise for parties and formal dinners. Amelinda was therefore favoured greatly by the people of Elsinby.

She was a large-eyed Jersey cow in the prettiest of fawn colours, with just a hint of white on her forelock between two small horns. Slender and delicate, she looked like a dainty picture of a picture-book cow; she walked like a lady, behaved like an aristocrat and produced milk that was the creamiest and most delicious anywhere within a radius of ninety miles. Some said the richness of her milk was due to the quality of the pure spring water which she drank in copious quantities from her own trough.

The second difference was that although Amelinda had a tendency to escape from Seamus's smallholding to go for long walks by herself, she was not trying to avoid death in the slaughterhouse. It seemed she escaped for no reason other than the fact she liked to go for a walk. Whenever she did escape, however, the alarm was quickly raised either by Seamus or by someone who encountered her on her perambulations.

Inevitably, Amelinda was speedily re-covered and returned to the paddock where she lived. She never objected to being escorted back to Seamus's smallholding at Beck Garth, with or without a halter. She was such a delightful animal that everyone liked her and virtually anyone who came across her wandering along the lane could approach her, turn her head back towards home, and encourage her to walk by giving her a quick slap on the rump. And she would walk contentedly by the side of the postman, policeman, schoolteacher or anyone else who happened to know her and who was willing to walk her home. She seemed to enjoy being escorted back to her paddock and never tried to avoid those returns. To my knowledge, she never caused any damage, she never invaded anyone's garden or private premises, never damaged a motor vehicle by kicking it or bumping it, and she never broke into a trot or a gallop. She enjoyed a very sedate and ladylike walk but the odd thing was that she always chose the same route.

The chief puzzle, however, was how she managed to escape. I don't think anyone was deliberately letting her out but she seemed to sense when the gate was insecure and capable of being pushed wide open. It was just conceivable that she had learned to open the gate herself. That was one suggestion. The gate's latch was of the type known as a hunter's sneck, hanging from the top bar of the five-bar gate, it comprised a length of wood which swung loose on two chains and which was deeply serrated to provide a kind of tooth. When the gate was closed, this sneck fitted into a catch on the gatepost and was held in place by the tooth-like projection.

It was a very dependable means of securing a gate, but when huntsmen were riding through, they could lean forward from their mounts, press the side of the latch with the end of their whip and it would open with the slightest of pressure. The horse could then breast its way through the gate; once the horse was through, the gate then swung shut with its own weight, and the latch clicked back into the closed position. It is not beyond the bounds of possibility that Amelinda had learned to depress the latch with her nose and then push open the gate, although the general feeling was that she knew when the gate was not fully latched. Visitors, children, and even Seamus himself might inadvertently leave it in a vulnerable position.

Whatever means she used to escape, however, no one knew why Amelinda continued to stage these escapes and there did not seem to be any pattern to her sudden desire to go for a walk. It did not happen at regular intervals such as the full moon or every Wednesday or when the weather was doing particular things – it seemed as if something suddenly prompted Amelinda to break out of her paddock and head along the lane towards Ploatby. That was always the route she took but, of course, she had never been allowed to complete her outward journey.

One morning I received a call from the telephone kiosk in Ploatby. It was a passing motorist who rang to tell me he'd seen a cow wandering along the lane from Elsinby towards Ploatby, and thought I should deal with it. I assured him the matter would have my immediate attention. I jumped into my van and headed for Elsinby – I had to pass through Elsinby to reach Ploatby – but my first stop was at Beck Garth where I hoped I would find Seamus.

The moment my van eased to a halt outside his back door, he emerged with a big grin and said, 'She's gone again, has she, Mr Rhea?'

'She has, Seamus,' I sighed. 'A motorist has just called me.'

'Same place?'

'Ploatby Lane,' I said. 'Come along, Seamus, hop in and we'll go and find her.'

As we drove along the lane, without any great urgency because we both knew how Amelinda would behave, he said, 'I've been thinking I should change the sneck on her gate, Mr Rhea. I think she's learned how to open it.'

'But that would defeat the purpose of the hunter's sneck, riders won't be able to open the gate so easily – and there is a bridleway through that paddock, isn't there? Horses do need to be able to pass and re-pass, so you can't lock the gate.'

'Yes, that's true, Mr Rhea. It might be riders not securing the gate properly, or the gate not closing itself as it should – but I've thought of all those possibilities, everything does seem to work properly.'

'I shouldn't worry too much. Amelinda never gets very far, someone always recognizes her and makes sure she gets home. But where does she go, Seamus? She always uses the same route.'

'No idea, Mr Rhea. She just sets off and heads along this lane. Sometimes she looks as if she knows where she's going, but she's always been turned back before getting too far.'

In dealing with his matter, I had no intention of threatening Seamus with the offence of allowing livestock to stray onto the highway; it carried a fine of only five shillings (25p) and besides, our usual action was to take any such straying animal to the pound where it remained until collected by the owner – at a small cost. It was a regular thing for animals to stray on country roads – on the open moors, of course, the sheep were always wandering across the roads because they were not fenced in. It seemed silly to penalize one man for something that happened without penalty among others nearby. The truth was that court cases and fines were rarely, if ever, resorted to on these occasions unless there were some fairly strong aggravating circumstances, such as a farmer failing to maintain his fences and hedges after several warnings. And it was as easy to take Amelinda the half-mile or so back home as it was to find the nearest animal pound – easier in fact, because the pound was about four miles away. If she was a danger on the road for her usual half-mile or so (which she was not), then she would be more of a danger on a four-mile trek. In rural areas, one had to apply the law with common sense.

On this occasion, we found ourselves behind Amelinda within a couple of minutes. She was plodding with some determination along the verge, sometimes halting to plunge her nose into the vegetation and sometimes chewing succulent titbits from the hedgerow. But, very quickly, we were at her side. Seamus got out of my van and I followed.

'Come along, Amelinda,' he said gently. 'Time to go home.'

Amelinda made a light mooing noise, tossed her head and turned around at the sound of his voice. She was like a well-trained dog, she required no force or bullying in order to persuade her to return. I watched and then, on the spur of the moment, said, 'Would it be useful to find out where she was going, Seamus?'

'Let her go, you mean? And us follow?'

'I've the time if you have,' I said. 'And it might solve a problem for you – and for her. And I suppose, for me.'

'Well, suppose she goes on for mile after mile – we'll finish up on Scarborough seafront if we're not careful, and that would cause a rumpus! Holidaymakers don't like cows wandering among them.'

'She might be going only as far as Ploatby,' I said. 'It's only a mile from here.'

'Tell you what,' he said, 'if you're agreeable, we'll follow her for a little while. maybe as far as Ploatby if she gets that far, just to see where she's heading.'

'Right,' I said. 'And I'll leave my van here; it'll come to no harm. The walk will do me good.'

And so the pair of us decided to accompany the cow on her walk. Or, to be very precise, we decided to follow Amelinda as she went upon her mission – we did not wish to distract her by walking too close to

295

her head. The patient cow, having been prepared to return to Elsinby, registered some surprise as Seamus persuaded her to turn around once again and to continue her walk in the original direction. But once she realized she was free to pursue that route, she set off at a medium pace and we fell into step behind her.

She moved steadily along the wide grass verge with her wide and beautiful eyes sometimes turning towards us as if to say she was pleased we were allowing her such freedom. We continued towards Ploatby, a strange sight I am sure, and then quite suddenly she turned right. There was a narrow green lane leading off our route; it ran between two dry stone walls and was little more than the width of a cart. Years ago, it had been a route over the hills, often used by drovers and their herds of cattle, but in recent times, through lack of use, it was no longer considered a road. I knew it led high into the hills, through forests on the slopes behind Ploatby, and then across the heights before descending, four or five miles away, into the Plain of York. In modern times, the green lane was used as a bridleway by horse riders and as a footpath by ramblers and hikers, but it was not a busy route. However, for reasons which we did not yet understand, Amelinda turned up that lane.

'She's not going all the way to York, is she?' muttered Seamus in some concern.

'This used to be a drovers' road,' I told him. 'Over two hundred years ago, that would be. I wonder if she knows that? Maybe she's got a sixth sense about this route? Perhaps her ancestors came this way – it was the Vikings who brought jersey cows to this country,' I added.

'Well, she's getting excited about something,' he said. 'She's going faster now' I wondered if I should persuade him to turn Amelinda around and head for home for I had no wish to finish my walk in distant York, but Seamus said, 'There's no stopping her now ... look, she's got her head down and she's off!'

And she was. Amelinda had accelerated her pace and was almost trotting now as we increased our speed behind her. The lane was rising quite steeply at this point and I began to find myself panting and perspiring in my uniform as the cow maintained her steady pace; Seamus, made fit by his outdoor life and manual work, had no trouble keeping up with his cow and then she reached a patch of level ground. There was a gap in the wall – a narrow gap – but it was not due to damage. Amelinda stopped there. She pushed her head through the gap which was not wide enough for her entire body and I realized she was drinking deeply. She had found a well.

It was a deep pool of cool, clear water which must have risen from a spring in the ground because there was no inlet stream; there was an outlet, however, where the overflow vanished down a hole in the ground. A small retaining wall of stone had been built around the well – it was circular, about five feet in diameter, and this was clearly the reason for the gap in the wall. People and animals used this ancient route and could still halt here for a drink, just as they had done in centuries past because the well was in a very good state of repair and was functioning perfectly.

Amelinda stood for a long time, drinking deeply from the cool water and then she emerged, looked at both of us with those soft brown eyes, and then walked back in the direction from which she had come.

'She's going home!' cried Seamus. 'Would you believe that? She's come all this way for a drink of water, and now she's going home!

How did she know where to come? She's never been here before!'

The cow was now moving steadily back down the hill with the pair of us following hard behind, and when she reached the surfaced lane, she turned left and headed back towards Elsinby.

'What do you think about that, Mr Rhea?' asked Seamus.

'One thought crosses my mind,' I said. 'I wonder if that well is the source of the water in her paddock back home? It's high enough in the hills for the water to find its way into your trough.'

'You mean she might have smelled her way here, followed its underground route, so to speak?'

'I've no idea whether cows are capable of that, but what other explanation is there?' I asked. 'She's never been here before, so you said.'

'That's right ... its all very odd, Mr Rhea ... very odd indeed.'

When we reached my waiting van, I bade farewell to Seamus and Amelinda and she continued to plod her way home without a backward glance. Later, Seamus told me she had gone to her gate but could not let herself in. He had opened it for her and she

299

had gone into her paddock where she immediately crossed to her trough to take a sniff at the water and then, as if satisfied with her day's exploration, settled down to graze.

The funny thing was that Seamus did nothing extra to secure his gate but Amelinda never escaped again. And that charming little well in the hills above Ploatby continues to produce an endless supply of cool, fresh water.

Lots of smallholders and other men in Yorkshire like to breed racing or homing pigeons and others enjoy bee keeping, particularly when the latter results in jars of delicious honey produced from the moorland heather. One would rarely expect antagonism or rivalry between followers of these quite distinct and separate interests, but that is what happened one summer in Aidensfield.

One Sunday lunchtime, when I was off duty, I decided to visit the local inn for a pint of beer before my meal. This was one lunchtime during the week when the bar was packed with local people all of similar mind and whose wives preferred them out of the house while the meal was being prepared. It was always a jolly occasion with lots of good-natured banter. Lots of local business was initiated and conducted at these gatherings, lots of news was exchanged and, of course, lots of leg-pulling went on too.

As I enjoyed the relaxing drink, I became aware of two men having what might be described as a heated discussion at the end of the bar. It was not an argument which sounded angry or threatening in any way, but voices were raised with the inevitable result that everyone else lowered their own voices because they wanted to know what the fuss was about. The characters in question were Harry Hutchinson, a keen pigeon-fancier, and Edward Chance, known as Ted, who was a noted bee-keeper. Harry worked for the council and Ted worked for a construction company. Both lived along East Lane in Aidensfield where they were neighbours in adjoining cottages, each cottage having a spacious and well-kept garden. Harry's pigeon loft backed onto that part of Ted's garden where he kept his beehives.

So far as I was aware, there had never been any friction between the men; indeed, they were good pals as was indicated by their presence in the bar that Sunday. Usually, they accompanied one another for their Sunday pints unless either had some other commitment, but on this occasion, it seemed that their banter was rather more high-spirited than usual. In the early stages, none of the other drinkers was taking much notice of their conversation, consequently no one really knew what the fuss was about, and it was George Ward, the landlord, who became the third party in their discussion.

'Well, there's only one way to settle it!' George's voice sounded in one of those moments of silence that sometimes occur at a gathering of people, and his words galvanized the rest of us into silence. We wanted to know what was happening.

'Settle what?' The distinctive tones of Claude Jeremiah Greengrass now sounded from the opposite end of the bar.

'It's nowt to do with you, Greengrass! Or anybody else for that matter,' snapped Ted. 'It's between me and Harry.'

'What is?' asked someone else. 'What's going on, Ted?'

By this stage, everyone was looking at Harry and Ted as if awaiting words of great wisdom or some form of enlightenment, and then Harry said, 'Oh, it's nowt.'

'It can't be nowt if it's creating such a fuss,' said a voice from the back of the crowd.

'Aye, come on you two,' Claude challenged them. 'Let your mates in on the secret...'

Harry looked at Ted and Ted looked back at Harry, and then George Ward stepped in once again.

'Harry was saying that pigeons can fly faster than bees,' he told us. 'And Ted reckons he's wrong. He says bees can fly faster than pigeons. And I said there's only one way to settle it.'

'How's that?' asked Greengrass, perhaps sensing there might be scope to organize some betting on the outcome.

'Have a race,' said George.

'A race?' laughed Greengrass. 'Between a pigeon and a honey bee? How can you do that? It's impossible!'

'It's not.' George stuck to his guns. 'You take one of Harry's pigeons and one of Ted's bees up to the moors and release them both at the same time. Their homes are right next to each other so they'll both cover the same distance – all you need is independent judges to wait and check the contestants as they arrive back at home.'

303

'But there's thousands of bees in Ted's hive,' I decided to have my halfpenn'orth of chat. 'You can't tell one from the other; you'd never know which of them was the one that was supposed to be racing!'

'Dab one of the worker bees on its hairy thorax with some white emulsion,' said Ted. 'It won't harm ... I could catch one and do that, and I could take it up to the moors and let it go ... and when that white-marked bee returns, we'd know it was the racer.'

'It wouldn't work,' said Greengrass. 'How do you know your bee would come home? You can't train bees like pigeons. Wouldn't it want to go off looking for nectar or something?'

'Not if I released it at the right time. Bees do come home at certain times of the day, Claude, evenings for example, as the sun is setting.'

'How far can it fly?' I asked, wondering whether a bee could sustain a long-distance flight as pigeons are able to do.

'Up to two miles,' said Ted.

'That's not far for a pigeon,' said Harry. 'But it would be a fair match ... pigeons have to fly around a bit to get their bearings before they set off home, but once they get the direction worked out, they fly as straight as an arrow.'

'Right,' said George. 'All we have to do then, is find a starting point no more than two miles away; Ted has to select his champion racing bee and dab it with whitewash and make sure it likes pigeons – we don't want it stinging the pigeon so that it nobbles the race – and Harry has to select a pigeon that won't eat the bee. . . .'

'Pigeons don't eat bees, they're grain eaters,' snapped Harry.

'Just joking,' grinned George. 'Anyway, the two contestants will be taken to the starting point so we need an official starter, and we need an independent judge at the finish to clock them both home ... someone who will recognize the pigeon and the bee.'

'How about you, Constable?' grinned Greengrass. 'I reckon the law is independent, so you could be at the finish to see them home. To see fair play.'

'Right,' I said. 'So when are we thinking of doing this?'

'Today?' asked George. 'It's a fine day, there's no wind to speak of, it's light until seven o'clock...'

'What about me running a book then?' Claude asked, and then realized I was present, adding swiftly, 'Provided it's all legal and above board, that is.'

'Claude,' I said, 'I want to know nothing about that, but all I ask is that you don't do it in the pub! Betting on licensed premises is illegal.'

'Aye, well, I might think of something.'

And so plans were made. Due to the trickiness of standing close to a busy beehive to observe the arrival of a white-marked specimen, it was decided that Ted would have to be present at the return end of the flight. He would stand near his hive and give a pre-arranged signal to show that his bee had returned. Likewise, it was said that Harry should stand close to his pigeon loft to signal the return of his bird. As official judge, I would be positioned on the lane between the two houses so that I could see both owners; I could witness their raising of hands and record the time of the return of either the bee, the pigeon or both.

Trusted friends would release the competitors on the moor. The selected starting point was Griff Cross and a check on the map showed it was 1 mile 6 furlongs from each of the contestant's bases. It was reckoned the flight would take no longer than two minutes which meant that neither owner could witness the start of the race. It was to begin at 6 p.m. prompt.

At five o'clock, therefore, still off duty, I went to Harry and Ted's houses and, along with others, noted that he had selected a pigeon called Blue Boy. He showed this to everyone, placed it in a pigeon crate, and handed it to George Ward who'd been nominated the official starter. Ted had captured a bee; he had dabbed it on the back with a dot of white paint and it now buzzed around in a jam jar, looking far from happy.

'She's in training, doing circuits, flexing her wings,' he said. 'She's called Snow White.'

Ted said that George would have to lift the jar over his head as he removed the lid, because Snow White might be angry with him. By raising the jar, she would fly straight out, perhaps requiring a little shake or two. The pigeon was quite accustomed to launching itself into the air under racing conditions. And so George had to drive up to the starting point with his two charges and some helpers, and release the competitors together at six o'clock precisely. It was decided not to launch a flare to herald their departure, on the grounds that it might distract one or both of the competitors as well as create alarm in ships at sea or among passing aircraft.

Claude, meanwhile, was buzzing around the assembled multitude of racegoers with a notebook and cash box. 'How about you, Constable?' he grinned. 'Fancy a wager? I'm not doing odds, not with just two runners. It's a straight bet, you select either Blue Boy or Snow White. £1 a ticket. Winners share the proceeds. Losers get nowt. So there it is, pigeon or bee? You take your choice.'

'I'll have a ticket for the bee,' I said.

'To bee or not to bee,' he chortled as he made a note of my name in his book. 'Come fly with me.... It's about even bettin',' he added. 'Twelve have bet on the pigeon, and eleven on the bee so far. But there's more folks coming, see?'

'What's in it for you then?' I had to ask.

'A jar of honey, mebbe, or a pint of pigeon's milk ... I'll make nowt on running this book, if that's what you mean. Unless I pick the winner of course.'

'I believe you!' I said.

And so there was great excitement as six o'clock approached. As the parish church clock struck the hour, we all cheered in the knowledge that, high on the moor, the great race had started. Harry and Ted rushed to their posts to await the return of their precious livestock and I made sure my view of both was not obstructed while realizing that neither man could see the other. The bulk of the pigeon loft acted as a screen.

As the church clock fell into a silence, so did the assembled racegoers, all standing with their eyes raised to the heavens. There was not a word, not a movement, as we stood and gazed into the sky as if awaiting a vision of some kind, and then Ted shouted.

'She's here ... Snow White has landed ... here...'

I checked the time. 6.04 precisely and hurried to see the white-spotted bee crawling along the landing pad which was in front of the hive. And then Harry shouted, 'He's here. Blue Boy's here.' It was 6.05 and ten seconds. The bee had won.

There was great discussion in the pub afterwards because we all adjourned to the bar bang on opening time at 7 p.m. I won £1.15s.0d on Claude's scheme, George achieved a full pub at opening time, but Harry was not happy.

'I know my best pigeon can beat Ted's best racing bee anytime!' he was saying at his place in the bar. 'But Blue Boy took his time getting his bearings before he set sail for home while that bee just took off and made straight back to Aidensfield. I think Ted's had that bee of his under training without us knowing so I reckon we should have another race, Ted.'

'Next year?' suggested George.

'Right,' said Ted.

'Right,' said Harry.

And so the great Aidensfield race between a bee and pigeon was destined to become an annual event. It became known as the Milk and Honey Stakes.

9

In a remote and rustic area like the district surrounding Aidensfield, there were few opportunities for large-scale social functions. In fact, there were not many places, apart from hotels, where one could host what might be termed a smart but select indoor social event of a smaller kind. The use of marquees for weddings, dances and parties had not yet met with widespread approval, although some rural people did entertain at home. In this respect, the aristocracy were leaders for they had the money and the indoor space to host gatherings, large and small. Shooting parties, cocktail parties, large dinners and garden parties were examples of their ability to produce a memorable social occasion.

Many farmers also hosted large numbers of people in their homes, although this was usually a necessity due to their work rather than for any social-clambering reason. Helpers at sheep-sales, harvest-time or potato-picking, for example, had to be fed and watered, and I knew one farmer's wife who entertained the whole family to Sunday lunch every week – all forty of them! And she could accommodate every one of them in her vast kitchen.

Villages' halls were another focus for social gatherings, but the usual events in these were evening classes, whist drives, beetle drives, Women's Institute meetings, parish council meetings, village craft and horticultural shows and the occasional village dance or hunt ball. The pub was sometimes used for small meetings, too, and some country inns made rooms available for wedding parties, funerals and meetings of local societies.

In the late 1960s, however, important social changes were occurring. The after-effects of being conditioned to food rationing along with memories of the restrictions and self-discipline imposed by World War II, were finally being eradicated from the minds of the older people, and they were beginning to enjoy themselves with great freedom and with more money to spend. Lurking in the background of this social upheaval, however, was a sobering factor in the shape of the breathalyser. This was introduced in October, 1967.

In measuring the amount of alcohol a vehicle driver could safely consume, and in recording the intake of alcohol in a manner which could not be disputed in court, its impact on rural public houses was quite dramatic. Most of them abandoned their role as pure drinking establishments and began to develop a catering side to their business. Large rooms were set aside for this purpose so that formal dinners and lunches could be obtained in addition to substantial snacks in the bar. Quite suddenly, the village inn became the new focus for social events and organized outings, moreso because it developed into a place to which one could take a lady. Hitherto, ladies might be encountered in smart hotels, but they were rarely seen in pubs; only women considered to be of doubtful reputation were regularly seen in public houses. And with this rapid change in the perception and style of public houses, both in the town and countryside, came a corresponding development of the licensed restaurant. These were high-class establishments at which liquor could be purchased with a meal and many were created in isolated places where handsome buildings were transformed into romantic eating places.

Not surprisingly, some were former inns whose owners seized this opportunity to improve their clientele and attract new business. Quite swiftly, therefore, social opportunities for rural folk improved very dramatically. Meals were no longer a mere necessity, they were seen to be an integral part of an enjoyable occasion in pleasant surroundings and even townspeople began to migrate into the countryside for romantic meals. Even the smart set journeyed into the countryside for their leisure treats – quite suddenly, the countryside was *the* place to see and in which to be seen. Town-bred people were now beginning to realize just what the countryside had to offer, even if they concentrated upon man-made attractions rather than nature's mountains, moors and rivers.

And so it was that a very smart restaurant opened at Fieldholme. Andrew Brown, the former chef of an hotel in Manchester, had been holidaying with his wife in the Aidensfield district when they'd come across the former Fieldholme railway station which bore a large 'For Sale' sign. Dr Beeching's axe had removed the railway line and for a time, the station-house had been occupied by someone who'd bought it for reasons of nostalgia rather than common sense. As those feelings had waned, and as the moorland winters made travel somewhat difficult at times, so the owners moved back into town and the former stationhouse, with its offices, sheds, platforms, coal bunkers and water tank was again put on the market. Mr Brown, losing no time, talked to his wife, arranged a hurried meeting with his bank manager, explained his desire to fashion this old station into a smart new restaurant, and managed to buy it for a very reasonable price.

He and his wife then set about converting it into a famous restaurant which would become the mecca of the smart and wealthy set. Among the improvements would be extra bedrooms for customers of the more upmarket kind. And, of course, there was room outside in which to expand when his success demanded more eating or sleeping space – and so Andre's, as the establishment became known, blossomed into a reality in Fieldholme. It was a French restaurant of renown and style, it was *the* place to be seen and to both entertain and be entertained. Andre, as Andrew liked to be known, insisted on the right dress too – suits, with collars and ties for the gentlemen, and smart complementary outfits for the ladies. You did not go for a meal at Andre's while wearing sports jackets and flannels or sweaters and jeans; he even frowned upon gentlemen arriving in dark blazers and grey trousers, although he would tolerate such dress with a slight sniff and not-too-discreet turning away of his head. Sadly, Andre, or Andrew as the local people called him, had developed into something of a snob. Nonetheless, his establishment attracted the wealthy and influential.

For the ordinary people of the district, however, all this was rather too posh and pricey – they preferred fish and chips wrapped in newspaper, or chicken in a basket in the relaxed atmosphere of the bar of the White Swan or Malt Shovel. They liked to be comfortable while supping their pints or Babychams, and if they wanted something more formal, they would go to the dining-room of the Ashfordly Hotel which did a splendid mixed grill with chips because they had little idea about the niceties of fine wines, petit fours, tiers of cutlery and meals with peculiar foreign names.

Andre's, therefore, (both the restaurant and the man) acquired something of a reputation for being rather too snooty and far too expensive for down-to-earth Yorkshire country folk. Those with social pretentions and the money to fund their fantasies, however, did patronize the restaurant in the old railway station and some of them welcomed Andre's fawning behaviour as he ministered to their needs. The place was an undoubted success and within three years, Andre had expanded. He built a conservatory along the front of the house to form a beautiful extension to his restaurant and to make use of a portion of the former platform, and he added four extra bedrooms.

He and his wife, Renee, (Rene to the locals) decided to launch their new extensions with a large party to which all their regular patrons were invited. Andre, always with an eye to future business, also issued invitations to those who had not patronized his establishment but whom he felt were socially acceptable should they wish to honour him with their custom. Generally, those additional guests were people of local standing – some had titles, there was a former ambassador and his wife, an internationally known singer, a famous author and several local millionaires.

Much to my surprise, I was invited, along with my wife, Mary, and I think the only reason for our inclusion was that I regularly patrolled the area, often calling at Andre's with warnings about bed-and-breakfast guests who fled without paying in addition to ensuring the place enjoyed a continuing aura of peace and calm. I accepted, made sure my suit was cleaned and pressed, and wondered if I could afford a new dress and hair-do for Mary.

On the celebratory Monday night at 7.30 p.m. therefore we arrived at the function which was a drinks party and buffet. We were adorned in the finest clothes that could be purchased upon the pittance which was a constable's salary, were welcomed at the door by Andre himself and ushered into the close-packed throng. It is fair to say that I had never previously seen such a glorious spread of food nor so many drinks which flowed freely as waitresses and waiters fussed over the guests, ensuring that no one was ever left without a drink in their hand. Word passed around that we would be invited to help ourselves to the buffet at 8.30 by which time all the guests should have arrived.

And then, after about three-quarters of an

hour, there was a commotion at the door with Andre apparently in the thick of it. At first, few of the guests took any notice of the altercation thinking it was perhaps some good-natured banter, but as voices became raised from a loud to a very robust shouting level, most of us halted in our drinking and chattering and turned to see what was happening. Andre was at the entrance and there was a massive, thick-set, lank-haired man clad in a less-than-smart multi-coloured open-neck shirt and dark-blue trousers that did not seem to have been pressed for years. I recognized the fellow, although I had not had any close contact with him. He was a self-made millionaire called Tom O'Reilly, a dealer on a massive scale who specialized in agricultural machinery and equipment. He had depots throughout the north-east of England, ranging from Humberside up to Tyneside, and his home was at Seavham Manor, on the edge of my patch.

In addition to his agricultural dealerships, he had shares in many other businesses, from hotels to department stores by way of farms and grocery chains. I wondered if Andre realized with whom he was dealing.

'Our invitation was quite specific and it is

also a house rule,' I heard Andre shout. 'Smart ties and jackets must be worn. I have standards to maintain!'

'But this is a party, goddammit, and I've just got back from Scotland so I thought I'd look in before I settle down for the night ... I have my invitation ... O'Reilly's the name.'

'I'm sorry, Mr O'Reilly, but I cannot make exceptions. If you would care to return with a smart tie and, of course, a smart jacket, then I should be pleased to welcome you to my restaurant.'

There followed a moment of terrible silence as everyone present had now realized what was happening, and each of us wondered who the victor would be. I found myself wondering if my services would be called upon – there were occasions when police officers were invited to functions so that they were available to sort out disputes should they occur – but I had no wish to spoil my own night off with a confrontation or battle of any kind. I hoped one of them would back down – and as the seconds ticked by, it was clear that it was not going to be Andre. He stood in his imposing entrance with his feet apart and his arms folded across his chest, almost as if he was defending his castle against invaders.

'Then you've just lost a customer,' said Tom. 'Lots of customers, in fact.'

'I am sorry if you feel like that, but I am sure you will appreciate that I must maintain standards...'

But Andre was talking to himself because Tom O'Reilly had already turned on his heel and was striding across the forecourt to his parked Jaguar. There was a moment of hushed silence tinged with just a hint of embarrassment and then people began to talk among themselves as Andre took a deep breath, closed the outer door with something of a flourish and resumed his air of command. He had won that skirmish – but I knew that O'Reilly could have given him lots of future business.

The chatter and drinking resumed and then, after twenty minutes, we all heard the crashing of the outer door. It sounded as if an elephant was attempting to force an entry, but it was Tom O'Reilly; he was pushing open the door, with his body because both hands were engaged and then he crashed into the main area of the restaurant. By this stage, Andre was too far away to prevent him getting this far, but as a second hush descended, we could all see that O'Reilly was holding up a pair of dreadfully diseased and mangled rabbits. Each was dead and had been for some time; each had clearly been suffering from myxomatosis because their heads were swollen to grotesque sizes, their eyeballs protruded and in their blind distress, each had been killed by passing cars. They were a dreadful sight, and Tom O'Reilly dangled his fists as he held them aloft for everyone to see.

Even Andre halted at the awful sight, and then, as every single one of the party guests stood in silence, Tom flung the rabbits to the floor and called, 'Andrew, these are the last two you'll get from me until you pay for the others!'

And then he stalked out.

It is very difficult to assess the full impact of Tom's drastic action, but there were a few feminine screams at the awful sight, quite a lot of embarrassed laughter and some genuine hilarity but, later as we tucked into the buffet, there were some queries as to whether the chicken dishes were really chicken or whether they were rabbit with chicken flavouring. Tom had made a memorable statement, but he never patronized Andre's restaurant. I later learnt that Andre discovered the identity – and the wealth of that man – but he did not send an apology. Neither did Tom O'Reilly.

Following the incident, it must be said that Andre's Restaurant lost a lot of customers and for some time afterwards it was rumoured the place might close. It didn't however; it survived, albeit with slightly less rigid rules – but ties and jacket continued to be part of the scene. So far as that evening was concerned, most of us knew the prank was Tom's idea of a lesson-teaching joke, but it might never be known whether the loss of trade was due to Andre's stance against unwelcome dress standards or the possibility, however slight, that he might use diseased rabbits in his dishes. It had long been said that rabbits with myxomatosis were edible. However, I heard there was a decline in requests for his *Rillettes de Lapin* and also his famous rabbit, beef and pork casserole curiously known as *Sauce au vin du Médoc*, although some experts considered this to be *la grosse cuisine de la campagne* (the rough, coarse cookery of the countryside) – hardly the sort of dish for a sophisticated restaurant.

The Ashfordly district hosted two important social functions every year. One was the annual hunt ball in the autumn and the other was Ashfordly Section's annual police dinner/dance in the spring. Both attracted the elite of the area in addition to their own supporters and members, both were held in the fashionable ballroom of the Ashfordly Hotel and both were arranged to raise both the profile of their respective organizations and to raise funds. Much of the income raised by the hunt ball was spent on conservation of the countryside within the hunt's area and in the case of the police event, all profits were given to the Police Widows' and Orphans' Fund.

In the case of the police dinner/dance, planning was the responsibility of a small committee chaired by Sergeant Blaketon and it provided an ideal opportunity for him to display his organizational prowess and his social skills, particularly as the super-intendent and his wife were invited as guests and especially as the chief constable himself would very occasionally decide to grace us with his presence. Other high-ranking police officers from police headquarters would come too, such as the detective super-intendent, the superintendent i/c Force Administration and even superintendents from neighbouring divisions. Most of them would stay overnight in the hotel. There is no doubt the event was the finest of its kind in the county, hence the patronage we received from important people both within the Force itself and from the community – they included magistrates, county councillors, the coroner, forensic scientists and surgeons, solicitors and barristers, high-ranking hospital staff, important fire service and ambulance personnel, representatives of the armed services and even members of the local gentry and aristocracy.

The fine ballroom, coupled with the splendid dinner and overall happy atmosphere of the event combined to create a huge demand for tickets with the inevitable waiting list. Tickets were snapped up a year in advance; the number of guests was strictly limited but there was always an allocation for what might be termed 'the rank and file'- ordinary police officers and their spouses. Members of the public could attend if they could acquire a ticket and, in fact, the raffle at the dance always gave, as a prize, a pair of tickets for the following year's event. It was a prestigious and enjoyable occasion with the men dressing in their dinner jackets and the women in their long gowns. Mary and I always attended for we regarded it as the highlight of our social year – chiefly because one or other of our own parents came as baby-sitters and slept overnight but also because it was such a splendid, dressy event and an occasion to meet old colleagues and friends.

If there was an operational problem, it concerned the policing of Ashfordly and district while the dance was in progress. If all the local police officers wanted to attend the dance – which they did – there was no one to patrol the town or surrounding countryside. The answer was arrange for the town centre to be patrolled by special constables – most of the public did not know the difference between the uniform of a special or a regular member of the Force, consequently the deterrent value of a special was quite acceptable. Whether or not such a volunteer civilian could cope with a major crisis remained to be seen but such dramas rarely happened in Ashfordly. Besides, a special constable who required assistance or advice could always call Divisional Head-quarters if the need arose.

The countryside surrounding Ashfordly was patrolled by mobile officers from neigh-bouring sections and they were equipped with radio in their motor vehicles. They could respond rapidly to any major incident. Thus the policing of Ashfordly Section continued even if all its finest were letting their hair down on this one happy night of the year. And so it was that Sergeant Blaketon called each of his officers into Ashfordly Police Station for a meeting prior to the twelfth annual ball.

'Right,' he said. 'I want this particular dance to run as smoothly as all the others, and if possible, better. It is a very important event for me, more important than any of you realize just now. There will be some VIPs to look after, too, table settings to arrange, car-parking for official guests to be planned and a host of other minor tasks to perform on the night, from folding raffle tickets and drawing the raffle, to making sure all members of the dance band get their supper. I shall allocate tasks to each of you. But before all that, there is one important announcement: the new chief constable has indicated that he wishes to attend. Now, this will be his first social function of this kind in his new posting and he has chosen Ashfordly – it means we must all be at our most efficient and on our very best behaviour. I need not say how important it is to me, as the officer in charge of the section, to be honoured by such a visit. It places Ashfordly Section, and all the officers who serve it, very much in the spotlight.'

I could not remember any previous chief constable or even the deputy attending our annual dance, although I understood they had done so in the past, and so this was indeed a most prestigious event for Sergeant Blaketon – and for us all.

'Right,' he was saying. 'Policing of the town centre outside the hotel, in other words. Normally, as you know, this has been undertaken by specials, but on this occasion we are very fortunate. A new constable will be arriving at Ashfordly two days before the dinner/dance; he is a single man with a couple of years' practical experience to his credit and he has indicated he does not wish to attend the function.'

'Very neatly arranged, if I may say so, Sarge,' beamed Alf Ventress.

'Well, as the chief constable will be arriving I felt it was wise to have an experienced and capable person on duty outside the hotel. So PC Bellamy will be that man, David Bellamy. I shall brief him about his precise duties to ensure the chief is accorded the kind of welcome befitting his status. First impressions are lasting,

Ventress. Specials will patrol the outskirts of the town.'

It seemed that the new chief constable did not think it right that his official chauffeur drove him to social events, and so he would be driving himself and his wife to Ashfordly and he would stay overnight in the hotel to avoid having to drive home after a drink or two. Bellamy's job was to ensure there was a space for him and his wife to park outside the main entrance and alight from his vehicle immediately upon arrival; Bellamy would then indicate with hand signals to the constable on the door (an off-duty volunteer) that the chief had arrived, and this was the sign for another constable to step forward and escort these important guests into a small reception room for pre-dinner drinks. While all this was happening, Bellamy would drive the chief constable's car into the car-park behind the hotel and position it in a reserved place, return to the hotel and hand the keys to Blaketon.

Blaketon would pass them to the reception where a lackey would go out to the car and fetch the chief's luggage inside, then take it and the car keys to his room. Blaketon was aware that the chief and his wife might want to use the room prior to being officially greeted and contingency plans were made for that eventuality. Blaketon stressed how important it was to ensure those first few moments were achieved with perfection, style and grace. Blaketon himself would be inside the reception room to hand a glass of sherry or other aperitif to the chief and his lady when they entered; other VIPs would be shown into the room and introductions made. This was particularly important on this occasion, because the chief constable was new to the area and would be keen to meet as many influential people as possible.

The volunteer hosts for this important role in the reception area were specially selected constables from the Eltering Section; those from Ashfordly had other pressing duties within the hotel, the dining-room and the dance hall. Blaketon was sure everything would be all right on the night. After briefing us, he asked if we had any questions and after responding to one or two, he closed the meeting. The next meeting would be on the night itself, in the hotel an hour and a half before the dinner was due to start – PC Bellamy, whom I did not know, would attend that final briefing.

On the day of the dinner/dance, Mary and

I arrived at the hotel in good time. It was a foul night, bitterly cold and very wet. Heavy rain was pouring from a leaden sky and we had to make a dash from the car-park in all our finery. We hoped things would improve before the VIPs arrived, but the forecast was not good.

Blaketon had to make last-minute arrangements to borrow half-a-dozen large umbrellas to ensure the VIPs arrived from their cars as dry as possible. Then it was time for our final briefing. Those of us with responsibilities gathered in an ante-room on the ground floor. Apart from one man, we were all dressed in dinner jackets and black ties, looking more like waiters awaiting orders than off-duty policemen about to be briefed. I guessed the uniformed man was our new constable, Dave Bellamy, but no one introduced him. Without bothering with such niceties, Blaketon went through his checklist of duties and responsibilities. Most of us knew our role by this time, but he repeated his briefing, checking our understanding of important matters as he proceeded.

'Now,' he said eventually, 'this is PC Dave Bellamy,' and he invited Bellamy to step forward.

'Hello,' said the embarrassed young constable, a young man in his early twenties. With light-brown hair and a round face with a permanently happy expression, he appeared to be enjoying his temporary role.

'Bellamy is the newest member of Ashfordly Section. He arrived the day before yesterday and this is his first spell of duty. I have already briefed him in considerable detail about his duties outside the hotel, and we do appreciate you volunteering for this, Bellamy,' said Blaketon. 'It means we can enjoy ourselves for this one occasion in the year in the full knowledge that matters outside the hotel will be in very capable and professional hands.'

'Thank you, Sergeant,' Bellamy was slightly embarrassed at Blaketon's effusive gratitude. 'It's one way of meeting all my new colleagues at the same time and I'm sure there will be no problems.'

'Bellamy will meet the chief constable outside the main entrance,' thundered Blaketon. 'He will open the chief's car doors, ensure he and his wife alight (beneath umbrellas if it is raining) and escort them into the front entrance where it is dry. He will ask the chief for his car keys as he offers to drive the car around to the rear and into the hotel car-park. As he approaches the main entrance with the arrivals, Bellamy will signal to you – PC Gardner. You will open the door to admit the chief and his lady, then you will direct the chief towards PC Letts who will be hovering in the main body of the foyer. He will show the chief and his lady into our private reception suite for pre-dinner drinks.'

Bellamy nodded. 'Got it, Sarge,' he said with confidence.

'We must be aware that the chief and his lady may wish to go to their room before joining us and they may wish their luggage to be brought into the hotel immediately – in that case, PC Gardner, you will offer to carry the luggage to the hotel reception desk and you, PC Letts, will await his return from his room and then show him into our private reception suite. Now, any questions?'

'Just one, Sergeant,' said Bellamy. 'How will I recognize the chief constable?'

'You've not seen him yet?'

'No, Sergeant.'

'Has anyone seen him?' asked Blaketon.

Everyone shook their heads.

'Right,' said Blaketon. 'I have not seen him

either. He will be dressed in a dinner jacket and black tie like the rest of us, but he is not coming in the official car, Bellamy, so don't spend time looking for AJ 1.' AJ 1 was the registration number of the chief constable's official car. 'He will arrive in his private car which is a pale green Rover 2000, brand new, and the registration number is HAJ 575F. That should not be hard to identify. All I know from contacts at headquarters is that he is about average height with greying hair which is thinning on top, and a round face. Once the chief and his lady are inside the hotel, Bellamy, your main duty is over – you may resume normal patrolling duties, but, as a gesture, there will be supper for you in the hotel. Have words with the manager, he will be expecting you.'

'Right, Sergeant, that's great, thank you.' Bellamy wrote the car number in his pocket book.

'It might be prudent, Bellamy, as the evening is drawing to a close, to position yourself outside the hotel to deter any drunken drivers and other trouble, even at a dance of this stature.'

'Right, Sergeant.'

Having had Bellamy's identity revealed to us, Blaketon then outlined our duties for the night. While I was attending this meeting, Mary was with the wives of other policemen where they would enjoy a reunion and chat in the bar; she'd not miss me for the short time I was doing my part for the success of the evening.

My job was to position the place settings at the dining-tables – we had the names of everyone who had bought a ticket. It was that kind of event. Even the winner of the two tickets in last year's raffle was named – it was a Miss Esme Primton and because she had won two tickets, she had intimated she was bringing a male guest. Thus that ticket did not have a personal name – it merely said 'Miss Primton's guest'. As was customary, these guests were placed on the extensive top table, along with the chief constable, Blaketon and some twenty other VIPs.

After our briefing, I spent some time laying out the place names and checking them against the seating plan, after which I was able to rejoin Mary and the others. Much of our work had been done prior to the event, of course, and once we had performed our tasks for that evening, we were free to enjoy the occasion. Before joining Mary in the bar, I peeped outside –

the deluge was continuing and the streets were running with water, but at least the main entrance to the hotel was covered. People could stop their cars outside, hurry across the footpath, then fold their brollies before entering the hotel with some decorum, and it was under that canopy that Bellamy would await the arrival of our most important visitor. We had been told to expect him at 7.30 p.m. prompt.

Moments before that vital time, however, I noticed that Mr James Bullen was attending; he had arrived in the guests' reception suite with his wife, and I could not remember positioning a place setting for them at table. I rushed into the dining-room and scanned the tables, prepared to check every one of the 120 placings but happily soon found the names of Dr Adrian and Mrs Elizabeth Calder.

Dr Calder was coroner for the Ashfordly district – his name was on the official guest list, but Bullen had not been invited. It seemed, however, that he had arrived in place of his boss, for Bullen was the deputy coroner. I could not see Calder anywhere in the hotel but decided to have a quick word with Bullen, just to clarify the situation. I managed to approach him very quickly and said, 'It's nice to see you and Mrs Bullen here. It this your first time?'

'Hello Mr Rhea,' he referred to me very formally. 'Yes, our first time and we are looking forward to it. Dr Calder couldn't make it, he's got an unexpected family commitment in Kent, the death of an aunt I believe, and he asked if I could represent him and to convey his apologies. He did speak to the superintendent who said it would not be a problem.'

'Not at all! We're pleased you could make it,' and I tried to sound delighted by his presence, but I knew I had to amend the place settings. The superintendent had blithely agreed to the exchange without telling the organizers and so I sought Blaketon. I found him in a huddle with some guests, took him discreetly to one side, and explained what had happened.

'There's no real problem, is there, Rhea? It doesn't change numbers, does it?'

'No, no problem. It's just that his name is not shown on the place settings,' I said. 'I think we should amend that, as an act of courtesy. All I need is a couple of blank place settings, then I can write out the Bullens' names. It'll take only a couple of minutes.'

'They're in my brief-case, in the hotel office ... it's locked, my case I mean, so I'll come with you to get them. Good thing you spotted that ... come on, hurry, the chief's due any minute now. I can't hang about, I've got to be there to receive him and his lady.'

While Blaketon and I were thus engaged, I was to learn what had transpired outside during those very moments, so this is an account of what Bellamy eventually told me. As the starting time for the dinner approached, a succession of cars pulled up outside the hotel in the deluge, discharged their ladies under umbrellas and then were moved on by Bellamy to park behind the hotel. Due to the downpour, everything and everyone was rushed, and it was almost dark outside. The heavy rain and dark clouds added to the gloom, with the lights of the town reflecting from the footpaths and streets. After parking their cars behind the hotel, the menfolk galloped through the rain into the rear entrance, sometimes with brollies and sometimes without, there to spruce themselves in the gents' washrooms before joining the ladies. Out front, however, Bellamy was only interested in keeping a clear space for the chief constable's arrival. He was expected at 7.30 p.m. but Bellamy's work was not easy because cars tended to arrive in bunches and people tended to leap out of the line of parked cars in threes or sixes or nines or even more as they galloped beneath large umbrellas through the rain for refuge in the hotel. Spotting an unknown chief constable in such conditions and among such a crowd of running, umbrella-covered folk was difficult.

However, through the glistening lights and persistent downpour, there appeared a smart green Rover 2000. It arrived a few minutes before 7.30 p.m. with headlights blazing and windscreen wipers wiping and a quick glance at the front registration plate revealed the letters HAJ before it eased to a halt right outside the main entrance. Inside were the figures of a grey-haired man in evening dress, and a woman dressed in her finery. Surprisingly, in Bellamy's opinion, the woman was in the driving seat and the man was in the front passenger seat but this did not disconcert the gallant Bellamy as he leapt into instant action. Rushing out with a large umbrella at the ready, he opened the driver's door and said, 'I'll park the car, sir – er madam! You hurry inside out of the rain.'

The man replied, 'That's mighty kind of you, Constable. See, Esme, I said we'd get looked after!'

The woman just giggled.

With Bellamy hovering with his brolly, undecided whether or not to shield the chief first or his wife, the couple left their car, leaving the engine running as Bellamy covered the woman and escorted her to dry land. Then he went back to do likewise for the gentleman who struggled from his seat and then hurried, head down, into the hotel beneath the brolly, profusely thanking Bellamy for a quality of service he'd never experienced before. As Bellamy gave the thumbs-up sign to register the arrival of these major guests, the hotel door was opened wide by PC Gardner to admit them as Bellamy said, 'I'll park the car behind the hotel and will leave your car keys at reception, sir, er, madam ... and what about your luggage?'

'Luggage?' smiled the lady. 'Oh, no, we've decided not to stay, we'll go home after-wards. It's not far, fortunately, and I don't drink.'

'Oh, right, fine,' and Bellamy watched as his charges made their fine entry to mingle with the glittering throng of people.

'Thank you, my man,' said the fellow as he entered the lobby to be greeted by PC Letts, the next of the team of fully briefed constables. 'This is wonderful, isn't it, Esme? I told you it would be worth coming, didn't I? Aren't English policemen wonderful?'

Within seconds, after popping respectfully into the gents' and the ladies, to tidy their hair, check their clothing and preen themselves in readiness for their pre-dinner drinks, the pair were then escorted into the private reception suite. Blaketon, unfortunately, was not there to greet them. He'd missed their entry because he was finding the blank place settings for me but the waitress would ensure they were given a sherry or other drink. As I wrote out the names in the peace of the hotel's office, Blaketon said, 'I must get back, Rhea. Well done for thinking of that. It's that kind of attention to detail that makes a success of any venture.'

When he returned, he found PC Letts standing guard on the door of the private reception suite and said, 'Ah, PC Letts. All correct?'

'Yes, Sergeant. The chief constable and his lady have arrived, and I have shown them into this suite.'

'They're here?' Blaketon gulped. 'My God, they're early and I was not here to greet them ... how long ago?'

'Two or three minutes, Sergeant. That's all.'

'Right, thanks ... which is him then? I need to approach him and introduce him to the other guests, but I've never met him. Can you indicate him without making it obvious you are doing so? There's a good crowd in there, so just you open this door and point him out to me.'

Letts scanned the closely packed crowd and then indicated a fairly tall woman who was facing towards them.

'You see that blonde woman, Sergeant, quite a large lady, in her late forties, early fifties, with the round face and bright red dress, well, you can just see the top of a dress, dangling silver ear-rings, she's standing to the left of that second window ... well, that's his lady.'

'Ah, yes. So the grey-haired man with his back to us will be the chief?'

'Yes, sir, they came together. I recognize the back of his head.'

'I think I do,' muttered Blaketon, 'I'm sure I've seen the back of that head before but can't be sure where I can have seen the chief constable from that angle...'

And then he entered the suite, pushing his way through the crowd and apologizing for making some spill their drinks as he headed for his target. He found himself facing the woman, smiled and announced his arrival by saying,

'Sir, madam, welcome to Ashfordly Section dinner-dance, I'm Sergeant Blaketon...'

'By jove, Blaketon, you put on a good show for your guests,' said Claude Jeremiah Greengrass. 'I've never had such a welcome in my life. I know I'm one of your best customers but this is going a bit over the top. Lackies to park your car, brollies to keep your hair dry, sherry with the nobs ... by gum, Blaketon, you must be after promotion or summat.'

'Greengrass! How did you get in here?'

'I was brought in here, that's how. I was welcomed by a constable on the door and escorted all the way into this room, to join all these lovely people...'

'But how did you get a ticket?'

'I won the ticket last year, Sergeant,' said the lady. Esme Primton. 'And I decided to bring my old friend Claude along with me, as my guest. And I must say you have started the evening in a splendid way.

Wonderful, isn't it Claude?'

'I've a feeling it's going to end pretty soon,' muttered Claude. 'I might be turned into a pumpkin.'

'Nonsense!' said a plush voice nearby. 'I'm sure the sergeant will welcome you, Mr Greengrass. After all, you are one of my best customers too. Perhaps you don't recognize me out of court. Anthony Bridgeman, chairman of the bench.'

'Hear, hear,' said another voice.

'Oh, right,' said Claude. 'I see who it is now, we all look the same in these penguin suits. Well, I am a guest, I suppose, Esme's guest...'

'Be my guest!' Blaketon made a rapid decision to be gracious and accept his old adversary as an official guest, but followed it with, 'So where is the chief constable? And, more to the point, where is Bellamy?'

He looked at his watch. It was exactly 7.30 p.m. As he turned to walk out and find either Bellamy or the chief constable, a tall, smart figure appeared in the foyer, with a lovely woman at his side. Both were immaculately dressed with no sign of having dashed through stormy weather or of braving the elements or running in from the car park.

'Sergeant Blaketon?' the man asked.

344

'Yes?'

'Andrew Lindsey, Chief Constable,' explained the newcomer. 'And my wife, Linda. Nice to meet you. I do hope you haven't been waiting too long – we decided to arrive early, you see, because of the weather. I do like to enjoy a nice drive across the moors and we felt it would be nice to have an hour or so to relax in our room because it was such an awful night.'

'Oh, you've been here all the time? Well, sir, what a good idea ... do, do come in. I have my guests in the reception suite, so if you would like to follow me...'

And so, after a rather damp and shaky start, the evening got underway and the new chief constable charmed everyone, making them all relax and smile and feel happy. He even shook hands with Greengrass and had a long chat with him about second-hand oak furniture, something which it appeared he knew a lot about.

But we all thought that the presence of the chief constable was the reason for Blaketon's edginess that evening. It wasn't until his speech at the dinner that we knew why he wanted this particular dinner/dance to be such a happy, successful occasion. He began his speech by welcoming everyone, especially his guests and particularly the new chief constable and his wife, but then he stunned everyone, by saying,

'And finally, ladies and gentlemen, I have a personal announcement to make and felt that this was the right time. As you know, I have spent many happy years as the sergeant in charge of Ashfordly Section. I think the area has some of the finest countryside in England and I think we are blessed with some of the finest and most dedicated police officers in the country. It has been my pleasure to be associated with them over the years, and particularly as their leader. They have never let me down. And, I might add, we are blessed with some of the best members of the public I have ever met during my police service.'

'Hear, hear.' The voice of Claude Jeremiah Greengrass rose from somewhere among the gathered diners.

'However,' and there was a tremor in Blaketon's voice at this stage, 'there comes a time when every one of us has to move on. Now it is my turn. This is both a proud and sad function because it will be my last dinner/dance as the officer in charge of Ashfordly Section. You see, I have decided to retire.'

346

There was a deathly hush at his announcement.

Those of us in the Force could not believe what we were hearing, and when we did realize what he had said, we did not know how to respond. And then Claude Jeremiah Greengrass stood up, rapped the table for attention, raised his glass and said, 'Three cheers for Sergeant Oscar Blaketon – the finest and fairest man I know.'

And as the dining-hall resounded with those cheers with the band striking up "For He's a Jolly Good Fellow", Sergeant Blaketon sat down with tears glistening on his face.

The publishers hope that this book has given you enjoyable reading. Large Print Books are especially designed to be as easy to see and hold as possible. If you wish a complete list of our books please ask at your local library or write directly to:

Magna Large Print Books
Magna House, Long Preston,
Skipton, North Yorkshire.
BD23 4ND